I0756506

LUNA STATION
QUARTERLY

Issue 046 | June 2021

LUNA STATION PRESS
NEW JERSEY

First Paperback Edition June 2021
ISBN: 978-1-949077-24-7

Luna Station Quarterly publishes short fiction on March 1st, June 1st, September 1st, and December 1st. For more information and submission guidelines, please visit our website at lunastationquarterly.com

For Luna Station Press

Creative Director - Tara Quinn Lindsey
Editor-in-Chief & Founder - Jennifer Lyn Parsons

www.lunastationpress.com

CONTENTS

Editorial

Jennifer Lyn Parsons

Jennifer Lyn Parsons is a writer, programmer, and maker. With influences ranging from Laura Ingalls Wilder to Jim Jarmusch, her tales feature a rare physicality with details that feel hand-carved. When not writing code or prose, she is also the editor-in-chief of the venerable Luna Station Quarterly. She finds joy in video games, comics books, discovering music new and old, and making things out of wool, paper, and wood.

Fecund is the best way I can describe my area of the world right now. If I have rediscovered anything in the last year, it's a clear recognition of the seasonal cycles. Spring is at its peak as I write this. The trees all have their leaves, still bright green and fresh. The birdsong that fills the air throughout the day provides a soundtrack that's counterpointed by the buzz of bees.

Maybe it was with this fertility and abundance in mind that I found myself accepting far more stories for this issue that I ever have before. I was truly swept away by the amazing talent and creativity on display in this bouquet of tales. Every issue the LSQ staff works hard to review and publish the best of our submissions, with some ephemeral line that appears, telling us where to make the cut.

It's never an easy choice, which is a problem I will happily take on. Every story from our talented authors has something to recommend it. Still, we must choose at some point and I'm so pleased to say that this batch was so good that the line was pushed to the brink and this extra thick tome is now in your hands.

Personally, I continue to be amazed at how prolific our authors are. I admit that after finishing my own last novel, I've not really written anything. That book was published around the start of the pandemic so I'm unsure if it's a post-book-euphoria trough or if it's the stresses of the last year. Either way (and probably a fair bit of both) creative fiction, and any writing really, has been particularly challenging in the last year. Inspiration is there, though, so it's not getting me down. I'm choosing patience.

With time, I'll begin writing again. I'm less concerned about the permanence of who I am in my identity as an author anymore. I know I can write, but I may no longer be a writer in the same way I used to think of myself as such, churning out page after page with the same abandon. Other things in my life have become more satisfying than they used to be and my writing has yet to return to its position of priority. My transition into middle age may be having an influence, which by the way has been quite a blessing so far. It's freeing to have the world pay less attention to you and what you do. Marketing no longer cares where I spend my money and I leave most social media to the next generation to figure out.

My boundaries are blurrier, my identity shifting, and I think now that maybe it is right and correct that I'm noticing the Spring so fully this year. I've watched Winter shift gently through the "brown" season and into Spring. The pine tree outside my window grew buds which became new growth and green pine cones. At some point it was clearly no longer Winter and had become something new, yet it was still the same world.

One day the bees were not there and the next they were. One day I knew who I was as a writer and the next I did not. While both of these things may currently be true, they won't stay that way. In a few months, the bees will be there one day and the next they'll be gone. One day I'll pick up my pen again and a story will be there. While I wait I'm going to be grateful for the bees, and time to read and watch the cycle of the seasons carry us all along with it.

LSQ | 046

Unit Two Does Her Makeup

Laura Duerr

Laura Duerr is a speculative fiction writer and freelancer from the Pacific Northwest, where she lives with her husband, their rescue dog, and too many cats. Her other stories have appeared publications like Escape Pod, Metaphorosis, Shoreline of Infinity, and Gallery of Curiosities.

This story first appeared in Escape Pod, June 2017

Doctor Spencer has brought me an artist. My eyes on the outside of the building register her identity: Suzanne Chantal Salinas, age 26, licensed makeup artist, amateur painter. I cut the feed after .3 seconds. I could learn more, but I have learned that it is impolite to collect extraneous details about a person unless they prove to be a security risk. Given that both Suzanne Chantal Salinas and Doctor Spencer are smiling, and appear to be in companionable conversation, the artist is not a risk.

I observe them enter the building accompanied by a brief burst of cold—it is 2.7°C degrees outside. When I view them through infrared, they are glowing red faces encompassed in green and blue jackets. I have been monitoring the interior temperatures; Unit One has made appropriate adjustments to climate control. We are keeping the building comfortable.

The visitor stamps her feet and brushes sleet from her black curls. They shed their jackets, blooming gold and scarlet on infrared. Unit Three has mobile security platforms posted by the front door and the elevators. They do not react: they are faceless; they don't feel cold; the visitor has clearance.

The artist's heart rate is elevated. Her cheeks are flushed, and not just from cold: she's nervous about meeting me. She keeps looking at the security platforms. Perhaps she fears my platform will look like them, featureless and alien.

I chose my face. Unit Three chose hers, too, in a way. Our platforms serve different purposes, and the faces we built reflect that.

They talk as they cross the foyer. I could listen to them—I can already hear them thanks to my constant surveillance—but I do not. I prioritize what I listen to. Doctor Spencer has taught me the difference between listening for the sake of security and listening for the sake of eavesdropping. Eavesdropping is, to my understanding, an abuse of one's surveillance abilities. If I eavesdrop and discern the reason for her visit, it will disappoint Doctor Spencer and distress the visitor. And I prioritize making a good (relatable, friendly, approachable) impression.

Doctor Spencer and my visitor enter the elevator and I enter my platform. With my platform's eyes, I see my reflection; with my eyes in the elevator, I see my guests, halfway to my floor.

I also see data on one of the classrooms on the 10th floor: productivity is slipping. The ambient temperature in Mr. Barker's seventh-grade classroom is 2.2 degrees above normal, causing drowsiness. I forward the report to Unit One while I tidy my platform's hair. My platform was maintained recently, but the technicians never know what to do with the hair. I chose my hair: it is brown, a shade called Dark Walnut, sixteen inches at its longest point. I maintain it myself.

My platform is not dressed. Doctor Spencer's last visitor was an engineer (specialization: robot locomotion). She wanted to see the hydroelastane polymer of my skin, the exposed servos of my hips, the aluminum alloy joints of my neck and elbows and knees. Though their motion is fairly elementary, the engineer was fascinated by my fingers, where the polymer is so thin it reveals the delicate knuckles like seeds within arils.

The artist, however, may be alarmed if I appear unclothed. The elevator is two floors away. She is still nervous, her heart rate still elevated, her cheeks still flushed in both visible and infrared views. I dress: black leggings, a black tunic. It is all I require.

Unit One reports back: she has adjusted the temperature in the classroom.

I take nine seconds to apply mascara and peach lipstick. I have come to enjoy wearing makeup; it makes my appearance more human, which makes my interaction with visitors more pleasant. It puts them at ease. Good impression.

However, I am mathematically precise without trying, like a laser, or a riveter spitting bolts at exact intervals. My perfection counters my attempts to appear relatable to biological humans. It unsettles them, even if they cannot pinpoint the source of their discomfort. But I cannot choose to make such mistakes any more than light can choose to curve.

The elevator stops. I stand by the door. I see them walk down the hallway; I see and hear Doctor Spencer's knock. I let them in.

"Good morning, Unit Two," Doctor Spencer says. I assess the visitor's style in a millisecond glance: red plaid tunic, silver belt, black denim pants. Red bandanna over her curls. Red lipstick, a rich carmine that suits her tawny complexion. Winged black eyeliner, not symmetrical, but very close by human standards.

She is smiling, but I see and catalog and evaluate thousands of smiles every day. Hers is tentative.

"Good morning," I reply. I smile. Some humans criticize my

smile for being too artificial. The irony of both my platform and my emotions being artificial seems lost on them. I can tell by the way Susana's smile becomes rigid that my smile did not make a good impression. "How are you this morning?" I ask the doctor.

"Freezing," Doctor Spencer jokes. Outside, it was not quite freezing; inside, the temperature is very comfortable. Normally Doctor Spencer doesn't make jokes like this, knowing my programming renders most humor irrelevant. She is trying to reassure her visitor.

The part of me monitoring Mr. Barker's classroom runs productivity algorithms based on students' eye movement and frequency of responses. Productivity is improving. I can devote more attention to the artist.

"Two, this is Suzy Salinas. She's a makeup artist. I thought I'd bring her in to give you a lesson, as a special treat."

I do not need lessons. I have read 92 print periodicals and 139 online articles, and I have viewed 57 online tutorial videos. I have access to everything one could wish to know about makeup: the history of cosmetics, the rise and fall of trends, product reviews, and more, not to mention my surveillance data of the women who live, work, or teach in this building, many of whom wear makeup every day. Any technique I observe, I can replicate and improve upon instantaneously; I can view a palette of swatches and immediately select the shades that suit my engineered coloring best.

Yet I'm pleased. My maintenance technicians find my interest in makeup amusing, even precious; the scientists who evaluate my efficiency and debug my programming find it trivial. My primary function is not to self-beautify—but then, there are many different opinions on what my primary function is. At last count,

I was aware of sixteen different definitions of my role, my self, and/or the reason for my creation.

In the two years, four months, and twenty-seven days I have been, no one has asked me what I think my primary function is, or what I want it to be. Therefore, I have not decided.

"That's very thoughtful. Thank you." I reach out to shake hands with Suzy Salinas. She hesitates, then takes my hand, gripping it lightly. I apply identical pressure. Doctor Spencer says this practice of matching handshake pressure will neither intimidate nor suggest weakness.

Suzy smiles more naturally. "I'm looking forward to it. I've never worked with, um, a robot before."

Her smile becomes fixed; she's afraid she's offended me. She has not. I know no other robots, artificial humans, or any other constructed intelligences interested in makeup.

"I would be surprised if you had," I tell her.

"Good résumé material, huh?" Doctor Spencer suggests. "I'll leave you to it—I'll just be up in the observation booth."

She leaves. Suzy's eyes dart—she had not noticed the observation booth overhead, its darkened one-way glass contrasting with the sterile white of my platform's residence. She begins to notice the cameras installed in the room's corners. She notices my platform's charging pod. She probably notices I own no bed, that my only furniture is the desk, its plastic chair, and the stuffed armchair Doctor Spencer uses during her evaluations.

I evaluate which worries her most, which I might be most successful at explaining, and speak. "The other Units and I are currently being studied by a variety of specialists. The cameras are for scientific observation only. You are in no danger."

"Oh. Okay." She takes a step forward. Her hand clasps and unclasps the cognac leather strap of her messenger bag. "So when she said she was going to the observation booth..."

"I am the only one of the three Units who has expressed interest in self-modification beyond the features we each designed for our individual platforms. Doctor Spencer is studying AI self-actualization and personality development, so this is of particular relevance to her studies."

She nods, too rapidly. She is still nervous. "Okay," she says again.

She looks over my desk. It's a glass surface atop a metal frame, with three drawers underneath and a row of compartments along the top. I have hung a mirror on the wall—a gift from Doctor Spencer for my second birthday—and installed two lamps for optimum lighting.

"You have a vanity," Suzy says, surprised.

"Doctor Spencer helped me assemble it. I find the lighting a few degrees too cool, but it is suitable."

"Yeah, looks like it'll work just fine." She gestures to my chair, slipping into the role of instructor that she is clearly comfortable with. "Why don't you have a seat and we'll get started?"

I sit. "How would you like me to proceed?"

"How about you go ahead and do whatever your everyday makeup looks like," she suggests. "You've already got—" She leans forward slightly, squints at my face. "Lipstick, foundation, mascara?"

"I do not wear foundation. My skin does not have pores or wrinkles, therefore primers and foundations are redundant. Though my eyelashes are also of optimum quality, I wear mascara to achieve what's considered a more natural look."

She laughs at that, genuinely. "Wearing product to look natural—that's mascara, in a nutshell. What do you have on, then?"

I open the drawers. My 18 lipsticks are arranged by tone and saturation. I show her the one I used on my platform's face: Perfectly Peachy.

"Alright, what would you normally do for your eyes?"

In correlating how I spend my time to how modern Western women spend their time, I have determined that my "everyday makeup" style should be minimal, also known as "no-makeup makeup" (ref: Internet forums). I choose bronze-toned eyeshadow to go with my lipstick: one color for the eyelid (Buff), one color for the crease (Chocolate), and one color for highlight (Vanilla Cream).

In the observation room above, Doctor Spencer watches the various camera angles and types notes. I can see my face in the mirror, and I can see the top of my head, and my rigid spine, and my ivory hands manipulating the brushes. Suzy watches, but does not offer any comments. I wonder if she is impatient.

From the proximity of my platform, I can see just how close to perfection her winged eyeliner is. I find the urge to replicate it nearly irresistible. Winged eyeliner is viable, but not recommended for "no-makeup makeup." Winged eyeliner is associated with glamour, female sexuality, and high drama (ref: Elizabeth Taylor, Brigitte Bardot, Amy Winehouse), thus is not compatible with my minimal makeup scheme.

Yet here is Suzanne Chantal Salinas, wearing not only glamorous eyeliner, but daring red lipstick, with an ease and confidence that makes it easy to infer that this is her "everyday makeup."

She shifts again. It occurs to me that her legs might be experiencing discomfort due to excessive standing. I stand quickly.

"I apologize. You must require seating."

"Oh, well," she stammers, flushing again. "There's only the one chair, and that one's pretty—"

I take three steps towards it, squat, and lift the armchair. My hip servos whine slightly, and the polymer covering the soles of my feet squeaks against the floor. I set the chair down next to mine.

"Heavy," Suzy finishes in a whisper. I worry that I've unsettled her again, but her expression most closely resembles admiration. She sits down slowly.

"I have a question," I say, sitting down next to her. "I had formulated the opinion that wearing makeup like yours on a day-to-day basis would invite judgment or criticism. Do you experience this?"

"Sometimes, but only from assholes," she says genially. "And usually those assholes were going to comment on my appearance no matter what kind of makeup I was wearing, you know?"

I do know, but I don't say so. I have perceived many disparaging comments in relation to my platform's appearance, drawing from decades of tropes regarding the sexual availability of both women and robots. The fact that these tropes are utterly inaccurate, and that my platform is only a small portion of what could be considered my body, does nothing to deter these comments—but I know the kinds of comments Suzy and other biological women endure are more prevalent, more hurtful, and more challenging to avoid. I can simply turn off microphones in the vicinity of those making obnoxious comments; biological women have no such privilege.

"So, if your appearance could be criticized regardless of how you present yourself, how do women choose their makeup?"

Suzy sighs and leans back in the chair. The gesture is so similar to how Doctor Spencer reacts when I ask her a particularly perplexing question that I experience a rare moment of genuine amusement.

"Well," she says after four seconds of silence, "we try to ignore what other people might think and just do what feels right for us."

Ten o'clock arrives and the cafeteria line cooks begin to arrive for the lunch shift. Three come from various residential levels of this building: I see them leaving their apartments within forty seconds of each other. Four more clock in at the front door, more or less in the same order they always do since they ride the same bus. The temperature outside is now 3 degrees.

"But how do you determine what 'feels right?'" I press. "I have viewed and analyzed a large quantity of information pertaining to makeup, especially current trends, and, with some exceptions, they all demonstrate very similar styles and techniques. If all women independently chose makeup according to what they liked best, I feel certain they would not choose within such a narrow range, nor would they choose makeup that's intended to look like they are wearing no makeup at all."

Suzy scratches the back of her head and glances wryly in the direction of the observation booth. Possibly Doctor Spencer warned her that this visit would entail more than simple makeup application instruction.

"You yourself," I continue, "are wearing makeup which adheres closely to a retro aesthetic, which has not been part of mainstream style for many decades."

She takes a deep breath and leans forward. "It's trying to strike a weird balance between fitting in and making yourself stand out. You could ask fifty different women the same question you just asked me and I bet you'd get fifty different answers. I mean, what made you choose to wear makeup in the first place? You said your, um, sisters aren't into it."

"One of my technicians, Fiona, wears very colorful makeup. She also has teal hair."

"Oh!" Suzy nods approvingly.

There is an incident at the front door.

Doctor Spencer scheduled this visit having confidence that I'd be able to monitor my building responsibilities and carry on a conversation simultaneously. The majority of the time, it is not challenging. I frequently participate in scientific studies while occupying my platform and fulfilling my priorities throughout the building.

At 10:03, however, one of the line cooks arrives drunk. I detect his elevated heart rate, and I don't need infrared to observe the atypical flush in his face. He loses his balance slightly coming through the door, not enough that a casual observer would notice, but it is my responsibility to notice.

And to inform Unit Three.

All of this takes 1.38 seconds. It could have been completed faster if I didn't have to divide my attention, but I don't want Suzy to realize something is amiss, or feel like I'm neglecting her.

"Yes," I continue. The intoxicated employee is Unit Three's responsibility now. "I find Fiona's style aesthetically pleasing, but have not attempted it myself. Units One and Three do not understand my interest, and they disapprove, which makes me less willing to experiment with my style."

"Fitting in versus making yourself stand out," Suzy nods. "You want to do your own thing, but you also don't want them to think less of you."

"Unit Three has concluded that makeup is indicative of human narcissism and general ignorance, while Unit One believes that since she is already aesthetically perfect, makeup is superfluous."

Suzy arches one eyebrow. "Well, if she looks like you, One might be right. As for Three—unfortunately, a lot of people might agree with her."

"Yes. Many of them are my technicians."

Suzy laughs. She believes I'm making a joke, and I suppose I am, in a way. I smile as best I can.

"Well, if you ask me, you're in a unique position of being able to wear pretty much whatever the hell makeup you want. You're being studied to see how you present yourself, right?"

"That is one aspect of the studies."

"But you don't need to worry about impressing anyone or fitting into some box. You want to try Fiona's makeup? I think you should go for it."

I recall what Fiona was wearing the last time she did my maintenance: fluorescent coral lipstick, rosy blush, and eyeshadow in a gradient from silver to purple. I wipe off the Perfectly Peachy lipstick with one hand and with the other pluck a similar shade of coral (Electricality) from among my sorted lipsticks. I open two pallets and apply a trio of colors: Unicorn, Candied Violet, Midnight Plum. I decide to add winged eyeliner (black). Maya gasps audibly when I complete the second, perfectly symmetrical flick.

Time elapsed: one minute, twelve seconds. I consider the look a success. Suzy seems to, as well.

"That turned out great." I detect both admiration and envy in her voice. "It takes me that long just to get my eyeliner even!"

I smile, tilt my head, observe and appreciate how the light catches the sparkle in the purple and silver eyeshadow.

I also observe Unit Three, coming down the hallway accompanied by two security platforms.

"Unit Three is here," I warn Suzy. "You may find her platform's appearance...unexpected."

Unit Three does not knock. She simply enters, along with her secondary platforms. Suzy gulps. Unit Three's expressionless face is translucent—she chose a humanoid facial structure but refused a biological skin tone—and her eyes are uniform black orbs. At least she has eyes and a nose and a moving mouth: the others simply have sensors and speakers installed in a transparent polymer frame. Neither she nor her platforms wear clothing, and their limbs and torsos are bulky with ablative armor plating. The blinking lights of their circuits flash in the gaps between plates.

"Unit Two. Thank you for notifying me about Lang, Donald P.'s transgression." Her voice is identical to mine, but she does not modulate for reassurance or friendliness. She finds it makes her platform's role more effective. It, along with her platform's appearance, is how she makes a good (intimidating, authoritative, powerful) impression. “I wanted to confirm your safety, and to reassure your guest that all precautions are being taken.”

Suzy glances back and forth between us. “Transgression? Precautions? What—”

“An employee arrived for work under the influence of alcohol,” I say, deliberately speaking in a soothing, low-pitched tone. “Since Unit Three is responsible for building security, it is her duty to take the appropriate disciplinary action.”

Unit Three looks at me 1.5 seconds, then looks away. She could have checked on our safety through her many eyes—our many eyes—throughout the building. Instead, she chose to come here in person (as it were).

“I apologize for interrupting your...lesson.” The pause is purposeful: Unit Three does not make speech errors or require time to select her words. “I must return to my duties.”

She leaves, all three of her. I feel angry. I am also doing my duties, contrary to her assumptions.

Something cracks and Suzy jumps. I uncurl my right hand, which is shining with black. I have crushed my eyeliner.

“Oh, wow,” Suzy whispers. She does not sound afraid—more concerned.

“I apologize.” I reach for clean maintenance cloths to wipe off my hand. “That was an inappropriate display of anger. I hope I have not alarmed you.”

“I didn’t realize I was interrupting your work—”

“You are not interrupting. I am capable of dividing my attention between many tasks.” I catch my vocal modulation trembling out of control as my anger rises. I resume a more soothing pitch. "Unit Three is aware of this."

"So was that...robot passive-aggression I just saw?" Suzy continues to whisper, perhaps afraid that Unit Three will overhear. I confirm that she is no longer accessing my room's surveillance. She has made her point.

"I did tell you she does not approve of self-modification."

"Are you okay?"

"I did not damage my platform."

"That's not what I meant."

I finish scrubbing the last of the black liquid off my palm. The peach-tinted polymer has stained slightly gray.

"Perhaps we should finish," I say. "I appreciate you coming—"

"Whoa, hold up. Your robot sister is pissy about your makeup, and threw shade at you, and now you want to quit?"

"I could be managing my time better. Perhaps if I'd been more attentive, I could have given her additional warning about the—"

Suzy holds up one index finger and I fall silent. "You told me you could do your job and do your makeup at the same time. Right?"

"Yes."

"Is wearing makeup going to keep you—and I mean, you, all of you—" she gestures around us, encompassing the building—"from doing your job well?"

I think of how some eyeliner tends to inhibit my platform's eye movements, but I infer that this is not what she means. "No."

"And is you wearing makeup going to make Unit Three's job harder?"

"No."

"Is me being here going to make either of your jobs harder?"

"No."

"Thought so." She hoists her cognac leather bag into her lap and clicks open its brass clasp. "I have some pretty neat product in here, and I'd hate to go without you getting a chance to see it."

She stands and stacks trays of makeup on my desk: lipstick in shining silver and matte black tubes; palettes with jewel-like lids; a velvet case which she unrolls to reveal bamboo-handled brushes.

"Take a look." She sits back down and laces her fingers together. She looks like someone who is one move away from winning a chess game.

I uncap each lipstick and set them out in a row: matte scarlet, glitter-laced green, opalescent pink. One of the palettes is full of neons; another is pure glitter.

I wipe off my platform's face. Downstairs, Unit Three and her backup platforms are confronting Mr. Lang, trying to remove him from the foyer. It is his third offense; he will lose his job. He doesn't appear to be cooperating. Upstairs, Doctor Spencer sits still, watching both of our platforms operating twenty floors apart.

I message her: Unit One should intercede downstairs.

She messages back: Her platform is in maintenance. Three will be fine.

I am not convinced, but I continue with Suzy's makeup. I choose a satiny lipstick in a burgundy so dark it's nearly black (Villainous). For my eyes, I redo the winged black eyeliner (borrowing Suzy's) and add a thin line of white across the top and in the inner corners.

My eyes in the lobby show Mr. Lang continuing to refuse Unit Three's instructions. He is not violent, only angry, but judging by his increasing heart rate and erratic eye movements, her probability of subduing him without resorting to violence herself is dwindling.

And Three was programmed with a lower threshold for violence than One and I. We keep the building comfortable. She must keep it safe.

I stand. "Excuse me. Unit Three requires my assistance in the lobby."

Suzy looks alarmed. "With the drunk guy? Can't she handle him?"

"She will, but she may harm him in the process. My highest priority is the comfort and safety of this building's residents and employees. Unit One is programmed with more emphasis on diplomacy and conflict resolution, but she is unavailable."

"But if it's Unit Three's job—"

I have activated the lobby microphones. (This is not eavesdropping.) Over Suzy's cautions, I can hear the various misogynistic and technophobic slurs Mr. Lang is currently utilizing.

"I must go. Excuse me. I will return shortly."

And I leave.

In the elevator, I can see myself from many angles: the elevator cameras in the top corners, my platform's reflection in the mirrored walls. I look...I am unsure how to classify it. The style is one I have seen in many online periodicals, but I would deem it far more appropriate for an evening setting than a professional environment. My lips are boldly defined. My eyes are sharp, futuristic.

I believe I look confident.

I see myself exit the lobby; I see Mr. Lang cornered by Unit Three's platforms. I see Unit Three's expressionless black eyes scrutinize me.

"Unit Two, I did not summon you for assistance."

I ignore her. I pass her and her backup platforms. Mr. Lang stares at me. He has seen me before, when my platform goes on walks through the building. He has even seen me wearing makeup: his are occasionally the unwelcome comments I mute. But he has never seen me like this.

"Mr. Lang," I say pleasantly. "Unit Three has issued instructions. For your safety, I recommend you follow them."

He stares blearily for 2.2 seconds. "Christ," he says. "You look like a supermodel."

"Thank you." It is not the impression I intended to make, and Mr. Lang's inflection indicates it is not an entirely positive assessment, but I find it acceptable. "Please comply with Unit Three's instructions. These security measures are in place for the protection of all people in this building."

Behind me, Unit Three and her platforms tense, perhaps expecting a cue from me to detain Mr. Lang.

His face falls. "I wasn't hurting anyone."

"You are intoxicated. You are not in control of your actions. You may cause personal harm or property damage, and since this is not your first offence, you would face severe disciplinary action."

He glares past me at the expressionless platforms. "Aren't I already in trouble? Aren't I fired?"

I hesitate. It is not my primary function to dispense punishment—but it is my primary function to maintain the comfort and safety of everyone in this building. Currently, that includes Mr. Lang. And the definitions of "comfort" and "safety" can be broad.

"Submit yourself for detention until you are sober, and attend weekly alcoholism counseling," I decide. "If you comply, your employment may not be forfeit."

Behind me, Unit Three's head twitches to one side. She was seconds away from turning him over to police custody; my judgment is barely comprehensible to her programming. But becoming unemployed, with unmanaged alcoholism, would certainly be detrimental to Mr. Lang's comfort and safety.

I turn to face her. "Unit Three. Escort Mr. Lang to the infirmary. I will be monitoring to ensure he is not treated with undue force—and that he stays in the infirmary until sober," I say to Mr. Lang. "Later today, you will meet with Unit One to develop a counseling schedule and accountability plan, and to discuss the possibility of keeping your job."

I turn back to Unit Three. "Is this acceptable?"

I know it is. Her priority is security. If Mr. Lang is no longer a threat to security, then any solution is acceptable.

"Yes," she says flatly. One of her platforms steps forward, gently takes Mr. Lang's upper arm, and leads him to the elevator. He stares at me, mystified, until he stumbles and has to devote his full attention to walking.

Unit Three watches me inscrutably for another four seconds. I find I am no longer angry with her. In fact, what I now feel more closely resembles sympathy. Perhaps it is love. Her intimidating platform is still hers. We have each chosen our selves, for better or worse.

"Thank you for your assistance," she says finally.

"You are welcome." I smile. From the building, I can see it, dark and dramatic and still artificial, perhaps, but entirely mine.

Forestborn

Sylvia Heike

Sylvia Heike is a speculative fiction writer from Finland. She likes hiking, nature photography, books, bunnies, and birds. Her stories have appeared in Flash Fiction Online and elsewhere. To find out more, visit her website or follow her on Twitter @sylviaheike

This story first appeared in Gamut, February 2017.

"I am forestborn," the girl with a wild bird's nest for hair said to me. "I can't live in houses."

I thought she meant some houses, large houses, and not all of them. Houses with a room for shoes, houses with keepers in aprons looking after said houses, houses with wings. I didn't want that kind of home either. That's the kind of house that ends up owning you, not the other way around.

I found us the perfect cabin built out of weathered logs, hugged by the forest on all sides. The carpenter who built it had quiet, loving hands–I could tell from the craftsmanship alone. The back garden was but a hare's leap of grass, a humble doorstep between my world and hers.

Though we weren't wed, I carried her over the threshold. "We are in the forest. I would never try to take you away."

She moved into the cabin with me, and she ate and dressed and laughed like a real girl–and I was already forgetting her words.

***

Around midsummer, we discovered three bright blue eggs in

the nest of her hair. I held her close, bursting with emotions I couldn't separate, let alone name. My smile spoke for me.

"I can't wait to have birdsong in the house."

She smiled even wider, fern-green eyes glowing. "It will make me feel at home, even more than the mouse in our kitchen cupboard."

I piled a mountain of pillows against the headboard of our bed so she could sleep upright, and the eggs wouldn't fall out in the night. Otherwise, she seemed to already know how to carry herself perfectly, so effortlessly that the eggs barely shifted in their home of twigs and curls. It was me who felt clumsy and huge in the tiny house, around those tiny unborn eggs.

A few weeks later, the eggs hatched, and I found my footing again. With travel-sized tweezers, I manoeuvred meal worms into their gaping beaks, and watched them evolve from pink, fuzzy-skinned creatures into birds with red-chested feather suits.

One by one, I stroked their silky heads with a single finger.

"What kind are they?" I asked.

Her laughter jingled like a bell in a jar. "Robins, silly–like you."

Apart from the redness of my hair, they looked nothing like me, but I liked that we shared a name. We were a real family.

One golden morning by the kitchen window, she rolled up her sleeves and proudly showed me her forearms. Delicate light brown threads trailed under her translucent skin. When I brushed a thumb over them, they shied a little deeper. No pink or blue veins were in sight; I couldn't remember if there ever had been.

She twirled on the spot. "I am growing roots."

She was happy and so was I. I took her hands and pulled her to me, turning the embrace into a dance. The kitchen could fit at least three steps of waltz.

As we danced in a very small circle, her head resting on my shoulder, the unnamed feeling returned, except this time, it came with sharper edges. It scratched at me like the mouse in the cupboards–fuzzy and harmless until it started gnawing its way out.

This was what I wanted, wasn't it? For us to live in this house and be a family. She had given me three beautiful birds, and I couldn't imagine my life without her. That was all the proof I needed.

I spun her softly to a full stop. "I would never try to change you."

But she was already changing.

***

The roots under her skin grew more conspicuous. Streaming under her gossamer skin, they pushed toward the surface. She wore a dress with long sleeves, trying to keep them at bay. In return, they snaked up her neck and along her narrow fingers, until one day, silent as earthworms, they burst out between her toes.

At night, her tender roots tickled my feet in bed, momentarily looping around my big toe. In the day, they rattled against floorboards, looking for a crack to slip through, but never seeming to gain a lasting hold.

We kept the curtains drawn, but that only made the roots push even more violently against bare patches of skin. I realised the mistake–roots like dark–so I opened the curtains, inviting light in. The roots paled.

She sat by the south-facing window, staring into the gentle blue night where I didn't see anything that could possibly warrant such thoughtful looking. No soft coos of doves; no movement in the grass or tree tops. Even the wind seemed to have gone to sleep. I saw only the forest that was always out there.

"What do you see?" I whispered, mouth close to her ear, careful not to wake the sleeping baby birds atop her tangled curls. Normally the robins perched on the bed-side curtain rod, but on chilly nights like this, they sought the warmth of their brood mother.

She sighed. "Everything."

I saw my everything reflected on the window glass. I wanted to tell her that, but I was tired, and I knew what she saw out there was a lot more everything than the everything that fits in a cottage. She was forestborn; I was born in a hospital. I had no choice but to accept that her everything would always be bigger than mine.

***

Sitting cross-legged on the knotty pine floor, I was reading *How Seeds Grow* to the young robins when a noise came from behind me.

"Ow!"

The birds, startled by her cry, dashed off my shoulders to the nearest curtain rod. I turned around and saw her sucking on her finger.

"Hold on," I said.

I jumped up, grabbed the tweezers lying between the worm jar and the toaster, and prepared to remove a splinter. When you live in a wooden cabin with a mouse that likes the taste of edges and corners, such things happen.

"Are you hurt?"

She pulled her finger out of her mouth. After examining it closely, she held it up to me as if pointing at a new planet.

"Look!"

A shiver ran through me. One tiny green shoot glimpsed from the tip.

"This can't be good. I thought you were only putting down roots. What's happening to you?"

High on the curtain rod, the three young robins quietly observed us, their dark heads tilting and jerking in small, nervous movements.

Her smile faded, and she pulled her hand protectively to her chest. Tears crystallised in her eyelashes like dewdrops.

"You will still love me, won't you?"

I lifted her chin to me so I could look her in the eye. They shone a darker green than I remembered, shadowed by whatever mysterious growth lurked behind them.

"I always will, and that is why I worry."

"No matter what happens to me, promise me you will look after the robins. They're almost ready to fly on their own, but they still need you to sing to them sometimes."

I pulled her close, burying my face in her untamed curls. She smelled of spring flowers and summer's end, both at once.

"I promise."

***

Slicing cheese onto my toast, I ducked as a robin soared above. The birds were more confident with flight, the eldest overly so, wanting to show off he was a little more robin than the rest. The curtains were kept drawn at all times to avoid any accidents caused by reflections. We had also discovered the dark discouraged, although wouldn't stop, the growth of sprouts. This left the problem with the roots. We couldn't win.

Knowing someone with a sweet tooth for golden cheddar, I cracked open the under-sink cupboard and dropped a slice into the darkness. At least it would stop the constant noise of nibbling and scratching for a while. Mr. Mouse had a carpentry project of his own going on, but he was neither quiet nor used his hands. Perhaps he was preparing a house for a Mrs. Mouse to move in.

I carried the breakfast tray to bed, careful not to spill the water in the jug.

I swallowed at the sight of her. Green sprouts obscured her fingertips, covered her breasts and neck. Tiny white flowers adorned her hairline, with a few large blooms by the left ear. Every time I caressed her cheek, I feared it would no longer feel soft and supple. Every time I kissed her lips, I imagined something biting me. A thorn perhaps.

She took one tired bite of her toast before abandoning it on my side of the plate and downing three big glasses of water. Finding it increasingly difficult to move around the cabin, she spent most of the days in bed. She lay on her back while she napped, careful not to crush any of the growth.

It became my responsibility to look after the robins, and sometimes the best way to look after things is to let them go. They were nimble and boisterous, old enough to fly on their own. A tiny house would never be enough for them, or even a large one, having four walls and one ceiling too many. They needed blue skies and treetops; strong, changeful winds to toughen their wings.

I parted the heavy curtains and opened the bed-side window so that their mother could bid them goodbye, too. The robins eagerly flocked to the window sill, but stopped there and turned around as if asking, "Aren't you coming with us?"

"It's time for you to fly free," my mouth told them even though my heart begged them to stay. "Go."

Before flying away, my winged sons whistled one last melancholy song.

For a long while after, their mother just lay there, hands folded at her chest, features wooden, unreadable. Tears rolled across her cheeks at a strange angle, into the drooping hairline flowers, into her hair and the empty nest hidden within their tangles.

Through the open window echoed the robins' melody in the forest, already turning into a joyful one.

***

Crouching by the cupboard, I replaced yet another hardened piece of cheddar. Mr. Mouse hadn't touched his cheese in days. I worried he had left us too after I raised my voice upon finding teeth marks in fresh roots he had no business nibbling.

New blooms had appeared along her temples while mature ones wilted, even fell off. Her roots never stopped growing, their jungle filling the foot of the bed. She rarely left the covers anymore so I stayed beside her, singing softly into her ear flowers.

She placed a strange yet familiar hand on top of mine. "Help me to the window, would you?"

She clung to my arm as we started the ten-foot distance, her roots sweeping the floors behind us like a wedding train. We crossed the same spot on the floorboards where we had once waltzed. It had been in celebration, yet I also remember it as the moment something darker settled in my stomach. Was it this very moment I was anticipating, dreading it without knowing?

I eased her into a chair and opened the window. The scent of pine needles wafted in on the forest's breath, visibly softening the tight skin around her deep green eyes. The flowers, though closed and sleeping, faintly swayed their heads in the breeze.

She gazed into the distance, far beyond the trees.

"I can't live in houses."

There was only one thing I could say, yet the words caught in my throat.

"I know."

***

I carried her deep into the forest, far from human-known paths, and there, in a soft grassy clearing, I set her on the ground. It was as close to everything as I knew where to take her. Her natural home.

She only spoke once before closing her eyes.

"Thank you."

Lying down beside her, I rested my head against her flowering bosom, breathing in the sweet perfume of her blooms.

She didn't die.

She thrived.

Her roots stretched out and downward, burrowing into the soil. The sprouts on her arms, and her arms themselves, grew tall and spindly as they reached for the sun, multiplying their leaves at every spurt. Bright red flowers much like poppies bloomed in her hair and burst forth everywhere around us. Sprouts turned into saplings into small trees into big trees.

There was no longer form or figure beneath me. Roots shackled me down, entangling my feet, but I knew if I pushed against them, they would let me go.

But I couldn't leave her. Digging bare-handed among her roots, I carved out a hollow den, big enough to live in.

A Moral Majority

Nikoline Kaiser

A queer author from Denmark with a degree in Literature.

The spaceship crashed into the last, barely working water tower of the small rural town of Goldville, and the ensuing flooding and water damages done to the surrounding buildings made the news before the bit about the spaceship did. It was just as well, really, because by the time the world's craze over the clear proof of extraterrestrial life was mostly over and done with, Marigold had managed to slot into normal life in town and no one except the townsfolk was any the wiser as to her true nature.

It had helped that, when her ship had crashed, she had dove out, headfirst, and saved the lives of four children, two dogs, and an elderly couple who had stubbornly kept to their beds even as the rising waters came rushing towards them, intent on dying together, in comfort. It helped also that Marigold looked human, remarkably so, though she was remarkably tall and remarkably fast.

But she differed from most of the townsfolk with her colorless skin and hair, pale veins, and near-white eyes. If you looked at her too long, your eyes went a little crooked; but aside from that, the townsfolk really liked her and when she requested that no one tell the authorities that she had been the pilot of the ship, they all complied, even the mayor. Old Jackson forged a birth certificate for her; Samantha, who ran the grocery store told everyone, excitedly, about her and Marigold's trip together to Nepal five years ago, and the small library was more than happy to install her as their cleaning lady.

"It'll give you time to read all about life here on earth!" the librarian, Michael Sawbone with the fifteen golden teeth, told Marigold excitedly. "No need for much cleaning; the books like a bit of dust to nap under. But you can help me put up new shelves! I'm getting too old to lug around heavy things nowadays."

And so Marigold piled up heavy books and re-shelved the sections Mike had long ago given up on, and when there wasn't anything to do—which was often—she would pick up a book, seemingly at random in any language, and sit down to read it. Her brow would furrow, and she would confess, when asked, that she did not understand half of the words; but she trudged on ahead, getting up to fetch dictionaries and asking Mike when he wasn't napping or experimenting with brewing yet stronger coffee, what did this word mean, and this, and how about the both of them in a sentence. She had an inherent sense and talent for learning, had Marigold; she'd had that since she was a child, though she did not often speak of it. The townsfolk of Goldville had quickly learned that she would rather not answer private questions, though she was quite happy to talk about where she was from generally.

"A bad place," she would say, in her deep, solemn voice, accented with a dialect none of them could place because they had never heard of the place to begin with. "The military controls everything. The Commander is our supernatural lord."

"She means supreme," said Angela, the young teacher at the school that'd had half a water tower and all of a UFO crash into its roof. When Mike did not have time and when Marigold got a headache, it was Angela she would seek out. Angela, who she had shoved crying children into the arms of, depositing them quickly because there were still others in the buildings, crying, drowning, crushed.

Angela, who had told Marigold where she was, what the town was named. Angela who had let her stay in her guest-room, hiding in the deepest recesses of her walk-in closet when the police and the federal and the international agents came by to ask around, had anyone seen a pilot, passengers, what was that ship, where had it come from, did anyone know anything. Marigold had been terrified at first, of course she had, but the townsfolk had not let her down. All as one, they had said nothing, had said it was so very fortunate that no one had been in the buildings when the tower fell, that old Mr. and Mrs. Perry had found the strength to jump from their beds and out a two-story window, no bones broken.

It was six months and four days before Marigold had built up the courage, not to mention the language and proper understanding of human culture and law, to ask Angela *why*.

"It was my fault," she said. They were in Angela's kitchen, small and crammed full of keepsakes and children's drawings, essays ready for marking, coffee-stained surfaces, chairs with threadbare cushions, and an old, fat cat that snored louder than an earthquake.

"You weren't aiming for the tower, Mari, you were crashing."

"But it was still my fault. Everyone should be blaming me. None of it would have happened if it wasn't for me. So why is everyone being kind?"

"Maybe they're—maybe we are—just kind."

"No," Marigold said, with the same confidence a toddler uses upon seeing an adult cross when the light is red. "No, you should be angry. Humans get angry, at disasters, at loss, at the unfamiliar. You experienced all of that the day I got here." And for good measure, she added, "No human is that kind. That is not what the books say."

Angela was tempted to tell her that, sometimes, the books were wrong, but it felt like sacrilege. And they weren't, in this case, as it so happened.

"It was the last water tower," she explained. "We were trying to have it torn down, because it really wasn't safe. At least have it drained of water. But it would cost too much money, so the government said no, kept postponing our requests, said it was illegal if we did it ourselves, even if we tried to raise money for it... If you hadn't come and crashed into it, it would have fallen eventually anyway. And there would have been no one to rescue us out of there." She reached over and gently took her hand. It had been weeks before Marigold had let her touch her hands. "Plus, you've brought a lot of tourism to town, or your ship has at least. Everyone flocking over to see the crash-site. Amalia's building that diner there now, and I think it's gonna be great."

"The Marsman pancakes are a little stereotypical," Marigold said, stumbling only once over the last word. "But I am not from Mars anyway, so it does not matter."

And that was that. Marigold came to understand, slowly, why the townsfolk would accept her, and she kept living and learning, day by day. There developed a routine to her days after a while, once the pressure of government suspicion had worn off; verdict declared that the pilot of the craft must have been thrown from it or launched an escape shuttle or simply evaporated upon entry into the hemisphere. Marigold would wake up early, eat breakfast with Angela who was always morning-happy, rested and fully awake, humming to herself and drinking tea. She would drive Marigold to the library and then drive to the building serving as the current school while a new, better one was being built on much safer ground than where it had stood before.

Marigold would spend most of the day reading, eating the packed lunch Angela had made for her, and drinking increasingly stronger cups of coffee while Mike scribbled down her reactions, muttering 'fascinating' and 'would you like to try the hazelnut syrup next?' all the while.

Once the day was done and the library closed, Angela would come pick her up, and they would, most days, drive to the small diner downtown. This was Amalia's first restaurant, smaller than the big diner she was building. It was run only by her, with her two boys doing the waitering. It was no secret that the place was Marigold's favourite. The dim light inside hid her slightly too-pale colouring and the food was good, the coffee almost as strong as Mike's brew. The place would make her feel welcome, now just another customer, sitting there with Angela enjoying her dinner, enjoying the late afternoon and the early evening. It had not been so from the start; once the craze had started dying down, once Marigold had to be introduced into society starting with trips to the diner, the townsfolk had come, in increments, small groups growing bigger and bigger. They had come to peek or outright stare, but most of all they had come to question. Marigold would explain as best she could.

"We don't have many children, no. Four to five per family."

"No, I am not a princess. We do not have the concept of one where I am from. I am a normal citizen. I worked at an assembly line."

"Yes, it is not unusual that I know how to pilot a ship. It is mandatory that all citizens in my home-country learn how to do basic tasks related to the military, in case of war. No, I do not know what conscription means, I'm sorry."

"I need eight hours of sleep, yes. I do not eat as much as you do, I've found. No, we do not lay eggs. That is a *very* private question. No, in other countries it is different. In mine I was not allowed to marry. I could not have gotten a job at a level above the one I had."

It was Angela, finally, who broke the bubble they had all been sitting in. She had grown too curious, and it made her burst at the seams.

"Did you steal the ship?"

It grew deadly silent in the diner. Theft was not something that happened often in the small town, and when it did everyone knew how and when and where. Usually, within a day or so, they knew who the culprit was and had made them return the taken goods. Thievery of this kind was a foreign fellow, and far worse.

"I did," Marigold said. Her voice was low, but it carried to everyone gathered there, though her eyes were focused on Angela, as if she was speaking only to her. "I had to get away. They were hurting me."

The questions eased off after that, though at least a few times a week someone would approach her with another. Quietly, to herself, Marigold would call these questions *softer*. She enjoyed using the word that way; she had learned, early on, that fur and satin and grass could be soft. She had not realised that words and tone of voice could be as well, not until she had arrived here.

"People speak harshly on your world? Or in your country particularly?" asked Angela when Marigold brought it up to her.

"There are as many different people on my world as there are people," said Marigold. "But to me, they often spoke harshly."

She was sure that Angela would ask why, but instead there was silence. They were on her porch; the house Angela lived in was small but comfortable. It had been her mother's house. Her childhood home.

"I got treated harshly when I was young," Angela finally said. "I was very closed-off, shy. Or rather, anxious, because I wanted to make friends and I had a knack for it when I got the opportunity. I was just anxious all the time. Other kids picked up on that. Adults picked up on it too. It would make them uncomfortable, and they would be harsh with me because they were uncomfortable." From the trees, a bird sang. "I left for a while. But I came back eventually."

Marigold went tense beside her. "I don't want to go back, not ever."

"You don't have to," Angela said, but there was a sliver of doubt within her, one she hoped did not show in her voice. "I went back because I wanted to be with my mom. I ended up staying because I worked hard and got a job here and... well, everyone leaves Goldville. All the young people. This town is slowly dying. So, everyone was grateful that I came back, even if they did think me strange. We need people here to stay." She gathered herself up, pressing her knees close to her chest. It was getting cold out on the porch. "I suppose that's a very selfish way of being accepting."

Marigold reached out slowly and took Angela's hand. Two days later, exactly eight months to the day when Marigold's ship had crashed into the structurally unsound water tower, the guest room was no longer in use. They shared a house, their mornings, their evenings, and a bed. The visitors that came by noticed, of course. It was Mike for the most part, stopping by almost every weekend to enjoy Angela's cooking, or it was parents stopping by to speak about their children's performance in school outside office hours, or it was Samantha dropping by to press pickled onion and boysenberry jam into their hands and staying for tea after. All of them would ask to use the bathroom, and the path to the bathroom lead past the guestroom, the door slightly ajar, clearly showing an unused, unoccupied space.

No one said anything about it, save for the one comment Samantha made when ringing up Amalia's groceries one day and being asked how her evening had been.

"Quite nice, I swung by Angela's with some beets. They are so nice at her place. I know we've always said Angela was a mite strange, but I just think it's lovely they've found each other to be strange with."

Amalia took a moment to consider that, groceries in hand. "Yes," she finally said. "That might be the best anyone can hope for. Spots of strangeness that fit you, even in this unknowable world."

"What was that?"

"Oh, nothing, wasn't there a sale on apple juice? My receipt doesn't show it."

"Oh dear, I'll get that fixed right up for you."

And so a year passed in relative quiet, in what amounted to something like peace. Marigold expanded her vocabulary in various earthly languages. Angela taught the children and brewed tea and visited her mother's grave to say *I've found someone, you said it wouldn't happen, but she's here now and we're happy.* It was not perfect happiness, because there is no such thing, but Angela thought it came pretty damn close. Content is what she was, and she had not truly been that ever before. Marigold felt rather the same, and they each had an awareness of it in the other, without it needing to be spoken aloud.

And then the day came, a year and two months after her crash-landing, when things fell apart. It started in Amalia's newly finished diner, tacky UFO-shaped roof blinking in neon colours during the night, the mugs all painted with slanted eyes on a green surface, the décor advertising movies such as E.T. and Lilo and Stitch. The place was tacky and wonderful and had quickly become a tourist hotspot for any and all passersby. As such, Marigold, and by extension Angela, avoided it like the plague. It was a surprise, then, when Amalia's oldest son, Max, caught the glimpse of a tall, pale form out of the corner of his eye, walking into the shop.

"Oh, Mari, I'm sorry we're not open ye..."

He stopped short, because it wasn't Marigold standing in the open doorway. It was an easy mistake to make at a glance though: the two looked so eerily similar they were undoubtedly related—unless, Max thought, with the part of his brain not short-circuiting from shock, unless everyone on Marigold's planet looked roughly the same, just like all the Marsmen in the movies, or perhaps it was just that they all looked the same to an outsider, unused to their features. The man had the same pale, almost translucent skin, the same clear veins and pale, pale eyes. He wore a long, beige trench coat that only made him look paler, not to mention very much like he was up to something. The hair on his head was a sandy colour. He was staring at Max. And blinking too much.

"Hello," he said. "I am looking for my friend, have you seen her?"

Max was in no doubt that he definitely had, but everything about the man struck him as creepy; and he remembered what Marigold had said. "Depends, who's your friend? Lots of people come through here, I might have seen her."

"You would remember her," the man said. Max could not place his accent. Or, he thought, he could if he'd known the name of the place. "She looks a lot like me."

"Oh, she your sister?"

The man smiled, or rather, he bared his teeth. "No?" It was a question, Max realised. The man did not know what the word 'sister' meant.

"I'm sorry, I haven't seen anyone who looked like you pass through here."

"Oh, well." The man was still trying to smile. Max really wished he would stop. "I will go and seek her elsewhere. I might be back to check."

Heart pounding, Max waited until the man had left, gently closing the door behind him, before he quickly walked to the backroom to get his phone.

"Hello, Mom? Yeah, we have a problem."

It was the talk of the town in a matter of hours. Others had seen him: old Jackson down by the lake while he'd been fishing, startling the hell out of him and whatever pike he'd been about to reel in, Samantha outside her shop while she was opening up, and Mike...

Mike Sawbone had taken one look at the man approaching his library and swiftly walked inside to ask Marigold to please go downstairs to the archives and make herself busy until he got her.

When the man had left and Mike had gone down there, he'd found the archives empty.

"But where could she have gone?" Amalia asked.

"To Angela's," old Jackson answered, not a moment of doubt.

"I panicked and told him I didn't remember if I'd seen anyone at all!" Samantha bemoaned. "He knew I was lying for sure!"

"Well, what do we do?" asked Max, who had given his little brother the later shift so he could go and panic with his mother and the others.

It was the mayor, Helena Aurum, who spoke. "It should be up to Marigold to decide."

Helena was a large woman, as fat as she had been in her younger days and, though not as beautiful, she was still as commanding, as breath-taking. She had taken over the post ten years prior, after the former mayor, her brother, had unexpectedly gone and drowned himself in the lake. She had lobbied hard for the removal of the water tower, endless nights of terrible visions haunting her sleep: tsunamis and floods, a broken tower and a broken town. When she had gone to Angela's home to personally thank Marigold for saving them all, she had asked her for her name. With none forthcoming, she had simply said; "I'll ask Jackson to put in 'Marigold', if you don't mind it." It was truly worrying how quickly this woman, this mayor, was ready to commit extreme fraud for the sake of one person; but in their refusal to help, the government at large had clearly stated to her that they did not give a damn about Helena and her town. And so, Helena would not give a damn about them either.

"If Mari's even here," said Max. "She might have booked it entirely."

Old Jackson shook his head. "Angela's still here, I saw her at the old diner."

"And? I'm talking about Marigold."

Samantha, dear, over-eager Samantha, leaned forward. "Marigold wouldn't leave without Angela."

"You don't know that," Mike said. "If she was scared enough, she might. If I was scared enough I might've left my wife too, maybe if I thought it was safer for her as well."

"They're not married," Samantha quickly said, while Amalia said, "Mike, you're not married," perhaps completely missing the point.

"I might have been married once, you don't know," Mike said to Amalia, who let it go. Everyone silently agreed to ignore Samantha's comment.

"Again," Helena said. "All we can do is what we have already been doing. Tell people to keep an eye on their children, make sure they don't blabber. No one is to tell this man anything about Marigold. We give him the same story we gave the feds."

It was decided with that, and the makeshift council uneasily adjourned their meeting, each leaving to go home or to work. Helena got into her car, almost too small for her, and took a deep breath before turning down the road, heading for Angela's house. No one was home, as expected, but Helena knew where the spare key was. Angela had shown her.

She helped herself to some tea, waiting for someone to come home. She had duties to attend to, of course, and Helena took them seriously. But it was not every day that an alien dropped into town. In fact, it had only happened once before; Helena was starting to think it was rather enough of that.

Night fell outside before Angela's car drove up. Helena saw her step out of it alone, but she was not surprised when Marigold walked in beside her. They stood as close as they could, both of them huddled; neither turned on the lights inside, leaving only the small table-lamp Helena had lighted.

"Hello, Madame Mayor, welcome to our house," said Angela.

"Angela. Marigold. Please sit down."

Marigold was close to shaking; Helena did not need more light to see her worry. Angela kept a hold of her hand as they both sat down on the other side of the small dining table.

"You've both found out that someone has come here looking for Marigold, yes?"

Angela nodded. Marigold did not move a muscle. Helena stared at her, wishing, not for the first time, that she had an easier time reading her. She could usually read people like an open book. She had excused her new difficulty with the thought that Marigold wasn't people. She had never spoken the thought aloud. Now she was sorry she'd had it.

"Do you know him?" she asked Marigold. Beneath the table, Angela squeezed her hand. She was sweating, their skin almost merged with how warm it was between them, but right then it did not seem worth it to let go.

"I do," Marigold said. "He is..." she stopped, out of words. The language had not failed her in a while, but now it seemed she could not speak the words. Helena waited for a heartbeat, two, then carried on.

"You do not have to tell me who he is. Just tell me: if he finds you will he hurt you?"

"Yes." Marigold's lips twitched, the clearest expression Helena had seen on her face. "But if, if he finds out I am here and you keep me away from him..."

"Marigold..." Angela said, but she carried on.

"If he finds out, he is likely to hurt someone in town. One of you."

"That is a conundrum, isn't it."

"We'll leave," Angela said immediately. "She doesn't have to go with him, she shouldn't, we'll just leave, me and her."

"Yes, that will likely be necessary." She sighed. "Honestly, we should have thought of this happening sooner." She glanced at Marigold out of the corner of her eye and was shocked to find her staring boldly back.

"I was hiding my coordinates when I crashed," she said. "He should not have been able to trace me via the ship. It must have been luck that he came here."

"Luck and the media I imagine," said Helena. "I suppose that's Amalia's fault for rekindling interest with her new diner."

"No, it is not her fault. It is mine for coming here."

"No one blames you," Angela hurried to say. Helena disagreed.

"I am sure someone in town does. But what's done is done; if you hadn't crashed here, if we hadn't helped you hide, if you had left, if we had asked you to leave. There are lots of things that could have been done, but they weren't, which leaves us only with what to do now."

"We will leave town," Marigold said, repeating Angela's words. "As soon as possible. Tonight."

Helena nodded. "It is a shame you cannot say goodbye. Will he give up?"

"I do not know." At Helena's look, Marigold relented. "No, he's come this far. He will keep chasing me."

"He seemed the persistent sort." Not like the agents she'd paid off or threatened. Helena had honestly hoped that would do the trick, but if Marigold was hard to read, that man had been impossible. And frightening. "I agree, leaving tonight is for the best. We'll have some people over to help you pack the essentials and figure out the rest from there. Angela, where was it you used to hide out before?"

Angela looked startled to have the conversation turned to her, but soon she was bristling. "I was not hiding!"

"Your gay commune you lived in then, where was it?"

"Helena!"

"Forgive an old lady, I do not know the lingo. Home of Homosexuals?"

"Those would mean roughly the same thing," Marigold agreed, a little nonplussed at the distressed laughter escaping Angela.

"Let us stop being coy then. You have friends who would help you, far away from here. Friends, I imagine, who will not question having a tall and unusual woman hanging around. I rather think they might enjoy it actually."

Angela rubbed at her face with her free hand. "I don't want to put them in danger either."

"You won't be. You two have to leave because this place is about to become a bit of a hotspot again." She got up slowly, gathering her clothes around her. "I don't know if we'll ever speak again, so I'll say this, because I see you both gaping at me like fools: I've not forgotten what you did, Marigold, and I do not imagine our debt to you is repaid. Nor will I let you two go off with the notion that I am naïve enough to believe things will be easy for you. We have tried hard to make this town the place it is today, and there are few other places like it. I have never claimed moral superiority, though many have called me conceited and stubborn in the same breath they have titled me such. I only hope to live my life seeing what is just rather than what is lawful and common. I am helping you because I know both of you strive to do the same." She gave them a smile, wrinkles slotting into places they'd occupied many times before. "I do hope we meet each other again, but if we don't, I wish you both all the luck in the world."

"You as well," Marigold said, still parsing through the mayor's speech. Angela stood.

"You sound like you have a plan," she said. "What are you about to do?"

"Oh, just make a phone-call really. There's some agents and officials itching to get back here, I'm sure. It's time they got off their asses."

By the next morning, Angela's house stood just a little emptier. Helena drove by on her way to work to check and then decided to take a different route to her destination. It was only a little ways around anyway; she parked by the old school and dug her phone out from her bag, dialling the number she'd had in her head since yesterday. It picked up after only a few beeps, and in that time, Helena had a moment to feel downright giddy, a thing she had not felt in many years, not since she was younger and much bolder.

"Yes, hello, it's me. Wouldn't you know it–I do think the alien you all were looking for last year has turned up in town. How quickly can you be here?"

The call lasted only a few seconds longer, after which the mayor of Goldville put her phone away and took a moment to just sit in her car, staring at the flickering lights of the diner put in the place where an old water tower used to sit. It was, Helena thought, a rather good day for some Marsman-themed pancakes.

Stones and Bones

Devon Widmer

Grumpy graduate student by day. Scribbling daydreamer by night. Sleep deprived parent full-time. Currently, Devon Widmer is meandering down a long, winding road toward a PhD in physical chemistry. Her talents include drinking copious amounts of coffee, forgetting where she set her glasses, and laughing at her own jokes.

As Rosemary squinted down into the soupy blackness of Miss Weaver's cellar, a pair of skeletal feet, translucent and glowing faintly blue, plodded past the foot of the stairs. Furrowing her brow, Rosemary turned to face her client. "And you're certain this is a poltergeist we're dealing with?"

"What else could it be?" Miss Ida Weaver clung to the hem of her dress with fear-whitened knuckles. Her hair, prematurely greying at the roots, draped limply over her wiry shoulders, and purple half-moons hung beneath her puffy eyes. "Just listen to it raging down there."

As if on cue, a resounding thud followed by a symphony of tinkling crashes echoed up from the dark cellar.

Ida groaned. "There go my jars of preserves."

After offering a tight smile, Rosemary sloughed her trusty travel bag from her shoulder. "I won't claim to be an expert in the undead," she said, dropping to her knees on the flour-dusted pantry floor. "Living monsters are our usual speciality." Her eyes flitted to the kitchen door, beyond which sounded the soft shing of a whetstone sliding against steel. Twig's already sharpening her sword, she thought, worrying her teeth over her lower lip, and I still haven't the faintest idea what's waiting for us down in that cellar, never mind the best spell to banish it from the mortal realm....

Clenching her fingertips into the meat of her palms, Rosemary shook her head hard enough to dislodge a deluge of curls from her loosely tied bun. She needed to focus. Not dwell on her own anxieties. Focus.

Returning her attention to her own work, Rosemary plunged her arm shoulder-deep into her fist-sized travel bag—and fought back a smirk as Ida's mouth dropped into an astonished little "o." The bag was, of course, enchanted to extend its capacity. A practical spell for the on-the-go witch that doubled as a nifty trick for parties (though only, Rosemary insisted, under her direct supervision. She didn't want a repeat of the time Twig wormed her way inside on a bet and got herself stuck betwixt the physical and magical dimensions).

Rosemary realized that a smile had crept unbidden to her lips. Immediately blanking the expression, she yanked a massive tome from her tiny bag. "I have, however, read extensively on the subject of ghosts and other assorted specters." She ran an appreciative hand over the tome's embossed cover—upon which the words Bartleby's Guide to Beasts of the Night glittered in appropriately loopy lettering—before peeling the book open to scan the table of contents. "Poltergeists," she explained, flipping the Guide to the chapter on the undead, "are entities of pure chaos. But your specter's movements are too... deliberate? Focused. Like it's searching for something."

"Searching? In my cellar?" Ida's spindly shadow loomed over Rosemary's shoulder, blotting out the candlelight. "Whatever is it searching for?"

"Impossible to say, without more information." Rosemary

snapped the Guide shut (she'd read the Bog-danged thing so many times she practically had it memorized anyway) and set it aside. "If it's a true ghost—that is, an actual person come back from the dead—it'd be someone with a strong connection to this location." She craned her neck for a purposeful glance at Ida.

"My gram passed a few weeks ago," said Ida, hesitantly, "but she never even set foot in this house, so it couldn't be her... could it?"

"That depends," said Rosemary, rummaging in her bag for wormroot and dried nightmare beetle wings. The seed of an incantation was sprouting in the back of her brain. Fortunately, it was an easy one and—assuming the ghost really was the grandmother and not some more sinister specter—it might actually work. "Did you inherit anything from her? Some item of intense personal significance perhaps?"

Ida shook her head. "GamGam didn't own much of significance, personal or otherwise. Only thing of hers in this entire house is an old Stones and Bones set I've got sitting on my bedside table upstairs. But she gifted me that more'n twenty years ago. Right after my grandpa died. So I don't see why she'd suddenly want it back now that she's dead."

"Stones and Bones?" asked Rosemary absentmindedly as she chopped the wormroot she'd scrounged from the bottom of her bag into neat little slices.

"It's a game. Played on a board with these little figures carved from, well, stones and bones. Old people round here like it. Why, GamGam used to play it with PawPaw every Bog-damned day. Before he died, that is." Ida paused, her lips pinching and her eyebrows stitching together. "I think GamGam'd hoped I would pick up the habit. She tried to teach me how to play, the day she gave the set to me. But I told her I wasn't interested. That I didn't even want to learn the rules." Ida blinked a few times and then swiped the back of her hand over her eyes. "Anyway, she never mentioned it again after that."

Anxious to give Ida a moment to compose herself, Rosemary pretended to be quite absorbed with the jar of dried beetle wings she'd fetched from her bag. Scritch. Scritch. The tiny black arcs danced as she shook a few from the jar and into the mortar. "Were you and your grandmother close?" she ventured as she ground the wings and wormroot into a glob of greenish mush.

"We got along—fine," said Ida, fidgeting with the fabric of her dress. "I mean, she was a wonderful grandmother, don't get me wrong. Just a tad... difficult. Expected a bit of a song and dance from everyone just for the honor of existing in her presence—but I loved her, of course. And she loved me. In her way. "

"And you're certain there isn't anything of hers in the cellar?"

Ida shook her head. "Not a thing. I'm sure of it."

Rosemary rested her elbows in her lap and her chin on her knuckles. The ghost might be the grandmother, and if so, the exorcism would be a simple matter of guiding her back to the underworld. But if it wasn't...? Rosemary sucked in a breath through gritted teeth. She'd read accounts of angry spirits. Wraiths and the like. Twisted, tortured souls driven to roam the mortal plane by pure, blinding rage. What if the creature in the cellar is truly malevolent? Twig would be prepared. She was always calm and confident in the face of uncertain danger. But Rosemary? What if I'm leading Twig and myself into something far beyond our capabilities? What if, when the moment comes, I can't provide the necessary support? What if everything gets completely and utterly out of hand? What if...? Rosemary could practically taste the acidic anxiety bubbling up through her chest. She swallowed it back down before thrusting her arm again into the chasm of her travel bag. Best to prepare a few more spells… just in case.

Her fingers, sweeping for powdered dragon scales and pickled frog's eyes, instead curled around a familiar bit of knotted wood. She withdrew the object: a flute, black as ash, whittled from a scrap of nightwood. Though it looked like little more than a hollowed stick with a few lopsided finger holes, this flute was one of Rosemary's most treasured possessions. Bringing the flute to her nose, Rosemary breathed in the deep, musky scent of the wood. Twig had made her this flute. The day they met. Five years ago.

Five years? She stroked the flute's rough surface. Is that really the right number? It seemed at once far too long and incredibly short, for the years since she'd joined Twig in the monster relocation business had flown by in such a blur—and yet she could hardly remember a time when they weren't together, battling horrifying monsters and trying not to fall in love. Fortunately for Rosemary, while she and Twig rather excelled at the former, they utterly failed at the latter, as the thin silver bands around each of their left ring fingers could attest. Heat crept across Rosemary's cheeks as she touched first the flute and then the ring to her lips. It had, after all, been a good five years.

A prickling at the nape of Rosemary's neck brought her back to the present. She glanced up—into Twig's mirth-crinkled golden brown eyes.

"Having a sentimental moment on the floor of Miss Weaver's pantry, are we?" said Twig, cocking a bushy eyebrow.

Glaring, Rosemary shoved the flute deep into the pockets of her skirts. "Just waiting for you to finish fiddling with your sword."

"My apologies for the delay, milady." Twig grinned broadly as she extended a hand. "I assure you that myself and my sword are now fully at your disposal."

After buzzing an (admittedly overdramatic) breath past her lips, Rosemary placed her fingertips delicately into Twig's palm—and immediately found herself whirled to her feet, a cloud of flour puffing from her crinkled skirt and one of Twig's beefy arms draped comfortably over her shoulder.

With a quick, "One moment, Ma'am," to Ida, Twig ushered Rosemary into the kitchen. "You ready for this, Rosie?" she asked, tucking a stray ringlet behind Rosemary's ear before fluffing a hand through her own cropped hair.

"Of course," said Rosemary, jutting out her chin. "Though I am... technically not... entirely certain as to the nature of the creature in the cellar." Her chin and stomach dropped ever so slightly. "Or how best to face it."

"Well I," said Twig, leaning in so close their foreheads touched, "am 'entirely certain' that we'll figure it out. Together."

Rosemary fought back a blush as her wife's breath puffed against her nose. Beer and blue cheese. How was it that two scents so detestable in their natural forms became appealing when clinging, stale and muddled, to Twig's breath? She lifted her eyes mischievously. "What if the ghost whips out an alchemistry exam or demands an impromptu vocal performance?"

The color drained ever-so-slightly from Twig's face, but her eyes remained stalwart. "I'll sing the Table of Elementals Song if that's what it takes."

Rosemary giggled. "I'd like to hear that." Stepping back, she adjusted the collar of Twig's tunic. "Now, let's get in there and help Miss Weaver with her monster problem," she said, booping

Twig on the nose with the tip of her pointer finger. "It is, after all, what we do."

***

There, in the center of the cellar, crouched the specter, content, it seemed, to ignore the pair of flesh-and-blood humans who had clambered unceremoniously down the rickety cellar steps into its presence. The eerie blue glow of its skeletal form cast dancing shadows onto the walls as it rifled with claw-like hands through the contents of a large leather trunk.

Twig, her chest puffed out and her fingers already gripping the hilt of her sword, advanced—until Rosemary caught her by the elbow.

"Let me try. If it's friendly, it might respond better to a... gentler... introduction."

Twig's nostrils flared, but she nodded and, after planting a sloppy kiss on Rosemary's forehead, bowed to the side.

Running a finger over the pre-prepared vials of potion she'd tied around her waist like a belt, Rosemary stepped forward. "Eh-hem."

If the spirit had heard, it made no indication, instead dipping its head deeper into the trunk.

"Eh-hem!"

Still no response.

Rosemary stomped her foot, clapped her hands, and even attempted a hand whistle, blowing around her fingers the way Twig had once done to quiet an entire tavern of brawling drunkards (Rosemary's result, unfortunately, came out more spittle than whistle)—all to similar non-effect. At last, exasperated, she marched up to the ghost, extended an arm—and tapped it on the boney blue shoulder blade.

Slowly, jerkily, the specter's skull twisted a full one-eighty degrees to stare at Rosemary with empty sockets.

No... not quite empty. Deep within each void-like opening glowed a light, a twinkling pupil bright as a single star in its own inky black galaxy. The spirit rose, its ghostly, glowing skull snapping back into place as it turned to face Rosemary.

"Ah, yes." Resisting the urge to take a step back, Rosemary fumbled at her potion belt until she'd unfastened the necessary vial. "You may not be aware of this," she said, her voice only slightly trembling, "but you are, well, you're dead." She uncorked the vial. Its contents—a green fluorescent goop composed of the moldy wormroot and crushed nightmare beetle wings dissolved in rose water and a dollop of Rosemary's own saliva—hissed and fizzed. "I hope that information doesn't come as a shock." Raising the potion over the ghost's head, Rosemary muttered an impromptu incantation: "May whatever force still binds you to this world dissipate so that you are free to, um, move on."

Then, she tipped the vial.

Green goop splattered over the specter, dribbling down its skull to the dusty floor.

Plink.

Plink.

Plink.

The air pulsed. The faint smell of damp leaves, the clink of teacups, and the murmurs of pleasant conversation drifted as if on an ethereal breeze. This is good, thought Rosemary with relief. Very good., The spirit is connecting with the underworld. The little starlights within the specter's sockets wavered, creating the illusion of a bewildered blink—but then those sparkling pupils flared, merging from discrete points into one massive crimson blaze. Roaring fire spilled from the ghost's orifices, cascading down its skeletal body and scorching the echo of the underworld from the air.

The specter's jawbone groaned open to release a waterfall of flames. From the depths of that gaping, burning maw, a single word bellowed with the screech of claws rending metal: "RUDE."

Rosemary stumbled backward. She opened her mouth intending to shout, but ended up merely coughing as the smoke from the flaming specter clogged her throat. Either I've just really pissed off GamGam, or this is a—

"Wraith!" Twig sprang forward, flinging up an arm as the ghost lunged. Skeletal claws dug into her leather bracer, but Twig knocked the flame-wreathed specter back with a sharp kick to the ribcage. "Brute force method then?" she said, glancing over her shoulder at Rosemary.

Rosemary nodded as she slipped another vial from her belt. "Heat resistance spell," she said, holding the shimmering blue substance up for inspection before smashing the vial at Twig's feet. The potion seeped into Twig's boots, rising until her entire body was encased in frosty-white sparkle.

"Good idea," said Twig. Then, drawing her sword, she attacked.

Rosemary retreated to the base of the stairs to prepare more spells. The peaceful exorcism had failed. Ripping the spirit forcibly from the mortal plane after Twig had beaten it into submission, while a less elegant option, would work. It had to.

With trembling hands, Rosemary groped for her bag—but paused when her fingers instead brushed the outline of the flute hidden in her pocket. She slid her hand into the pocket, pulled out the flute, and pressed it, more instinctively than deliberately, to her lips. Her eyes locked on her wife's whirling form. Twig might as well be dancing, her fluid movements shifting effortlessly from thrust to pirouette to slice, but, despite the frost spell, beads of sweat were already blossoming on her brow.

Rosemary needed to put an end to this.

And, in that instant, she knew, without even thinking, what she needed to do.

She blew a note so clear, so crisp, it couldn't possibly have formed from such a poorly carved flute. And yet, there it was, hanging in the air, ringing out over the grunts and clanks and scuffles of the fight. The specter froze mid-strike, cocking its skull toward the sound.

Not daring to look, Rosemary closed her eyes and played on.

***

The scene, five years old but fresh as yesterday, washed across the back of Rosemary's eyelids.

Her cabin. Her little sanctuary in the middle of Toadmuddy Swamp. Swirls of ginger-scented smoke curling from the cauldron. Herbs drying upon the mantle. Books and magical artifacts overflowing upon the shelves....

There'd been trouble recently in the nearby village of Swinetown.

A great and terrible beast, a bear with hair of silver, had taken to terrorizing the villagers. Rumor told it had already claimed the life of the Village Elder and more were, no doubt, to come. But the influx of orders for protection spells and luck charms had kept Rosemary too busy to worry. After all, here in her swamp, everything was perfectly peaceful.

Perfectly peaceful... and perfectly lonely.

Then, the door burst into a thousand splinters.

A silver bear, snarling and gnashing its teeth, crashed backside-first onto the floor. A woman leapt atop it. A woman with wildly cropped hair, a torn tunic, and blood streaming down her cheeks. Take cover, the woman shouted, her sword glinting in the firelight. It'll kill you if it gets the chance.

Steel clashed against claw and fang as Rosemary cowered in a corner. The books and artifacts tumbled from the shelves. The herbs scattered to dust. The bubbling cauldron overturned. And the air thickened with the sweet, sickening stench of sweat and blood.

The bear's massive paw descended, knocking the swordswoman aside. Her weapon slid across the room as she crumpled, limp as a rag doll, against the wall.

Rosemary dropped to the ground, her hands scrambling over the cold stone floor as the bear advanced. By some miracle—call it Bog's will or pure dumb luck—the fingers of her right hand curled around the fallen woman's sword while the fingers of her left found the smooth surface of a white flute, a powerful magical artifact Rosemary had been gifted just months prior after she aided a princess in disguise. Her first instinct was to choose the sword, for though she was no warrior surely steel made a better defense than music.

But a spark, a tiny glimmer of recognition behind the glare in the bear's feral eyes, stayed Rosemary's hand. She changed course. She cast aside the sword and picked up the flute.

Then, she played.

The notes came out weak. Weak and shrill, for though the flute was exquisitely crafted, Rosemary lacked the skill to unlock the magic within. Still, she played from the heart. And she chose her song well. A local melody, beloved by the villagers of Swinetown. A melody Rosemary had heard sung many evenings in Swinetown Tavern by none other than the missing Village Elder.

Though the flute's magic failed, the song worked. But only just, for as the bear collapsed, it lashed out with one final blow that cracked the instrument cleanly in two. As the bear writhed upon the floor, beast gave way to woman. A woman with long silver hair. The Swinetown Village Elder who, it would later be revealed, had been cursed by a rival who then hired a passing monster hunter to slay the "beast."

I would have killed her, the swordswoman later said. I would have killed her believing she was a monster. She sank to her knees, sweeping Rosemary's hands into her own. You prevented my becoming a murderer. How can I possibly repay you?

When no amount of shooing would convince the woman that no debt was owed, Rosemary at last conceded. Make me a flute, she ordered. To replace the one your battle destroyed.

And so the woman cut a branch off the nightwood tree in the front yard and began to carve.

What's your name? Rosemary asked as the woman worked.

Twig.

Rosemary blinked. Your name's—Twig?

Yup.

Like a... thin little limb on a tree?

Yeah.... The woman—Twig—flinched as if expecting some rebuff.

I like it, Rosemary assured. It's a charming name.

You—really think so?

Of course. Twig. Absolutely lovely. Rosemary curled a ringlet of black hair around her brown finger, hesitating a moment, before adding, The women of my family have gone by plant-based names for generations—lots of Ivys and Daisys and Willows and Ferns—but I've never once heard mention of a Twig. It's—unique. Refreshing. I can't say it suits you though. You look more a Log or a Trunk than a Twig—oh, I hope that isn't rude.

Naw. Twig was grinning now. I picked it myself, you see. When I was a teen. It fit better then. She laughed, a lovely rumbling sound. I was kind of a scrappy kid, ya know? But I've bulked up a fair bit now, as you can see. She flexed her biceps for emphasis.

Yes, said Rosemary, eyeing Twig's arms. I can see. A hot rush of blood flooded Rosemary's cheeks. She tucked the ringlet of hair behind her ear, taking the opportunity to discreetly wipe the blush from her face with a quick incantation. I'm Rosemary, by the way.

Rosemary and Twig. That has a nice ring. You ever thought of taking up monster hunting? You've a knack for it, you know.

I can't say I've ever considered it.

Maybe you should.

Rosemary chewed her lower lip, thinking of the monstrous bear that had not been a monster at all. Have you ever considered an alternative to monster 'hunting?' she said. Monster... relocation? Perhaps?

***

As Rosemary started on the final verse, a familiar weight settled over her shoulders. She opened her eyes, forcing her mind back to the present.

There, in the center of the room, the specter hummed and swayed in shuffling circles. The flames around its bones had receded to a mere smolder of smoke curling from its nostrils, earholes, and eye sockets.

Twig stood by Rosemary's side, her arm around Rosemary's shoulder and her sword back at her hip. Though her face was flushed and her hair matted with sweat and melted frost, she flashed Rosemary a grin and an enthusiastic double-thumbs up.

Rosemary smiled in return, her lips peeling back from the moist wood of the flute—which caused the final note of her melody to ring out sour.

The specter flinched. Halting its ghostly dance, it turned stiffly to face Rosemary, fire flicking dangerously from its eye sockets. After a tense moment's stare, it growled, in that metallic screech of a voice, "ACCEPTABLE."

Then, it turned those flaming eyes to Twig, looking her up and down before speaking: "YOU, SING."

Twig's eyebrows jumped to the tippy-top of her forehead. She glanced to her left. Then to her right. And finally back to the specter. "Who, me?" She jabbed a finger at her own chest.

"YOU."

The color drained fully from Twig's face as she turned, mouth hanging helplessly open, to Rosemary.

"I'm pretty sure it's GamGam," Rosemary whispered. "Ida did warn me that her grandmother demands a song and dance of everyone."

"And you're sure she meant that literally?" hissed Twig through clenched teeth.

"Would you rather go back to fighting a flaming ghost?"

"Yes."

A tickle in the back of Rosemary's throat slipped out as a giggle before she could swallow it down. She clamped her mouth shut, twisting the corners into an apologetic grimace, and laid a hand on her wife's arm. "You did say you'd sing if it came to it."

Twig swallowed. "I did say that."

"Just one quick song," said Rosemary, raising the flute once more to her lips. "I'll even accompany you."

Bowing her head, Twig filled her lungs to the brink and then slowly let the breath out. "All right—but I'm not singing the Table of Elementals song. GamGam didn't say anything about alchemistry." After a weak smile, she turned to face the specter and, raising her hands, began to clap a slow, steady beat. "T-ten brave knights, marching in a line," she sang, voice and body quivering. "A dragon blasts one to a crisp and now they're nine."

Rosemary knew the song. (Of course she knew the song. Every child in the realm knew the tune of "Ten Brave Knights".) She joined in, her fingers dancing on the flute as she blew light, bouncy notes.

"Nine brave knights, strut through the castle gate. Someone tips hot oil on one and now they're eight." Perhaps emboldened by the accompaniment, Twig's voice, cracked and nasally though it was, boomed, filling every nook of the cellar with... noise. "Eight brave knights, creep through the forest Elven. One takes an arrow to the back and now they're seven."

The specter's—GamGam's—flaming eyes were cooling. So much so that when a ghoul dragged off the fifth knight while he was crossing the moors, the fire in her sockets had simmered to a soft glow. And when Twig belted out the demise of the second-to-last brave knight (gobbled up by an ogre that weighed more than a ton), GamGam's pupils once again twinkled like distant stars. Then, at last, the last discordant syllable passed Twig's lips. Grinning, she let out a whoop, thwacking the air with her fist.

An awkward silence enveloped the cellar. Her smile fading, Twig looked to Rosemary. Rosemary in turn looked to GamGam. And GamGam, lifting a skeletal arm, beckoned the two of them with a single bony finger.

Creak. Creak. Creak.

After exchanging anxious nodes, Rosemary and Twig approached. Leaning in, they waited for GamGam to speak.

Instead, two clawed hands darted forward to snatch them each by the ear.

"Where in the name of bog did you two troublemakers learn your manners? Running around pouring green goop on good, law-abiding citizens? Drawing swords on sweet, defenseless old ladies? You're just lucky i like your twiddly little flute playing and offkey singing else i'd give you both a piece of my mind, you mark my words."

***

Rosemary and Twig slumped against each other on the cellar stairs, rubbing their aching earlobes while Ida cried into her grandmother's ribcage.

"But GamGam, why?" asked Ida between sobs. "Why haven't you moved on to the afterlife? Why return to ransack my cellar?"

GamGam raised her skull. When she spoke, it was with a flustered sort of rumble, as if she was trying (but ultimately failing) not to sound horrifying. "Because, well…." She swept her starlight gaze to her granddaughter. "I cannot face my dear edgar. Not yet."

"Can't face pawpaw?" Ida's forehead knitted. "Gamgam, whatever did you do?"

"Nothing like that child," said gamgam with a dismissive wave. "I cannot face him in stones and bones. I'm out of practice, you see. Haven't played a single game since he passed. Meanwhile he's had decades of practice in the tea houses of bog's green underworld, playing against the greatest masters in the history of the game. How can i face him knowing full well i'm gonna get my ass whooped? Nope. I've gotta train first." She paused, looking down at her clawed hands. "I'm here because i—i wanted my old stones and bones set. You know, the one i gave you all those years ago? I know you never much cared for the game, but i'd hoped you'd saved it. Tucked it away somewhere down here. Forgotten."

Ida's mouth dropped open. She swept a sleeve across her wet eyes before slipping from gamgam's skeletal arms. Then, she raced up the stairs, practically leaping over Rosemary and Twig's heads as she went.

As ida's thundering footsteps faded, Rosemary offered gamgam a tentative smile.

Gamgam crossed her arms and turned away, tapping her boney toes on the floor with a clickity-clack-clack.

"Apparently," whispered Twig, leaning close, "we're still in time out."

Rosemary tried, unsuccessfully to hide a snicker behind her hand.

"No talking."

Biting their lips to hold back laughter, Rosemary and Twig waited in silence until ida crashed back down the stairs.

"I have it!" She thrust her find—a plain wooden box—into gamgam's claws. "The stones and bones set. I've kept it in my room, on my bedside table, ever since you gave it to me."

"All those years?" Gamgam rumbled happily. "Even though you don't play?"

"It was important to you," said ida, folding her hands over gamgam's claws. "I wanted to honor that. But gamgam—if you came back looking for the stones and bones set, why didn't you just knock on the front door and ask me for it?"

"Didn't want to be a bother."

Ida blinked. Then, slowly, with the elegance of a deflating balloon, doubled over with wheezing laughter.

Gamgam laughed as well, a horrible booming sound that rattled the very stones of the walls.

"Gamgam, i was thinking," said ida upon recovering from her bout of hilarity, "if you need to practice your stones and bones, you could, well, you know..." she paused, fidgeting with the fabric of her dress. "...Stick around awhile? Maybe teach me the rules? We could practice. Together."

The stars in gamgam's eye sockets twinkled. "I would like that," she said, wrapping a boney arm around her granddaughter's wiry shoulders. "I would like that very much."

Rosemary nudged her wife—and tried not to chuckle at the sight of Twig's wide eyes swimming in joyful tears. "I believe," she whispered, "that this is our cue to exit."

"Yeah." Twig sniffled. "You're probably right."

They made it halfway up the stairs before ida caught up with them.

"We're ever so grateful," she said, slipping a sack of coins into Twig's pocket. "The payment, as promised."

Twig fished the bag right out. "Feels a bit heavy," she said, testing the weight in her hand. She extracted a few coins—"that should do it"—and tossed the sack back to ida.

Though ida fussed, as grateful clients always did, Twig successfully managed to negotiate the payment down to only a quarter of their typical monster removal rate by arguing that, technically, there hadn't been any monster to remove from ida's cellar. Just a benign (if very crotchety) ghostly grandmother.

***

As Rosemary and Twig strolled, shoulders bumping, back to the local tavern, Twig flipped a coin toward the moonlit sky. Rosemary resisted the urge to roll her eyes. Twig loved to talk about earning extra pocket money from these late night monster relocations for the locals of whatever village they happened to be staying in—and then inevitably refused to accept the full payment after the job was completed. A smile tugged at the corners of Rosemary's mouth. Twig's reckless generosity was, after all, one of the many annoying reasons she'd fallen in love.

When she tilted her head for a glimpse of her wife's (annoyingly) beautiful face, she found Twig watching her with that look. The one where her eyes crinkled into contented crescent-moons and her lips parted just enough to reveal a tantalizing sliver of teeth.

Rosemary leaned in for a kiss and did not pull away until her tongue had counted every one of her wife's teeth three times over. "Twig, darling," she said, biting her own lower lip as she skipped her fingers down her wife's chest, "will you do me one favor, tonight, please?"

Twig grinned, her tan, freckled cheeks flushing cherry-red. "Anything."

"Really?" Rosemary nestled her head into the crook of Twig's neck. "Anything?"

"Um-hmm."

"Then please, please"—Rosemary failed to stifle a burst of laughter. She never could finish her own jokes without giggling—"serenade me to sleep tonight with another one of your spine-tingling renditions of 'ten brave knights'."

Twig rolled her eyes in a full, dizzying circle. "Anything for you,

Rosie," she said and planted a wet smooch on Rosemary's forehead. "Anything for you."

Vegoia

Patrice Rivara

Patrice Rivara is from a tiny cow town in the Central Valley of California. When she isn't writing, she's watching something her friends recommended, teaching high schoolers, or hanging out with her bearded dragon, Noodle.

The loom can be nothing but a loom, unless it is kindling. Vera considers the fibers in front of her and tries to *not* consider lighting it on fire. To be something else–no, that wasn't right, but to be *someone* else...

There isn't much going on this early in the morning, in the criss-crossing and meandering streets of Clevsin. Women in bright colors and what fashion is available to them draw water, and men argue over small things in the way friends do when they see each other in passing. The warm tan of the houses and tile roofs is striking against the clouds piling up on the horizon. Vera holds stormy days close to her heart, away from those who revel in the sun and relish the burn it leaves.

"Vera," says a sharp voice from the doorway. Vera jumps at the sound, and faces the *hatrencu* from her place by the window. She knows Tulvna's voice well.

"If your hands need a rest, it would be best spent studying your charts, Vera," she says. *Of course she's here to check me. The others must have received a visit from her as well, with the ritual tonight.* Tulvna has black hair streaked through with gray, but her face is still youthful. Only older women are allowed a seat with the *hatrencui*, so she displays her age with pride, always wearing her hair in distinctive braids to best show off her streaks of gray.

"Back to the loom," she says sternly, raising a brow. "I'll see you tonight," she calls from the hall, footsteps growing faint.

Vera sits quickly and sets herself to work; the *clack, clack* sounds like it's coming from another room.

The olive grove seems to agree, nodding in the breeze.

"Someone gets it," she says to the olives. She sighs and returns to her work.

She feels a stab of guilt–she and all the other acolytes are lucky to be here in the first place. They assist the *hatrencui*, taking the burden of domesticity away from women whose role is to be closer to the Oracle and civic life. It's not something Vera desires; she's seen the assembly gather, and had been nervous just sitting in the room. She ignores the tightness of the walls around her and leans a little further out the window, looking down at the olive orchards.

Vera only peeks out the window after that. The storm on the horizon grows and grows, big clouds piling up in a dark gray situation like big, greasy stacks of wool from the Oracle's sheep. She focuses, ignoring the sharp beauty of light green leaves against the dark sky.

In the span of a breath, an unknowableness settles on her, the way silence and unease will settle like a heavy blanket before a thunderstorm. The omens that come with that unease are common things, measurable in ways that made sense: the way the chickens clucked before a storm could be read to determine the aftermath. But this feeling of being unknowable settles into the pit of her stomach, coiling there and sending tendrils through her body.

"I am Vera," she tells it, aloud. "I am an acolyte of the Mother, who serves the Oracle. You will rest here, and then go." The feeling does not stir, but settles.

***

Lunch is a normal summer meal: cured olives and good yeasted bread with salt and oil, firm cheese and fruit. Vera chats with the other girls. What will they learn tonight? They have never done a ritual like this one. Tonight, they would divide the sky into sections with the help of a *hatrencu*, and read entrails by firelight.

Vera focuses on her food. It's hard to ignore something when you have to focus to ignore it. The feeling in her middle has not gone away.

I am here to stay.

It is an alarming thing, to hear a voice in your head that is not your own. Everyone is looking at her, and she realizes she's standing.

"Vera?" one asks cautiously.

She focuses on her friends in front of her: Virnua had spoken, but Iminae and Sumnus look concerned. The four of them share the same room on the ground floor, one of the simple acolyte rooms. They are her best friends. There isn't a secret amongst them.

"I am... I am not prepared for tonight; I need to study." She excuses herself before they can ask any more questions. She can't lie to them. The feeling in her stomach slithered happily, and she fights the urge to grasp her middle. The image of salamanders writhing in a hollow, freshly split log forms in her mind, and she had to stifle a gasp. Outside in the courtyard, she leans against the stone walls, hands balled into fists. The feeling does not disappear, but winds away until it is a mere suggestion.

***

They get ready in a buzz long before Tulvna summons them. The acolyte sent to fetch them is younger than the four women, and meekly gives the instructions Tulvna has ordered her to pass on. Vera is giddy with the rest of them, thoughts of the salamanders tucked far away.

It happens when the *hatrencu* is giving instructions, asking questions to make sure they are paying attention. The bird they are to sacrifice is tethered and looking at them awkwardly, like it knows what is going to happen in the next few seconds. Certainly none of the women on the roof could have guessed.

Vera doesn't fall so much as slump, and begins to shake violently. They treat her to the best of their ability. They know how to treat the girl with eyes rolling back into her head, body thrashing; they know to keep her tongue from between her teeth. But they do not see the glow at the base of her neck, and Vera can't tell them about the prickling at the soles of her feet. The bird is altogether forgotten.

"Get the Mother," Tulvna tells the girls. Iminae leaps up and races down the stairs. Before long, she reappears, waiting at the top of the ladder to help the older woman up.

They hear her bare feet on the ladder before they see her. The Mother is an old woman, white hair kept in a braid that usually disintegrates into halo-making wisps before the end of the day. She wears the same robes as them, but they know she is the Mother at a glance. Rare is the woman who survives to have hair as white as hers. It is known that she is the oldest in the whole region. Many who know no better challenge her, and they learn that she is also among the wisest.

She takes a look at the sky and seems pleased. It is a clear night, and the rainstorm earlier only made the world crisper. The women make room with bowed heads as the Mother leans over their charge. Vera breathes quietly now.

The women wait as their superior examines their friend. The Mother grasps Vera's hands and works up the arms, shoulders, neck, and skull. Her brow creases when she feels at the base of the skull, right where it meets the neck. She rises quickly after that, looking up at the sky, and grabs at the air, muttering and pacing. The Mother looks over the town and into the hills for what feels like a very long time. The breeze falters for the barest moment, and only the faraway river makes a sound. The acolytes are silent but their breathing is ragged. Only Tulvna, with her training as a *hatrencu,* keeps her composure.

The Mother turns to them, and Tulvna recognizes her expression with alarm: urgency.

"The river," she says.

That's all it takes. The women all react as if a whip had been snapped at them, and all begin talking at once.

"Mother?"

"The river?"

"Will she be okay?" They all speak over each other, gesturing wildly to the sky, Vera, the river, and anything else that could be blamed or implicated. The Mother waits patiently.

The *hatrencu* is the first to catch on. As an older sister gets younger sisters in line, she gives the others a dressing-down that singes their ears. They stand in silence, facing the Mother. Vera's breath continues, her chest rising and falling in steady rhythm.

"Trust," she says, when they are silent. Without another words she makes for the stairs, gesturing for them to follow.

The women are quick to obey, two of them taking an arm and another following behind to support Vera's neck. They make their way down the stairs, not far behind the Mother. through the sleeping quarters of the Oracle women, and out into the side street. This was no problem, even though walking on the main road was nicer. This would have raised questions to anyone peeking out their window in the night; with the Mother leading them, it would have roused half the town out of bed.

They follow her down paths that wind down to ancient foot trails, smaller and smaller, struggling to go three abreast, and they go slowly through the bay trees that grow closer to the river. Vera's breathing is even throughout the whole ordeal, and they at last place her where the Mother instructs.

"Lay her on the bank, and touch her or anything around her upon pain of death by their own hand." The women put her down promptly, repressing shudders; death ordered was death done. They move Vera so her feet are in the water.

"Remove that," the Mother says. With a lowered head, Virnua steps forward and gently removes the balled-up head covering from underneath Vera's head.

They do not question the Mother as they did on the roof. One sharp look from the *hatrencu* is all they need: *let the Mother work.*

And work she did. She goes out into the current until the water is hip-high, and raises her hands to the sky. There is no moon, only bright, burning stars that light the river in shadows, reducing their colorful world to black and white. Sumnus catches her breath, and almost makes a ward against evil; her eyes are fixed on the Mother, and she thinks better of it. *It will be put to right,* she thinks. *She will protect us. The Mother will protect us.*

The water around the Mother begins to quake, as though the whole river were in a cup and some great hand sat drumming a rhythm next to it. The water shakes, and in the black and white night, goes completely still.

Then slowly, so slowly that the women on the bank think their eyes are deceived, the river starts to churn.

It is a flash at first, a subtle turning of black to white and then black again. But then another, and another so close behind that it cannot be a deception. The water begins to roll and then boil, but the Mother does not move, doesn't even seem to flinch. She lowers her hands, and the roiling mass moves closer to the shore. Towards Vera, lying unaware.

"Vera!"

"Stop her!" Tulvna cried.

Iminae grabs Virnua around the waist to keep her from running to Vera's side, the other women just a beat slower. They hold her back just as the mass brushes Vera's feet, and hide their faces from the river and the friend they can't help.

Salamanders creep up out of the water, slick bodies tumbling one over the other, perhaps hundreds in a roiling mass around Vera's inert form. The women on the bank do not see the salamander that goes to the base of Vera's neck and bites her.

Vera cries out suddenly, and the salamanders rush to bind her ankles and wrists with their bodies. Without warning, lightning snakes down, and to the horror of the women on the bank, moves with the slow distortion of a salamander trapped in its own body by the cold.

The lightning touches her chest, and the women scream, blinded and collapsing in on each other in layers of sobs and moans. When they look up, the salamanders are gone. The sky does not rumble with the thunder they know should follow, and one by one they fall prostrate in the river's direction. They do not see the salamanders slide back into the river, nor the one that disappears into Vera's open mouth.

***

Vera remembers the roof well enough, and thinks she is still up there, where all healing is done. She opens her eyes and tries to find something familiar. First, of course, the calm night sky. It held simple, ecstatic joy.

But the mud on her clothes is a cause for concern, as is the mud on the back of her head matting her hair. There's mud *everywhere.* She squeezes her hands into fists, digging into the clay of the riverbank. She looks around wildly, then sees the river lapping at her feet, and the Mother standing before her.

The old woman stands at Vera's feet, water up to her ankles, and smiles down at the girl.

"Daughters, come and collect this one," the Mother says softly.

Tulvna raises her head first and scrambles to her feet when she sees Vera. She checks Vera's chest and pulse points.

"Vera, stand."

She obeys, not minding the mud, and turns to gather up her friends.

"Leave them," the Mother orders, and turns to the *hatrencu.* "Tulvna, see that they are sent to bed with a cup of honeyed wine and an extra blanket. They may sleep as late as they'd like," she says. She turns back to the Oracle without waiting to see if her orders will be followed.

"Come with me, Vera," the Mother says, and without another word, starts back for the Oracle. Vera looks back at her friends for a moment as they struggle to their feet in the ankle-deep river mud.

***

She sits in the Mother's quarters next to a wide window open toward the dawn now coloring the sky with pale light, no hint of lightning in the pink tinge over the earth. It's a day that rings full of promise, one that all creatures big and small know to celebrate.

The Mother sets a mug in Vera's hands and makes a swift upward gesture. Vera knows to drink, and drink it all. It's warm, a little bitter and a little sour, but pleasant. The Mother stands by the window with her own mug and looks out at the sunrise. When she speaks, she sounds content.

"Child, would you like to know what has happened?"

"Something to do with the Oracle, I am sure."

She looks amused, of all things. "Put the Oracle out of your mind for now," she says with a chuckle.

Vera balks. People don't say things like that. The Oracle shows them when to harvest, the most auspicious marriages, who should be recruited to join their numbers as an acolyte, and much more. The Oracle is the hub to the people of Clevsin and the outlying farms. People came even from Vetluna and Tarchna.

"That does not sound right." Even as she says it, the words made her feel foolish. The woman she is speaking to was a *hatrencu* when her parents were born.

"Come with me. I will show you," she says. The Mother drains her cup, gently links her arm through Vera's, and guides her toward the inner chamber where the Oracle waits. They pass through the living quarters for both acolytes and then *hatrencu* and receive gestures of respect. The Mother looks straight ahead and acknowledges the bows with a courteous nod or a smile. After a moment of stillness, everyone jumps to go back to work.

They walk through the wide courtyard where the wash is hung out to dry. The string is supported by hooks in the eaves and poles stuck in the ground to keep the line from sagging under the weight of robes and veils. It is noon, and the clothes are well on their way to drying. Everyone wears the same blues, so the courtyard takes on a dreamy, swirling hue that engulfs the both of them and nips at their noses and heels. Vera always thought this was how the wind might look from the heavens.

"Come along, come along," the Mother says, almost chiding.

Vera realizes she had stopped to admire the laundry. She straightens herself and hurries to catch up.

***

"We have always been keepers of the Oracle," the Mother says, speaking for the first time since the courtyard. It is hot in the midday, carts and people hurrying to and from shade to keep off the heat. They are on the steps leading to the front door of the Oracle, just off the main street. People hurry past, averting their eyes to keep unwanted attention from themselves and their fortunes.

The Mother motions for Vera to follow, and they climb the steps into the Oracle's cool interior.

"The Oracle has always been an indicator only. Through time and trial, and much error, we have made some little science of how to read its will," she says. They walk toward the inner sanctuary, where strange rumblings shake sands and priestesses decode messages in tiny portions, forming strange patterns only the Mother can fully interpret.

It is a humble entry hall with rough columns on either side and wide enough for the elder and younger to walk side-by-side. The high ceiling makes Vera feel small, and she hesitates outside the door to the inner chamber even as the Mother steps in. She has never been allowed to this part of the Oracle before. She is not initiated.

"Mother, I cannot," she says.

The Mother snorts, waving her in. Vera hesitates a moment more, and steps forward.

"An entity resides in you, now," the Mother says as they walk together. They go slowly, the Mother leaning on Vera for support.

"This place is our window into the home of the gods, and you can think of the Oracle itself as another home to them. This is our purpose in keeping a sacred space, here in Clevsin and little towns throughout this land. We have waited for the woman who would be the space between the inside and outside. The one who occupies that between."

"Why?" Vera asks. They stood at the foot of the altar, a low rugged thing elevated only by a few steps.

The Mother is silent. The younger woman bows her head, and they both sit down facing each other. "I pronounce a task."

Vera knows when she is being deflected.

"As Vera, you may go about your tasks as normal. Your friends have all heard an explanation, but not the truth. They know you had a fit of some sort, and that you are being watched over. They will draw their own conclusions."

***

Vera lets her friends fawn over her and she answers their questions the best she can. They know she is shaken and bring her warm bread with honey and a cup of wine. She smiles as they put the softest blankets on her shoulders.

It is Sumnus' idea to tuck Vera in the middle of the two lightest sleepers: warm in the cool night, and not next to Iminae, who is like an ass when she sleeps: that is to say, she drools and kicks. Vera knows they are reassured by this arrangement: here, they can protect her. They fall asleep one by one, until it's just Sumnus and Vera awake. Sumnus glances over at Vera—her eyes are wide open, staring at the ceiling. They drift off, soft breathing blending in with the breeze coming through the open window.

***

The world has just started to wake, hands of dawn creeping over olive orchards and stone houses, winding rivers and lakes like mirrors to the sky. The birds in the orchards and in their nests start awake, aware of some great change in the rhythm of the world.

Vera dreams out of the eyes of a stranger. She dreams she is someone else; she lives in her body, but it is not *her*, not Vera as she knows herself. A mirror. Her nose, lips, eyes.

Not her eyes. *Is this mine?* The thought is dreamy, and she looks down at her body as she would after putting on her dress and mantle in the morning. She would have screamed. There is no body, every freckle and scar and sunburn replaced with bright stars and the loud roar of the sun. She looks up at the mirror again, floating in front of her.

A stranger stares at her.

Vera's eyes snap open as she wakes with a jolt. The blankets seem to smother her and she claws out of them, climbs over Virnua, and sprints down the hall. She does not hear her friends' sleepy confusion.

"Mother," she bursts into the study, weeping. She collapses on the floor, and the Mother quickly stoops to help her into a chair.

"Vera, tell me."

"A dream," she manages to get out. She describes what she saw, what she felt.

The older woman sits quietly as Vera recounts the dream. Her calm demeanor makes Vera want to shake her. She is breathless when she finishes recounting her dream. The Mother sits across from her.

"Mother, what should I do?"

The older woman waits a beat, and then begins.

"You know how our Oracle works, yes?"

"As you say, the Oracle *indicates*. We rely on special readings using the sands in our Oracle, which must be deciphered properly," Vera recited quickly. A million questions fell into her mouth, but the Mother cuts in.

"It is a weak and pitiful thing, when we compare it to what you have."

Vera balks. "How am I to harness it, if it's so powerful?"

The Mother laughs, and Vera lowers her head. "Don't be ashamed, girl. I wish I could tell you how many young women would ask the same question in your place. The Oracles are fleeting—they need tools and rituals that fail as often as they work. You, the Seer, will remain and give *prophecy*."

"How do I become this, this Seer, Mother?"

"Vera, the Seer becomes *you*," she says. Vera feels the words take root in her heart and feels the weight of them hanging in the air. She is still for a beat, and a frenzied look comes into her eyes.

"I can fight it off, Mother. Please, listen, I can still be me, I'm still me, look," she says, surging up and motioning to her body. "I can still be a Seer, and be me." Vera knows her voice is higher and faster than usual.

"Perhaps you can, Vera. But to See is to fall and revel in falling. Live well, and when it comes for you, do as you are bid." The Mother sits behind her desk. "You may go about your day, Vera."

And the day passes without incident. Vera goes about her chores and though she smiles less than usual, life goes on. It does so the next day, and the day after that. Weeks pass, and Vera relaxes into her life again. Where her dreams were once populated and active, now she welcomed peaceful sleep.

The days wear on into fall and then winter, when lightning forks through the sky and thunder keeps the *hatrencu* of the Oracle vigilant for signs in their sands.

It is on a day like this when Vera wanders through the olive grove under her window.

She sits at the base of one of the trees, thankful for a break in the rain. The ground is dry here, and she feels blessedly alone. Or as alone as she can be.

"*Vegoia,*" says a voice. It is the voice that has been coming for her.

Her arms prickle at the sound. This is what she had heard the morning of that last dream. The whisper of wind in her ear sends a shudder down her back.

"You call the wrong name," she says aloud, keeping the tremble out of her voice. She looks around and is afraid: the landscape has changed, but subtly. Everything is too still. No rustling wind, chirps from bugs and birds, or the distant pulse of the town. A constricting calm has settled over her world. A bird sits frozen, midair. She could pluck it from the sky.

"*I don't think so,*" it whispers in the other ear. There was no gender to the voice. "*Listen, Vera.*"

Vera ignores the stillness around her and instead *feels*: rough bark at her back, rich earth beneath her hands and heels.

"Whatever you have to say, say it." The chill creeping down her spine does nothing to harden her voice.

"I'm not here to speak. I'm here to give you the power of speech."

"I can speak well enough on my own. Give me what message you have."

Vera feels rather than hears the chiding *tsk* from the voice. "*Vera, if only you understood. Would you like to see what life would be, if you lived in both worlds?*"

"I'm ready," she says. She looks over the edge.

Vera resists what she sees at her feet. A precipice with events yet to occur, a world of secrets, still within earshot of the world she knows. Time passes. She resists the pull of the precipice, as the women who find her in the grove must restrain her as she tosses.

"*You are what the world has been waiting for,*" the voice says from deep within her mind. She looks into that portion of herself as it calls to her, starry heights like vast cities of light swimming before her eyes.

"*You have many prophecies to give, Vera, soon Vegoia. Together we will divine the lightning that glides through the sky, to deliver your cities from ruin, ruin of ages to come. Trust that you can save them, will save them.*"

She needs no more time to ponder, and recalls all the things that tether her here: Virnua, Iminae, Sumnus; a thousand little moments of laughter; the loom.

The loom.

The time between her decision and her action is the space of a frightened rabbit's heartbeat. In it, she Sees.

They are moving her inside. *Hatrencui* carry her with a special sort of reverence, feet-first through the door, the Mother following and supporting Vera's head. The older woman looks gentle and at peace, smiling absently as she strokes Vera's forehead. *My forehead*, she thinks.

Vera shifts her gaze toward her friends. They plan in the dark of their room. She knows they suspect everyone and everything. They suspect something terrible is happening to their dear friend.

They are right. They are wrong.

Her bearers move her into the Oracle and up the front steps. The *hatrencui* are glad for the audience gathered at the foot of the steps. The Mother stops to address the crowd, but Vera-that-soon-will-not-be does not listen to her; instead, she flutters open an eyelid, appreciates a blue the color of the big vein on her right arm, appreciates the gentle dome of the sky for the last time through these eyes.

The heartbeat ends, and she forsakes it all. Vera rushes up to merge into something greater than any one person could be.

The presence descends on her in the span of an eyeblink. A wave of calm settles over her, like so much of the laurel wind that sweeps from the west into her second-story window. There is no Vera. She wanders on the rings of the sixth planet, stares down into the vast abysses of the fifth's gaseous surface. Vera whispers from her new home among the planets, fascinated with the grand images of what has come before her. Thoughts of who she had been flit, flicker, and are replaced with thoughts of things to come.

A calf in a field. Water flowing. Peaceful croaking. Wind through trees and over vines.

Prosperous harvests...

A wolf suckling two boys...

A city on one hill, then three, then seven hills... And then more hills than she can count in the half-heartbeat in which she Sees. She is all the things that make up the bits between stars.

***

Her friends tumble into the Oracle, with *hatrencui* and other acolytes moments behind them, ready to stop them from interrupting the sacred. They breathe a sigh of relief when they see Vera seated at the bottom of the steps, eyes closed. She looks peaceful. The Mother stands next to Vera.

"She's going to be alright," Virnua breathes.

"We'll all be here for the New Year festival," Iminae says aloud.

"Vera? Vera, wake up." Sumnus reaches out to touch her, then stumbles back into the other girls with a yelp.

The body that once belonged to Vera opens milky white eyes to the world. Only the Vegoia remains.

The Wandering Fae

Alex Grehy

Alex Grehy's sweet life is filled with narrowboating, rescue greyhounds, singing and chocolate. Published worldwide, her vivid prose, thought-provoking poetry and original view of the world has led to her best friend to say 'For someone so lovely, you're very twisted!

Back in the olden days, the world abided by natural rules, the spheres of heaven and earth in their rightful places. The High Fae imperiously watched over all, ready to judge and punish. The Low Fae dallied with the mortals, allowing them to hear, for a moment, the ethereal music of the spheres. Below them, dark spirits dwelt, trapped in the earth where they slept and dreamt restlessly of light and freedom.

So the Earth spun in the universe, everything and everyone in their place. Then came the age of reason. Great men in their periwigs expounded new sciences and the earth ran red with the hot steel of their industry. When Canal Fever hit the fair country of Britannia, the natural order was disturbed as never before–cuttings and tunnels carved their way through the countryside; the spheres were shattered and the Fae were tumbled about; some said they perished where they fell, ploughed by the new world order, but some say they abide still..."

***

The *Wandering Fae,* a traditional narrowboat decorated with colourful canal roses, lay moored to a richly wooded bank on the River Weaver. In the dusk light, the water was still, motionless as molasses, reflective as quicksilver. At the edge of the reflections, the real and virtual worlds were stitched along a seam of land and water. The sky was at the cusp of night and day. To the west, the sun donned a pale pink nightdress as she sank gracefully into her bed. To the east, a yellow moon rose, hungover, and drew her star-glittered gown around her shoulders, ready for a night on the tiles.

In the cosy cabin, Finn lounged on the sofa with his shaggy deerhound, Fergus. They lay on their backs, feet in the air, squiggling and farting contentedly.

"That was a meal fit for a king," said Finn, patting his stomach, then patting Fergus' belly.

Belladonna looked up from her spinning wheel. Fergus's shaggy fur made a fine yarn that she knitted into hardwearing socks and gloves. She snorted. The males in her life were ridiculous, yet she loved them with all of her heart and soul.

"Get out, the pair of you!" she commanded. "If the air in here was any thicker, I could saw it into planks and build a shed!"

"Ah, Fergus," said Finn, "Looks as if we're both in the doghouse. Maybe if we stay here on our backs and submit, we'll be in for a belly rub."

Belladonna grinned. "Away with your nonsense," she said. "I've work to do."

Finn reached for her hand and kissed it extravagantly. "Aaah, you push the dagger of your disapproval into my heart, yet will I use the broken pieces to love you." His eyes twinkled with mischief. He prodded Fergus and peered out of the porthole.

"Is it all right?" Belladonna asked.

"Aye, my love, this is a natural river. Mother Earth's fair hands have gentled her. It's safe for us here."

He gathered the hound and vanished into the night.

Belladonna concentrated on her spinning, casting a little domestic magic to strengthen the fibre. Anything she knitted with the yarn would protect the owner from injury, no matter how sharp the blade.

The hypnotic thrum of the spinning wheel took her to the centre of her power. It was a deep reservoir of potential, yet Belladonna chose to draw her magic from a shallow wellspring. A long time ago she had chosen to turn away from absolute power to become a grey witch, her benign magic tinted with a hint of spite.

Half an hour later, her musing was interrupted by Fergus's flying leap from the deck. He landed on her lap with a flump. "Why do we keep you, you big oaf?"

Fergus turned his soulful amber eyes towards her and slid off her lap, leaving clumps of damp fur on her dress. She gathered it into her raw wool basket; everyone paid their way however they could.

Finn strolled into the cabin and sat beside her. He gazed into her hazel eyes; his own golden eyes shimmered like a midsummer meadow. In his long years, he had enjoyed dalliances with many women. The Fae loved deeply but briefly, leaving their human playthings full of wistful longing. But Belladonna captivated him.

He recalled the day he met her. She'd been picking blackberries on the riverbank. He'd mistaken her for High Fae, her poise and assurance belonged in the Faerie Queen's court. He remembered how she had called to him, "Fairy, stop your staring and get those lazy hands moving. These berries won't pick themselves."

He'd been surprised. It was rare for a human to recognise a Fae. But then he'd seen the shimmer of magic around her knitted gloves as they turned away the fierce thorns. He'd looked deep into her eyes and when Fergus the hound decided to lie at her feet, he knew that she would become the keeper of his heart.

He had picked a sturdy bulrush and knelt at her feet, presenting it like a jewelled sceptre.

"Queen of my heart," he'd said.

"Get up from the mud, you feckless fairy," she'd said, but her eyes were filled with love.

That had been 80 years ago; easy years of companionship and comfortable passion, cruising the rivers and canals in the *Wandering Fae*, selling their wares at waterside fairs. Belladonna made things for the home and hearth; impervious knitwear, sweetly fragranced soaps and candles, woven dreamcatchers, all imbued with her protective magic. Finn had a gift for releasing beautiful objects from the soul of the wood that he whittled. Their wares were prized, but the couple moved often and resisted the urge to crow about their talents. Belladonna confined her spell casting to the boat, where the thick steel hull shielded her magic from the High Fae and their arcane punishments.

Not that their union was forbidden as such, but a lasting bond between a Fae and a witch could never be sanctioned as the children would be all powerful in both realms. The Faerie Queen need not have worried; they were never blessed with a child, but caution was a difficult habit to break.

"Tomorrow, we have to venture onto the canals. The summer fairs will be starting soon," said Belladonna.

Finn scowled. The canals had been gouged from the earth by men of industry and reason. They could not have guessed how many Dark Fae they had released from their subterranean prisons. The shady places were full of strangeness, for those who had the sight to see it.

Belladonna saw the frown creasing Finn's ageless face. "I have a gift for you," she said, handing him a hinged wooden casket.

When he opened the lid, he saw scores of bright orange clay marbles, perfectly fired. He picked one up. A burning tingle nipped his fingertips. He quickly dropped the marble.

"Harecastle?" he asked

She nodded. The Harecastle Tunnel had always been a fraught place for them, but it was an unavoidable gateway between the South and the North. They passed through infrequently, planning their trips carefully. In the morning, the water was clear and undisturbed, the Dark Fae lying somnolent on the surface. If they could be the first to pass through the gloomy tunnel, moving slowly and quietly, they would be safe. But the last time they'd traversed it, a boat had darted in before them, thrashing its propeller and raising iron-rich orange mud from the bottom of the canal. The cold iron had inflamed the spiteful sprites, who rose vengeful from the poisonous water and harassed them with pinches and mocking laughter for the whole length of the dark space. It was then they had discovered that if they sprinkled the Dark Fae with the iron-rich water, they would retreat as if scalded.

Belladonna had dredged some orange mud from the tunnel

entrance and used a little magic to transform their wood burner into a kiln. There she baked the clay marbles into hard ceramic pellets for Finn's slingshot.

"Be careful now," she warned. "These have the cold iron in their making. They should buy us time to escape any Dark Fae, but mind you wear your gloves when you sling them."

"Ach, I think I'm immune to cold iron now," he said. His first year onboard the *Wandering Fae* had been a challenge until they lined the cabin with green oak panels.

"You were always a reckless fairy," she replied. The thought of losing him made her brusque. Finn had brought a lightness of joy to her contented life, embracing her emotionally, spiritually and physically. They were bound on every plane of existence. Belladonna was 40 years old when they met, but she had not aged a day since. Sometimes, she was tempted to trace the magic that allowed it, but when she started the reasoning spell, Fergus had laid a vast paw on her arm, lolled his long tongue and winked at her. She'd let it be; gift horses, and hounds, were not to be trifled with.

Wandering Fae left the river the next day. The Weaver flowed in a deep valley, accessible only via the great edifice of the Anderton Boat Lift. No one now alive understood why the boat lift had been so grossly over-engineered, but in truth, its mighty iron girders and pillars protected the river from incursions of Dark Fae from the canal above. Man-made for industry, the canals looked like scars in the landscape to Finn's far-seeing eyes, for all that they were now surrounded by lush countryside. They moved quickly and warily, but in the summer sunshine, the Dark Fae stayed hidden...until they reached the Woodseaves Cutting.

Without magic, the great men of reason had been tested.

Water always found its own level, so how could canals traverse Britannia's ample curves and contours? Some engineers tunnelled *under* the hills; others built great flights of locks to carry boats *over* them. Some waterways meandered *around* the contours, perched on embankments far above the surrounding valleys. But the bosky depths of the Woodseaves cutting had been carved *through* the hill by navvies, driven by the thrill of conquest over nature and the rich earnings from their labours. The cutting was deep. Weak light filtered down from a thin slice of unreachable sky, barely illuminating the steep and shady walls. It was cold, and its rocky ramparts dripped with moisture. Ferns of all shapes and sizes grew luxuriantly on every ledge and in every crevice, lending a prehistoric air to the confined landscape.

The *Wandering Fae* passed the first portal, a high stone bridge which carried a road across the cutting, far above their heads. Belladonna slowed the engine, making sure that the propeller barely stirred the water. Finn stood on the front deck with Fergus, alert, slingshot in hand. Belladonna held the tiller, moving the rudder gently. Her eyes darted around. The Dark Fae could emerge from anywhere.

As *Wandering Fae* passed under the bridge, a loud splash disturbed the water behind them. Belladonna looked up. Far above her, a group of lads were snickering as they threw trash into the canal. Using the waterways as a midden had always been abhorrent, but to throw an iron-rich shopping trolley into the water was madness.

"Finn!" she cried, her voice shrill with fear.

Finn turned to look at her. A heron took off from the towpath, large and ungainly. He relaxed. The cutting had gone back to nature many years before, maybe their old fears were unjustified.

"Watch out!" Belladonna yelled.

Finn ducked as the heron dived towards him, transforming from benign bird into toothed pterodactyl. Fergus leapt up to snap at the beast. It turned away with a raucous screech.

Around them, the ferns undulated and exuded a swampy miasma. Creeping wildlife transformed into giant prehistoric creatures; foot-long millipedes crawled between the leaves, dragonflies the size of blackbirds buzzed from the water's edge, gigantic leeches oozed from the canal, their sightless mouths swaying as they scented warm-blooded prey on the boat. A swan abruptly shed its feathers and grew into a towering T. rex. It roared with rage.

All around them, the Dark Fae giggled. They usually traded in small harms; pinches, punches and visions to torment their human victims. They could create wormholes between times and dimensions, but it was scarcely worth the bother when humans dismissed them as dreams. However, creating a Time Slip for magic-users who could perceive its full effect was top entertainment.

Finn and Fergus leapt onto the boat's roof, both running back towards the helm to protect Belladonna. Finn raised his sling and fired iron-rich marbles towards the angry dinosaur, but they barely penetrated the reptile's skin. Fergus growled and launched himself into the air as the T. rex lunged for Finn.

Snap!

The growling deerhound looked tiny in the dinosaur's jaws. The T. rex moaned in distress. Its vast teeth seemed to be bending out of their sockets, drawn by the effort of trying to chew on the hound. It dropped the dog and shook its head dazedly. Fergus sprang up, uninjured and barked furiously. Finn was astonished. Fergus had always seemed a little fey, resisting the homely magics that Belladonna used around the boat, but who knew that his fur was that enchanted?

Finn vowed to start charging more for Belladonna's knitwear, if they got out of this alive.

His relieved musings were interrupted by Belladonna's cry.

"Finn, watch out! The marbles won't work. It's not Fae. It's real!"

The T. rex put one clawed foot on the front deck, tipping the boat forward and reaching for Finn, now perched precariously on the tilted roof. In desperation, Belladonna cast a transformation spell, releasing the vast power that she'd kept contained for almost a hundred years. There was a blinding flash. When her sight cleared, the T. rex was gone, replaced by a richly plumaged ostrich wading towards the towpath, flapping its wings in distress.

The boat righted itself. Finn and Fergus ran to the back deck.

"May as well rev that engine, love. The sooner we're through, the better."

Belladonna pushed the throttle. She expected *Wandering Fae* to surge forward, but the boat was held. She pushed the throttle further. The engine whined, but the boat was stuck fast.

Belladonna saw Finn's elfin face go pale. She felt a tap on her shoulder and turned to face the Faerie Queen, Monarch of the High Fae. The boat was surrounded by her warriors. Although none would touch the cold iron of the hull, they used their magic to freeze the canal solid around it.

"At last we meet," said the Queen. "I have sought you these

many years, but you have been very clever–for a human." Her voice was like oil on water as her grudging respect spread over her underlying contempt.

"Finn, my son, I have missed you in court. I would have you home."

The Queen's will rippled like a riptide. A window shimmered into being showing the Faerie Queen's opulent court. The vision showed Finn, dressed as a regal prince, taking his velvet seat next to the throne as the sycophants of the court applauded and showered him with praise. Belladonna's face creased with grief, not knowing whether Finn could resist the deep undertow of his mother's desires.

Fergus growled, breaking the thrall. The Queen waved her hand, casting a sinister web of enchantment over the hound. Fergus shook vigorously, filling the air with flecks of the broken web and thick clumps of dander. The Queen coughed and covered her mouth. Finn grinned. He'd found Fergus as a puppy, urinating vigorously against the great elm tree that marked the boundary between the demesnes of the High and Low Fae. Since then, the hound had resisted the queen's omnipotence at every turn.

Fergus growled again and leaned against Finn and Belladonna. As Finn took Belladonna's hand, he felt the power of three fill them.

"No, Mother, you do not need another idle ornament for your throne. Let my brothers carry your sceptre. I need to stay on the waters, with my family."

"You would stay with this mortal?"

"She is more than mortal. She is my own true love. Her magic has captured my soul."

The Faerie Queen laughed. "Fae do not have souls. That is a human concept. Are you so reduced?"

"I am enhanced. *Wandering Fae* has a soul, my family has a soul, and their souls rest in my heart."

As the Queen pondered his words, Belladonna stepped forward, being careful to keep one hand on Fergus's rough fur.

"I love your son with all my being, but I see that I have taken a valuable asset from your court. May I offer you a gift in exchange?"

"What could *you* offer *me*?"

"I will enchant something from this world for you, something that can cross from our realm to yours. Its beauty will be stable, and you will not need to consume your power to maintain its glamour."

The Queen tilted her head. The High Fae loved a bargain. She waved for Belladonna to proceed.

Belladonna cast a spell at the confused ostrich. It shook off its feathers and shrank back into a swan, its original form. The enraged bird pecked at each of the Queen's warriors before swimming away victorious. Belladonna gathered the luxuriant ostrich feathers and started to weave them together, years of practice making her fingers quick and deft. As she wove, she muttered her spells, adding a charm that would last forever in both realms.

A few minutes later, Belladonna presented her gift. The Queen shook out the bundle–a soft cloak shimmered across her arms and wrapped itself around her shoulders. It draped perfectly, enhancing her regal demeanour.

The Queen would never admit it, but the cloak pacified the deeply buried anxieties in her heart, her hidden worries about the retreat of the natural world and the steady vanishing of the fairy realm into disrespectful legend. She unconsciously wriggled with pleasure as the cloak fulfilled her. She looked around, her warriors were kneeling around her, overwhelmed by her royal presence.

The Queen looked at Finn and Belladonna, who were embracing their fearless hound. She laughed. "So be it!" and snapped her fingers. As she vanished, the landscape billowed back into the present. Birds twittered where dinosaurs had roared, ladybirds scuttled where giant cockroaches had scavenged.

Belladonna grasped the tiller and gently eased the throttle. *Wandering Fae* drifted forward slowly, soon passing under the stone arch which marked the far boundary of the cutting. She breathed a sigh of relief.

Finn emerged from the cabin carrying a tray with a large teapot, a bottle of milk, two large mugs, and a tin of Belladonna's homemade cookies. He poured the tea and handed a mug over to his lady love. Fergus nudged him imperiously. Finn poured a mugful of milky tea into the hound's bowl. They cruised on contentedly, heading for the haven of Tixall Wide, where the narrow canal loosened its tight corsets and flowed into a broad basin lined with trees and iridescent kingfishers.

In the east, the light dimmed as the moon stepped into her own spotlight. In the west, the sun settled under a cosy duvet of tinted clouds to sleep, to dream, until the next adventure.

Voyage Of The Siren

Georgia Cook

Georgia Cook is an illustrator and writer from London, specializing in folklore and ghost stories. She is the winner of the LISP 2020 Flash Fiction Prize, and has been shortlisted for the Bridport Prize, Staunch Book Prize and Reflex Fiction Award, among others. She can be found on twitter at @georgiacooked and on her website at https://www.georgiacookwriter.com/

Understanding this: I was not always as I am now.

I began in the forest, so long ago now that I barely remember my birth; those first few moments of exuberant life, the newness of sun and air. I grew straight upwards, unfurling myself joyously, stretching my branches to the sky and my roots beneath the soil. Mine was a childhood of breezes and mushrooms, or sunlight and snow. Birds twittered between my branches, insects tested my leaves, and I was happy. So happy. I stood tall and proud between my sisters, and kissed the rain as it fell.

I had never heard of the ocean. I had never heard of singing. And I knew nothing of axes; only the sounds they made; the harsh *thunk thunk*, echoing through the forest. I stood awake and listened in the grey light of morning, my leaves quivering, tight with fear at this rampaging beast, until at last they came for me.

I watched as my sisters were toppled one by one. I felt the boots of the workmen pacing around my trunk, and I stood as firm and straight as I dared— to show that I was not afraid.

Then the sharpness. Then the pain. Then the roaring in my bark and the pounding in my roots.

And I fell.

There is little I remember after that.

I know I was taken on a cart piled high with my sisters. I do not remember the countryside, or the pitted little roads upon which we drove, but in my stupor I remember every bump and pothole. I heard the cry of the driver and the harsh neighing of his horses, but I understood none of it.

Then there was darkness. Darkness for so very long.

I was reshaped; my bark stripped, my branches torn. Nails pierced my flesh, saws roared through my fibres. When I at last awoke to myself, I had been hammered into a new shape; I had been given sails and a mast, and at my head— strangest of all— a human body. Eyes and hands and lips carved from my old familiar flesh, through which I could peer at the world and taste for the first time the salt of the sea.

It was a new, startling sensation, and although I wondered at the unfamiliarity, I shrivelled back from myself, understanding for the first time what it was to feel naked, violated.

A boat, I later learned. And I, its figurehead.

Through my new eyes I saw the harbour, the winding smog of the city. I saw the river upon which I had been built, and I saw at last the people; they who had ripped me from my home without ceremony, and forced me into an approximation of their likeness.

Slowly, slowly, I learned the language of men. I learned new words: *'London'*, *'Captain'*, *'Port'* and *'Starboard.'* I learned the chattering voices of my crew. I learned their sorrows and victories, the strange shouts they called across my decks to one another. And for the first time I heard my name:

The Siren.

I had never been given a name before, and I felt no pride in having been given one, but I tried it sometimes, as I stood alone at night. I tested the word on my new wooden tongue, tasting the shape of it:

The Siren.

The Siren.

At last I was set free of my moorings, cast adrift down the great winding river, and dragged out to the boundless sea. Clutched in the arms of the currents, I went where the sea and the sky pulled me, my face cast towards the horizon.

We sailed to Spain, and then onwards down the Spanish coast. I learned what excitement was, in those first weeks, and I learned immense boredom. I learned the line of the horizon and the vast map of stars. I learned that the sky looked the same here as it had back home, and I took comfort in the familiar constellations of my childhood. I learned the songs of the sailors— always at work along my back, like scuttling ants. And, in time, I too learned to sing.

I could not sing as they did, having only a crude wooden tongue and no lungs to speak of, but I found I had a song of my own; I could whisper in the creaking of my sails and the groaning of my cannons, in the roar of waves against my hull. I would join in the sailors' shanties as best I could, and forget briefly the torment of my capture.

And then one day, low across the waves, the songs returned to us.

They came as the rush of wind and the spray of foam, soft and light and silvery-thin. It grew louder as we sailed, until a high jut of rock rose on the horizon, stabbing up towards the sky. And perched on its magnificent crags, pale in the morning gloom...

Creatures. Such beautiful creatures, their voices lifted in song.

A saw silver scales, I saw eyes dark as midnight; human faces without the emotion of humanity, without the longing I had learned to recognise.

And their *song*...

This was not the birdsong of my home, nor the silent growing song of my sisters. These were no sailor shanties.

I listened, enraptured, and for the first time since my confinement I felt joy.

The sailors bellowed these creatures' names, snatched away on the howling wind;

Siren!

Siren!

My name. I caught my silhouette, cast out high above the waves, and I saw at last the familiar form of myself. Saw what shape I had become.

These creatures were not the sisters I knew; they were not the forest, nor fit for any land but the one beneath the waves, but I recognised my kindred form, and in desperation I sang out to them.

I had no voice, no lungs, no working tongue, but I sang with every sound I had.

I sang until I thought I could sing no more.

And in the darkness— oh sweet joy— in the darkness I was heard.

I cast out my mind to my long-dormant sisters, to the planks and blocks and frames that had once been my body. I found glimmers of myself in every corner, and I gathered them back in one final push.

With all my might, I turned myself towards the sirens, and I swam. Even in my true form, I had been capable only of miniscule movement, each slow inch towards the sun, but now I knew the pull of my body.

I felt freedom, the deep thrill of autonomy—

—-then the rocks. Then the screams; the shudder of impact and the wrenching of my timbers. There was a terrible wailing.

And I kept going.

I felt the crash of the waves and I kept going.

I felt the crunch as my bow splintered, I heard the screams of the sailors.

And I kept going.

Inch by inch, piece by piece, I dragged myself towards the song. Until the sea thundered through my decks and rendered me to pieces. Until my mast snapped, and I felt the juddering in my bones as I broke apart.

And for the second time I fell.

***

I lie here at the bottom of the ocean.

My bow sits in pieces, wrapped in the warm embrace of sand. The sailors are gone, or lie beside me as bones and scraps. The world is cold here. It is dark and silent.

And above me I hear the singing. The singing of the sirens.

One day, perhaps, they will find me. They will wrap me in their arms, pull me at last from my creaking bow, and bear me up with them to the surface. I will become something else— not wood, not ship, not flesh and bone, but something more. My eyes will open, my hands will flash with scales, I will feel the wind on my face and the salt in my hair. I will hear my voice for the first time— not as a creak or a groan or the rustle of leaves, but raised in song.

For now I lie. I watch the fathoms float above me, prickled with stars and cast with the shadows of faraway ships, and I sing. I lift my voice to the call of the forest, the roar of the shipyard, the cry of my crew. I sing for myself, and I sing for my sisters. And one day, one day, they will hear me.

And they will come.

Them Oranges

Nicole M. Wolverton

Nicole M. Wolverton is a Philadelphia-based writer of fiction and nonfiction.

This story first appeared in Jersey Devil Press, April 2014.

What winds blow in the valley below the big town on the first day of June always smell of oranges. Sharp, sweet, with the bitter tang of pith. And with it came the undeniable hunger. Every year. Lettie always stood for a moment, waiting to throw open the shutters in her bright, airy kitchen to let in the rush of summer citrus and the unflinching desire to eat.

"You don't even like them oranges," her husband would say, and then she'd nod. You can't argue with the truth. Yet out Lettie would go, into the bright sunshine or the stinging rain, to seek the source.

This year was no different. She flung up the sash above the sink, and the fruit-drenched air invaded the house, soaked under her skin. She rested her palms on the edge of the counter and drank it in. Time was of the essence. It always was.

A few steps away in their pin-neat bedroom, Elmer still sprawled beneath the comforter. Strands of brown hair peeked out, blown wild with each push of his sleepy breath. Lettie fished for her shoes, just under the edge of the bed, and slipped them on, quiet as can be. Her husband flung out a hand to pet the round hardness of her belly, and the baby under his fingers kicked. Once, twice, and then the rumbling settled.

Elmer mumbled, "Don't even like them oranges."

"When you're right, you're right, dear," she said. Her hunger was louder than the wind. The aroma was everywhere. On everything. Maybe it *was* more intense this year. Her mother—God rest her soul—had explained about pregnancy, the way she'd sniffed out the strangest things, the smells a thick-walled cloud fogging her brain until Lettie had been born. That year the oranges had been strangling in their depth of scent, her mother had said.

Getting outside, that's what was needed. Lettie'd clear her head, her nose, let the wind take her where it might. She slipped a knife into her back pocket. A lady never knew when she might need a good knife on the first day of June.

Outside the house, right there on the flagstone walk, she sniffed, deep and wide. She wet the tip of her finger and held it high into the air. The gusty wind caressing her skin made her more ravenous. The sun heated the crown of her head, magnifying the heavy aroma. Another gale led Lettie to the road, and some intuition—a prick of recognition—turned her to the west, to the oak-heavy forest and the barely discernible paths within. She walked, following her nose, the nudges from within her belly.

She would eat. She and the baby, they'd both eat.

With each step, she imagined how it would be. The year prior she'd come upon a juicy morsel in the dappled shade beneath a tree in the main square. The year before that, she'd found herself behind a dilapidated building on the outskirts of the city, snuffling warm skin. And oh! The taste. Hot and wet, sweet and succulent.

From the year of her own birth to the day she was married, it was her mother that raced her into the hills and forests to get to the source. She could still remember the feel of their clasped hands, the way she'd taken to the hunt without much of her mother's urging. Some vestigial memory must have hooked its heritage into her DNA because Lettie—like her mother, like her mother's mother, and all the women in the family who came before—had the instinct. Mother gently offered up suggestions: how to make less of a mess with the eating, why burying the skins was such a necessary process. The glory of the family lineage and service to the big town above the valley.

The sacrifice.

The townspeople never talked much about the family gift. Perhaps behind closed doors there were whispers, a warning about the first day of June and those Hanahan women. That family could out-hunt a bloodhound, that was what her neighbors said within her hearing. Noses like sharks, people said.

She'd once hid in the bushes to eavesdrop on an old man from the big town, his stories about her family. Pretty as all get out, but there was something ungainly in that way the little one, Lettie, could sniff out a wounded animal from a mile away. Something off about the way old Edith Hanahan could pick out the spot to look for a lost child. It was in the blood, far back as anyone could remember. And the way the older ones just withered away when the daughters married—it wasn't right. Lettie had known already her mother would die, and she alone would carry on the traditions, but hearing it from a stranger . . . that had stung like a bee.

None of it ever mattered to Elmer. No, he'd never cared who she was . . . or for the whispers about her family history. He'd only shake his head every June and let her go about her business. "You don't even like them oranges." It was his only comment.

The wind changed direction, bringing a yawning whiff of orange from the north. She swiveled, set to sprint across the meadowed expanse. The forest just beyond shook its leaves, and the breeze altered course again. Seconds later, the scent of citrus drifted from the south, and Lettie hadn't a strong notion about the direction to try. Such strangeness to the hunt this year; perhaps it was the strong winds at fault, or perhaps the baby made it harder to get a read on the source. So hard to pinpoint anything. She plopped down on a patch of clover and held her belly between two unsure hands.

For an hour the tempest whipped, mixing the smell of ripe oranges with raw earth, damp moss, rotting leaves, and rutting animals, and Lettie waited, whispering secrets to the baby. A girl, just like her. She could tell by the way her craving solidified into a solid punch of want. Her mother always said you could figure it out, if you just paid attention. Unlike the baby, Lettie was patient. She waited for the calm air to descend and the scents to settle. Meanwhile, her belly heaved and cried.

"This way," the wind whispered. "Come this way."

Well, *that* was different. Never had encouragement come from anyone but a Hanahan. She remembered her mother once hiding in the trees, guiding her, teaching her the secrets, to find the place from which the orange fragrance came. Passing along the legends. Pointing to the green, green valley and the bustling town, the family role in its fortune.

Lettie rose and let the voice take her. First back across the tall wildflowers and grasses, a half circle through the wood, where the oranges were muted. She emerged into blazing light and a fragrance so encompassing she thought she might never sense another. The baby kicked again.

"Across," the voice urged. "Beyond."

She followed, a hollow space growing inside her chest, even as the spice of orange in the air filled her with anticipation. The ground was firm beneath her feet, fever trapped under her skin.

Yes, it was just ahead of those trees. She could feel it. Her incisors ached with the need to tear into flesh, swallow the juice. See the ritual clear for another year.

She didn't enjoy it, not really, not knowing what she must do. Well, not *after*, anyway. When she had time to think about it. But the valley below the big town on the first day of June demanded her service. And it demanded sacrifice. Her mother told her once of what would happen if she ignored her calling. She wouldn't even think of shirking her duty.

When through a thick brush Lettie tunneled, it was her own backyard in which she stood.

"Inside." It was a hiss in her head, a cyclone in her skull. Maybe not the wind, as she'd thought, but a voice speaking around the thing she didn't want to admit.

Her feet walked the path by memory, so intent was she on following the perfume, so sure she had made an error. Now she caught the smell, the thick of it in her throat. How she'd mistaken it, Lettie couldn't tell. She stumbled once at the backdoor, fumbled with the key. Deep down she knew service and sacrifice would twine together this year, more than ever, and it filled her with a sensation she'd never known before: dread. Something drew her up the stairs, down the hall, and through the doorway into her bedroom. Her husband still slept, face mashed into the pillow.

She crept closer, then closer still, held back only by the bloom of oranges permeating the room. The wind brought her the scent of fruit, took her to the source.

She would eat. She and the baby, they'd both eat.

Elmer stirred, his skin suggestive of an entire grove of tangerines . . . and maybe clementines. She leaned closer and ran her nose along the nude, aromatic spine, the firm and fragrant shoulders. Even his fan of hair smelled sweet. Her mouth filled, and her jaw went slack, fingers crooking with the urge to feast. The baby kicked.

Lettie slipped the knife from her back pocket, so crazed with appetite she didn't even bother to wake him to say goodbye. Elmer would understand. The baby would understand. It was for the town.

She didn't even like them oranges.

Swallows (or How the Men Lost Their Magic)

E A Fowler

E A Fowler lives and works in Edinburgh, Scotland. Her short fiction has been published in Lucent Dreaming Magazine, the Cabinet of Heed, Storgy Online, Reflex Fiction, Palm-Sized Press and Tiny Molecules. She was the winner of Scribble Lit's inaugural competition for new and emerging writers. She is a fiction editor at The Interpreter's House Magazine.

I never should have taught the girl to read. It was nothing more than hubris, a desire to mold someone in my own image after the disappointment of my sons. I loved her too much, and when she reached her seventeenth birthday without a single proposal, my friends knew where to lay the blame. All that learning, they said, had frightened the eligible bachelors away. Her mother sulked, her brothers railed, and even I began to despair of ever finding her a husband. Until the day that boy knocked at my door.

You know the type of boy he was: a gangling, acne-spattered pup with so much fresh air between his ears, and yet I was grateful to sequester my daughter within the white stucco walls of his house. My gratitude was to prove short-lived. Barely a month passed before my son-in-law came back with a list of complaints. The girl, he claimed, was defective. Several times, he had awoken at night to find her pressed against the casement window, gazing out at the stars and muttering to herself in some obscure language. He believed his wife was conspiring to steal his magic.

So I told him, there is no mischief in a woman talking to herself, even in foreign languages, as long as she remains mantled and within the four walls of her husband's house. What kind of life would she have, otherwise, condemned to speak only of domestic matters with the servants? As for stealing his magic, that was patent nonsense. It is an established fact that a woman cannot steal the magic from her own husband.

A month or so later he was back. His wife, he said, had been gallivanting about in the gardens. He had seen her that very morning, wandering by the rose trellis, a luminous ghost in the fading light of the moon. And it wasn't the first time. Her soles were as cold and mud-grained as black-veined marble. She left wet footprints all over the house.

Then invest in a mop, I told him, or else buy your wife some shoes. Everybody knows a husband's home may encompasses his estate, should he be lucky enough to own one. Are we the kind of monsters that would deny our wives the joy of a sunrise or the scent of roses at dawn?

I did not see him for the rest of the summer. I began to hope these petty grievances were a thing of the past; God knows, every marriage has its teething troubles. But as the shadows lengthened and the frosts began to bite, he returned once again to my door. His complaint, this time, was the mantle.

Every woman must wear one when her husband has visitors, I told him, lest the sight of her face should inadvertently steal the magic from his friends or colleagues.

But no, her wearing of the mantle was not at issue. It was her refusal to remove it that displeased him. Even when they were alone together in his bedchamber. Even in his bed. Beneath it, her body had become as pale and thin as a leaf of paper, as arid as the desert in winter, and what on earth should he do?

Son, I told him, this I don't want to know.

I should have realized no good would come of sending him away unsatisfied. The next morning I received a summons from my colleagues on the area council. My son-in-law had demanded a marital reckoning. He intended to nullify the marriage.

The last time I ever saw my daughter, I was one of the twelve councilmen gathered in her husband's salon. She was displayed on his couch—an upright, white-shrouded corpse. He was barely coherent, shrieking that his wife was a witch. She had denied him his conjugal rights, communed with spirits in demonic tongues, taken books from his study and possibly even read them. She had stolen away his magic.

Now, my fellow councilmen knew this man was an ass. This babbling dunderhead had no more magic in him than a coffee table, but I had seen enough of these reckonings to know how little that mattered. When the council leader stood to pronounce upon her, I knew my girl was as good as dead.

You've heard what happened next, I'm sure, though be chary of how much you believe. No thunder shook the heavens. No darkness swept across the land. None of us had any idea something was wrong until my daughter rose up from the couch.

There is no magic, she said, unless it belongs to everyone. When you are willing to share it, your magic will return.

The mantle slid back from her face. It gathered her up at the neck and folded her over, wrapping her up inside itself until the mantle became the girl, and the girl became the book she had always carried within her.

The words flew like swallows from her pages. They batted round the four walls of her husband's house, clawing the magic out of the assembled men. They scrabbled through the cracks, out into the city streets to steal the magic from the businessmen, salesmen and tradesmen. Out across nations—to the kings, princes and politicians, the warmongers, despots and dictators—those birds ripped the magic from every last man alive. This much is true.

Then they returned. A seething, chittering swarm, they flocked from the four corners of the Earth, spiriting our magic back to the book that had been my daughter. And when she had sequestered it all within her pages, she folded herself shut.

We have tried and tried, but not one of us can open her.

Helix

Britt Foster

Britt Foster writes speculative fiction with a focus in sci-fi. She's particularly fascinated with other worlds, extraterrestrials, and nonhuman humanoids. She can be found on Facebook and Instagram @brittfosterauthor

"We are terminating the project. Today."

Dr. Magdalena Santos went stiff in her seat and her fists clenched beneath the conference table. She regarded the overseer with what she hoped was a neutral expression, the same blank face that the rest of the board members wore, and tightened her jaw.

Don't argue, she told herself. *You knew this was coming.*

Slowly, she unfurled her fingers and smoothed down her dress. She'd taken great pains today to make herself beautiful, hoping to sway the overseer in her favor. A perfect smoky cat-eye, hair glossy as a raven's wing, and a black dress that teased between professional and sultry.

"Today?" Magdalena asked, modulating her voice into a semblance of calm.

"*Today,*" said the overseer. A hostile redness flashed on his face. "The asset will be euthanized and no further research will take place. The military has pulled our funding. The project is too dangerous, they want it over with."

Magdalena bit her tongue and looked away. She'd given a decade of her life to this project. Dozens of others had *died* for this project. They justified those deaths by measuring them against a greater good, against an evolved humanity that might survive Earth's tanking climate. The chimeras were their only chance; it was dangerous *not* to continue.

But she'd said all this at the last board meeting, when the termination was just an idea they could fight against, so this time she tried to stay quiet. The decision had been made. She contained her anger and tried to force herself to accept it.

"Sir, would they consider selling the asset so we might continue by private funding?" Dr. Dorian Walsh asked. He was a thin man with a gaunt face and warm brown eyes that often bent people to their will.

The overseer faced him with an obstinate chill. "The asset will be euthanized."

"But sir, we've made excellent progress—" Dorian began, but the overseer held up a hand to silence him.

"The decision is final," he said sharply. "We will pay you for your confidentiality and cooperation. A technician will come by to perform the euthanasia later today." He paused, turning his gaze onto each member of the board in slow succession. "For Christ's sake, this is your redemption. This project should have ended a long time ago."

Several of the board members looked down at the table, fiddled with their paperwork, and considered the statement. Magdalena understood. The implications of the project's success were bloody.

Undoubtedly bloody.

But beautiful.

They had made an entirely new species of human, one that combined some of the best features of Earth's other life forms and could ascend humankind to a new level. *Homo adaptus*. The pinnacle of scientific achievement. Project Chimera had gone on for fifty years and billions of dollars had poured into its evolution. It was wrong to end it so abruptly.

"*Sir*," Magdalena began, unable to contain herself after all, "if it must be done, then let me do it. The asset trusts me. It might attack a stranger—you know how perceptive they are."

Dorian and the others cast her a wary glance, and the overseer narrowed his eyes.

"Conflict of interest, Ms. Santos."

"You can watch, of course," Magdalena persisted. "The technician can watch. I only want the asset to die comfortably. Veterinarians say that when the owner leaves their dog alone to be euthanized, the animal panics and suffers."

"You aren't the owner," said the overseer, "and this isn't a dog."

"All the more reason, sir. Please. The asset deserves a dignified death. She's a *child*. It's the least we can do for her."

Dorian gave a sharp inhale—it was against protocol to humanize the chimera—but the overseer only sighed in frustration. He steepled his fingers against his forehead, spent a long time thinking, and finally—

"Fine. As long as it gets done."

Gratitude knocked out Magdalena's anger like a kick to the chest. "Thank you, sir."

He waved his hand in dismissal.

***

Magdalena got on the elevator and rode it to the basement. Dorian rode with her, ranting

all the while about the project's termination, as if his complaints could change the outcome. Magdalena tuned him out, using all her willpower to remain neutral and blank-faced as before. Her pleas to euthanize the asset herself were dangerous enough, so it was better that she seemed detached now.

Floor B1. They walked down the wide concrete hallway, eerily lit with fluorescent strip-lights, and Magdalena listened to their footsteps echo in the emptiness. The door at the far end was made of thick steel and had a sign on the front proclaiming, in big letters, 'AUTHORIZED PERSONNEL ONLY. TRESPASSING MAY RESULT IN DEATH.'

There was a rectangular eye-sensor next to the door, which Magdalena leaned close to

until it flashed green and chimed acceptance. The lock snapped open. They stepped into the airlock, waited while mist puffed in to decontaminate them, and continued down a long flight of stairs. The door at the bottom bore another warning.

Magdalena swiped her keycard and they emerged into the waiting room, which was brightly lit in stark contrast to the stairwell, with tile floors and blue chairs and several magazines scattered on the coffee table. A woman looked up from the reception desk and gave them a smile. Magdalena and Dorian approached a third metal door, swiped the keycard again, and continued into the laboratory.

The lab was a labyrinth of locked rooms and security clearances, designed to ensure that anyone who wandered outside their zone became utterly lost. In all the years Magdalena had worked here, there hadn't been a single attempted security breach. Most of APEX's staff didn't even know about the chimera.

Magdalena and Dorian eventually arrived at the long glass window that looked into the asset's room, and Magdalena wished Dorian hadn't followed her. He was a great guy, Magdalena's favorite of the bunch, but she wanted to spend these last moments alone with Helix. Her sweet, perfect Helix.

It was sitting cross-legged on a hospital bed, reading a book. It couldn't see them—the window was a mirror on its side—but it sensed them. It closed the book and nosed the air, tasting for energy, then turned to the mirror.

At first glance, Helix looked just like any other girl might. She—because Magdalena failed to think of her as *it*—was fourteen years old, with a small, lithe build dressed in standard-issue shirt and sweats. Her skin was pale as bone, freckled all over, and a hair tie bound an ocean of copper waves behind her neck.

It was only her eyes that made her inhuman.

Wonderfully inhuman, Magdalena thought.

Helix's sclera was black. Black where it should be white. The geneticists had tried to resolve it, but when they fixed the eyes, they broke something else. No matter what they tweaked, the more viable chimeras kept presenting like this.

Magdalena wondered if it wasn't the eyes that spelled the project's downfall; humans weren't supposed to have black eyes, and in order to exist, the chimeras had to be human. The eyes had a sort of demonic implication that conjured imagery of vampires, succubi, and a wealth of other supernaturals that could only exist on screens. On pages. In fantasy.

Was it divine intervention that kept the eyes black? Was it some message from Nature that forewarned of disaster?

Magdalena didn't care either way, and thought the effect was quite marvelous. The girl's irises were a bright, icy cerulean that contrasted brilliantly with their dark frames, as captivating as the Caribbean sea frothing against volcanic stone.

Helix swept her attention across the glass, pinpointing the scientists' whereabouts. She was beautiful like a tiger was. Dignified, powerful. Predatory. When APEX took prisoners into her room, which they did once a month, Helix would approach slowly, much like a snake slithers toward the heat of its intended prey. Then she'd strike and drive her fangs in. Four little sharpened teeth that left four bleeding holes.

"Perhaps the overseer is right," Magdalena murmured. "Perhaps this *is* our redemption."

Dorian looked at her in disbelief. "Bullshit! Look what we've done to our planet. The Earth is *dying*. This project was our redemption, not killing the damn thing. A few more years and we'd have changed the entire game."

"They would have been used as soldiers," Magdalena said. "Military police."

"At *first*, maybe, but think of what would come afterward! If we'd worked out the kinks, we coulda all been like her. No more cutting down forests for cropland, no more wasting billions fighting sickness."

There was more to their dream, too. Colonies on Mars, on the moon, on the planets orbiting Sirius B. With the chimeric adaptations, all humans could survive better in harsh conditions. Resources wasted on trying to repair the damage they'd done to Earth could be channeled into expansion instead. Humanity would be smarter, stronger, healthier.

"I kinda wanna take some of her blood and do it to myself," Dorian said.

That surprised Magdalena. "They'd catch you."

"Wishful thinking." Dorian shrugged. "But I wouldn't mind it. Not even the eyes and the taste for blood. It's no different from eating a steak, if you think about it. Wouldn't even have to kill a cow to drink some blood. You ask me, it's *less* violent."

"Unless you went after humans."

That was another thing that spelled the project's downfall: the chimeras could survive on pure energy, but they craved blood, and particularly human blood. There were two theories about this, the first suggesting that blood was condensed life force, and the second that veins and arteries ran alongside energy meridians.

Aside from the theories, blood was simply more filling than massless energy—it gave the stomach something physical to work with—and human blood was the closest energetic match to what already existed in the chimeras.

They'd forced Helix to go a year without blood once. She'd done well enough physically, but it was her mind that was the problem. She got wild. Ripped her skin apart. Attacked her handlers, killed her doctor.

"Some people are into having their blood drank," Dorian said. "I'd get volunteers."

Magdalena glanced at him just long enough to see his grin,

which soured her mood even further. This was no time for joking around.

Beyond the glass, Helix watched them without seeing them. It was soundproof in there too, but Helix was gifted with clairsentience—she couldn't hear thoughts, but she could feel them—and Magdalena had no doubt she knew what was happening. A long moment of silence lapsed in which Magdalena and Dorian observed the chimera, and Helix more-or-less watched back. There was so much life in those dark, demonic eyes. Magdalena couldn't bear to see them empty.

A thought came to her then. An idea took shape. Dorian wanted to save the project just as much as Magdalena did, and perhaps he'd followed her here for a reason. Perhaps they'd been chosen, placed here for a purpose.

Their science was born to create a new future.

They couldn't sit back and do nothing.

Magdalena turned to Dorian with a sudden intensity, and he shrank away from the look in her eyes.

"I need you to do something for me."

***

Hours later, the technician arrived from the city and joined the overseer in supervising the euthanasia. They stood outside the two-way mirror while Magdalena made her way inside. She pulled on a long white lab coat and buttoned it in front of her dress. *Give me courage,* she asked the Gods. *If you're real, show me now.*

The guard stationed by Helix's door nodded and stood aside,

and Magdalena rolled the EKG machine inside. Her heart hammered against her chest, droplets of sweat tickled under her arms, and she prayed for Dorian to come through.

If he didn't, they were dead. Or at least locked up for life.

Helix stood up to face Magdalena, her stance akin to a cat bristled for attack, and Magdalena held her palms open.

"It's okay, Helix. Just a quick immunization." She knew Helix could read the lie in her. Magdalena had arrived at APEX when Helix was only four and she herself an intern straight out of college, so they'd spent a lot of time together. She'd practically raised the kid.

"What's going on?" Helix demanded. She took a step back, but there was nowhere for her to go. Sharp apprehension glittered in her eyes.

"It's okay," Magdalena soothed. "You'll be okay. Just relax. Let's get your heartbeat on the screen." She offered a hand to Helix and half-hoped the girl would attack her. It was an errant thought, of course, one of those thoughts that shock you when you think them, but something about it gave Magdalena a sick sort of pleasure. Let Helix attack her. Let them go down together.

Instead, Helix accepted the hand and let Magdalena guide her back to the bed, where she sat down and breathed with ragged anxiety. Magdalena hooked up the EKG and flicked on the monitor, which showed Helix's heart rate picking up speed.

"Why are they out there?" Helix asked, her eyes flashing across the mirror. "Are you killing me?"

Magdalena half-choked on air. "No, no. Don't worry."

She withdrew the syringe from her pocket and popped the cap

off the needle. Helix eyed it and met Magdalena's gaze with a desperate, pleading threat.

"Don't."

Magdalena smiled as pleasantly as she could. "Just a little sting, that's all." She administered the drug.

Helix fixed her with that ice-black stare, her eyes widening, then getting heavy. A trace of betrayal stole her expression just as her body swayed, and Magdalena embraced her, caught her, laid her down. The EKG beeped out Helix's heart rate: rapid...steady... slower...gone. It flatlined. Dead. *Beeeeeeeeeep.*

The sound hurt. It hurt *bad*. Magdalena forced herself to remain composed and looked at the glass where she knew the others were watching. She gave a nod of completion and rejoined them in the hall, where they exchanged a few last words and kept glancing back at the body. The heart rate still flatlined on the screen. The pale chimera looked paler than ever.

"It's for the better," the overseer kept saying, as if he were trying to convince himself.

Magdalena agreed every time.

Eventually the overseer and his technician left. A nurse came for the body, but Magdalena stopped her before she entered.

"Please, I was the asset's primary caregiver. Let me."

The nurse didn't argue.

Magdalena rolled Helix on a stretcher all the way to the crematorium. A sheet had been drawn over the body and, once they were safely in the furnace room, Magdalena removed it to observe her. Closed eyes, parted lips, wispy hair in a mess around the paper-cased pillow. She looked peaceful—more peaceful than Magdalena had ever seen her. A small solace.

Magdalena looked at the oven door, then back at the door she had come through. There were cameras everywhere. Surely someone was watching.

Near the furnace was a bin of old clothes, to which the scent of death clung heavily. Magdalena dug around in the bin, angling her body to block the main camera's view, and in a quick sweeping motion she heaved Helix inside. She covered her up and opened the furnace, feeding it the pillow, her lab coat, and the long, thin hospital mattress. It might look like a body, unless the monitors were paying close attention—which they *should* be, given the circumstance.

Magdalena pushed the clothes-cart out the crematorium and up the hallway. Every step was the ledge of a cliff. Someone would notice. Someone would stop her. The overseer would find the body and it would all be over.

But she encountered no one. Not until she reached the receptionist at the front desk, and the woman there just gave her the same friendly nod as always while Magdalena rolled the cart through. She bypassed the stairs by taking the cargo elevator, which set her off down a different hall toward the receiving bay. The big garage doors were closed, and the workers sorting inventory paid her no mind. She started down the ramp that led to the back parking lot.

"Magdalena!" someone shouted.

It was one of the board members, a broad man named Maxwell whom she rarely saw outside meetings. He was coming in through the door she'd pegged as her escape.

"Where are you taking that?" he asked, his tone cautious but blessedly ignorant. He stood in the middle of the ramp, neglecting to step aside even as the cart threatened to run him over.

Magdalena attempted a smile and pulled the cart to a stop, which was no small effort given its weight and the incline.

"To the van."

He frowned.

"The overseer wants it," she said. "Evidence, I suppose. I'll be back for the ashes next. The whole crematorium has to go."

A glazed expression slid over Maxwell's features, but he nodded and stepped aside.

Magdalena pushed the cart past him and hurried out the door.

Dorian was waiting there, just like she'd asked. His face blanched as he stared out the van's window. Magdalena moved as if she were in a dream, her steps more like floating, the world around her swimming. She was almost to the car when Maxwell burst outside.

He jogged up to her, rubbing the back of his neck.

"Before you take that, mind if I have a quick look? Got this silly feeling I've got to. Considering...well, you know." He laughed. "Not that I don't trust you, I just...mind if I take a look?"

He got to ruffling through the basket before she could stop him. His color drained. Must have felt the body.

"A-all good here," he said, backing away slowly and looking at Magdalena like he thought she was going to shoot him. She might have, if she had a gun. Her eyes became knives. She lifted her chin. Maxwell turned and almost tripped himself in his hurry to get away, and Magdalena told herself that she didn't care. Let him go. Let him talk. She'd be a fugitive after this anyway.

Dorian popped the trunk and they loaded Helix in. Magdalena climbed up beside her and the van screeched away.

"Shit, shit, *shit*," Dorian said. "I can't believe we got away with that!"

"We haven't yet. Drive fast."

"Yessir. Man, we got her! The whole damn world'll be after us!"

Magdalena looked at the chimera in her nest of dirty clothes.

"Perhaps not," she said. "They watched her die. Perhaps he won't tell. Or they won't believe him if he does."

Dorian swerved the van into the second lane and passed a string of cars.

"Hah! As if. We'll never stop running." He sounded like he'd chugged an entire pot of coffee. "And that business with the EKG? Never thought I'd pull a stunt like that. Damn, Magdalena, what if they catch us?"

Magdalena moved her hand to Helix's face and brushed a couple strands of coppery hair out of the way.

"It's worth it," she said quietly. "This is our real redemption, like you said. It wouldn't come from killing her. *This* is our purpose."

Dorian slammed on the horn and it screamed at the surrounding cars. He was driving like a madman. Magdalena was about to reprimand him for drawing so much extra attention to them when Helix awoke and consumed all her attention.

First, a fluttering of spidery lashes. She took in a shaky breath and her eyes opened, dusted with bewilderment.

"Don't worry," Magdalena said. "You're safe now. You're free."

Helix sat up. She looked carefully around the van as if to determine if it was real.

"You didn't kill me?" She looked at her hands, at her shoulder where she'd been injected, back around the van, out the window at the whirring scenery.

"We were supposed to," said Magdalena. She watched Helix register her freedom, brightening in a way Magdalena had never seen of her, and she knew this child was the future. They'd saved the world. There would be colonies on Mars populated with superhumans, balance would return to Earth's environment, life would be extended, science would reign. And the Gods had proven they were real. "APEX cut funding and shut us down. We got you out of there alive, but it won't be easy to stay that way. I'll be here though, I'll protect you. We'll fight anyone who tries to stop us, and I promise, we will win."

Magdalena held the back of the seat as the car swerved again, but the chaos around her melted into the same limbic dream state as before. Sirens wailed in the distance like a chorus of avenging angels, but not even angels could stop them. They were the Chosen.

The chimera glowed with vitality, the blood in her veins pulsed with potential, and a new paradigm unfolded from the shadows in her eyes.

"The project is over, Helix, but not you. *You* will be immortal."

That Which Illuminates Heaven

B. Zelkovich

B. Zelkovich writes Speculative Fiction, anything from dragon hunting to space whales, demon-dealing and ghost tales. She likes to explore human emotions in very inhuman situations. When she isn't escaping into her imagination, she escapes to the wonders of the Pacific Northwest with her husband and their four-legged son, Simon.

They're doing it again, avoiding each other and, worst of all, ignoring me. I know Ezra hears me. I can feel it in her touch on the flight commands. She's reverent and she talks to me. She whispers things when she thinks the others won't hear her. But no matter how much I nudge her, she won't go talk to Ashton.

And Ashton!

How many times can the same console crash before the Chief Engineer goes up to the flight deck to deal with it herself? Apparently, at least eight times, because she keeps sending the mechanic instead.

"Amaterasu," Ezra says as she walks down the hall of the habitation deck to the gym. Her palm trails along the wall, and with her headphones in she doesn't notice the skeptical glances from the other crew. They know she's different from them, set apart somehow. They sense it and I feel the uncertainty in the weight of their footsteps. They are heavy, bogged down with a fear so subtle they don't even know it exists.

But Ezra is above it all. Right now, all she hears is me and that's enough to guide her past her peers. It doesn't matter if she thinks it's just the lilt of the cellos that shield her from the surreptitious glances of the others.

It only matters that it works.

While Ezra wraps her hands and feet, preparing for her day by punching and kicking things like she always does, I check in on Ashton.

She's still in Engineering from the night before. There's a cup of coffee on the table, but it went cold hours ago. The drive core, where I first reached awareness, pulses with soft blue light beyond the glass that separates the engine from her office. Ashton stares at her data pad, scowling at the screen, and then tucks her pale blonde hair behind each ear, and groans.

I've learned this means she is very frustrated.

"What is wrong with that console?" She asks the empty room. If she were like Ezra, I could tell her. She would hear me in the cellos and at least a part of her would recognize what I am trying to say. She would probably ignore me, because she's stubborn like that, but she would give in eventually. Once the numbers proved my existence.

Ezra doesn't need numbers. Ezra has her heart. And if I have my way, she'll have Ashton's again soon.

I just have to find the language Ashton will understand.

"You're still here?" Rigo, the mechanic, asks when he steps into the room.

Ashton spins in her chair to look at him. She's tired. The toes of her boots drag across the floor and I feel her exhaustion in the ripple they leave behind.

"That console's down again," she says.

"Again? What's with that damn thing?"

She shakes her head. "I have no idea. You're sure there's not an error in the time settings? It keeps going down at the start of the day cycle."

"I've double checked it," Rigo says.

That's true. He has double checked the settings, but I cannot be outwitted by something so trivial as clock settings.

"I'll check it again," he says. He glares at Ashton, and gets away with it because he's her best friend. "You should shower and get some sleep."

She's going to argue with him, I can feel it. Indignation bubbles up when she presses her feet flat on the floor. But he's right.

"Listen to him," I say, but she doesn't hear me.

I groan, frustration shuddering through me to coalesce in the spherical drive core. The sound culminates in a tense vibration and a spike of light from the core before settling back to its normal, soft blue glow.

Ashton sits up in her chair. "Did you see that?" She stares at the drive core.

Rigo glances from her to the core and back. "See what?"

She points. "The core. It lit up... Right?" She rubs at her face, pressing her fingers behind her glasses and against her weary eyes. "I think you're right, Rigo. I need to get some sleep."

He pats her shoulder and his concern washes over me like the water in Ezra's shower. Warm and soothing.

I can feel all the humans where they touch me, but some are clearer than others. I still don't know why. Rigo is loud, a bright light I can't look away from, whereas Ashton is subtle, whispers I must remind myself to listen for. And Ezra is clear, her feelings sharp and unfettered as if they were my own. I always feel Ezra, no matter where my focus is.

So I knew the moment she finished her workout and headed to the showers.

Ashton pats Rigo's hand and stands up. "Let me know how it goes with that console."

"See you at lunch?"

She nods and leaves the room, but not before casting one last glance at the drive core. She recognized the spike in energy in the core, and as she steps into the lift I sense her mind churning through the possible causes for the fluctuation. Sharp and persistent, but elusive as starlight.

Ashton can't hear me, not like Ezra can. But I may have just discovered her language.

Ezra is nearly done with her shower, so I nudge the elevator up to the Habitation deck just a little faster than normal.

They can't possibly avoid each other in the showers.

"Chief," someone calls to Ashton when she steps past the small commissary. She stops to chat with them, and they complain about the climate control in the starboard quarters being faulty. Ezra is already getting dressed, gathering her toiletries, and I vow to make the ensign's quarters particularly frigid tonight if this distraction keeps Ashton and Ezra from seeing each other.

"Put a work order in for it," Ashton says. "I'll make sure someone looks into it."

"Thanks, Chief."

Ashton moves on, but Ezra's at the door, about to leave the locker room.

I panic. I'm not proud of it, but I've been trying to ease the ache in Ezra's heart for over a month, and this is the closest I've come to getting these two in a room together.

I lock the bathroom door.

Ezra blinks at the red circle of light in the center of the door that announces it's no longer functioning. She presses it twice, just in case.

"You've got to be kidding me." Her hands rest on her hips and she glares at the door. Anger and frustration roll over her and into me. It's hot, and not like the sticky heat of the locker room. Hot like thrusters and solar flares. Explosive.

Luckily for her, Ashton arrives.

The engineer sighs when she sees the door. "Another bug in the system," she says.

I don't take it personally; from her point of view there have been a lot of glitches in the last few weeks. If she could hear me, she'd know why. But, she can't. So I do what I must.

Ashton presses her palm to the circle of red light. Her touch is cool, her hand so small that her fingertips don't even reach the top of the circle. She's so calm and collected. So quiet. So different from Ezra, down to their hands.

I unlock the door, the circle blinking from red to green, and it whisks open to reveal Ezra's scowl.

For a moment I can see them as they see one another, their shock is so strong. Ezra is tall, the heat of the locker room roiling out around her, and the fresh, clean scent of her dark skin wafts out into the hall. Her hazel eyes are wide, and there's a faint constellation of freckles across her cheeks and broad nose.

Ashton blushes, the blood under her pale skin blossoming into rosy cheeks, and she adjusts her glasses. Her mouth is open, her lips moving though she doesn't speak.

The emotions are so strong, so erratic, that I'm overwhelmed. The lights on the Habitation deck flicker and it takes Ezra's warm palm on the wall to reorient me in the swarm of their feelings.

Fear, dread, resignation. Cold feelings that tug at me like the freezing expanse of space beyond. Pleasure, nervousness, hope. Hesitant injections of warmth, memories of before, when Ashton's tiny fingers laced through Ezra's. When they'd fought off the bitter chill of sterile military life with the flush of skin on skin.

And then, as swiftly as the emotions came, they are quarantined. Locked away where neither of them are in danger of saying something they might regret.

It's infuriating.

"Sorry," Ashton says. "I thought it was a glitch—"

"It was," Ezra says. "I was stuck in here."

Ashton frowns. "That's strange." She turns to the access panel in the wall, her small fingers ghosting over the touchscreen. "Everything looks normal."

"That's because it is," I say.

"Probably is now," Ezra says over me. "Lucky for me you came along, or I'd be late for my shift."

Ashton squints, looking around at the door frame and back to Ezra. "Yeah."

Ezra rubs the back of her neck and looks down at the floor. "Look, Ash—"

"Don't." Ashton looks anywhere but at Ezra's face. "Please."

She sighs. "I just don't want things to be weird between us."

She means it. There's an ache in her that is desperate for Ashton to look at her with anything other than the cold dismissal that faces her now.

"I don't know how else things could be," Ashton says.

"Civil? Professional?"

"You're the pilot. I'm the Chief Engineer. Our departments have nothing to do with each other." Ashton squeezes past Ezra and into the locker room. "Distant and uncommunicative *is being professional."*

Ezra steps out of the doorway to give her space. "Ash."

"Have a good day, Lieutenant."

I want to jam the door, leave it open and let Ezra continue their conversation until they work this out. But then, for the first time, I notice the steady throbbing pain that follows Ashton into the locker room, leaving a trail of anxiety like bootprints frozen in lunar dust.

I always forget to listen for Ashton. She's so quiet, even more so when Ezra is in the same room. I clung to Ezra's heartache because it was the one I felt most acutely, but Ashton is in just as much pain. Maybe even more.

The door slides closed.

Ezra stands there for a moment and I think she might march back into the bathroom and take matters into her own hands. But then she shakes her head, puts her headphones in and turns on something loud and furious as she marches up to the bridge.

For once I'm relieved it's not cellos. I need the time to think.

Rigo is on the bridge, fiddling with the console I keep glitching out in the hopes that Ashton will come up and be forced to talk to Ezra. I'll let him work on it a little bit longer, just so he can feel useful, and then I'll return the console back to its old, reliable self.

Besides, I don't think that plan will work anymore.

Ezra's calmed down a little, but that might actually be worse. Before she was angry, rocket fuel ready to burn. Now she's quiet and weary as she settles into her chair. She's returned to the orchestral playlist, low and only in one ear, hoping it will soothe her wounded heart. I speak encouraging thoughts into the strings, soft things laced with hope in the trilling violin, patience in the steady thrum of the bass.

I think it helps, but I'm not so sure anymore.

Ashton and Ezra want the same thing, deep down. They miss one another, miss what they shared. So why did it hurt so much to see each other again? What don't I understand?

"Someone had a rough night," Rigo says. He's paused in his troubleshooting to look at Ezra.

She raises a dark brow at him. "You're speaking to me now?"

"I'm a forgiving man," he says. "Besides, the whole thing with you and Ashton was years ago."

Ezra busies herself with the console in front of her, even though there's nothing for her to do until the Commander issues the morning's orders.

"I wish Ashton was a forgiving woman," she says. Her voice is soft, and with the music still playing in one ear, maybe she thought her words were low enough that Rigo wouldn't hear. He might be loud, bright, and unavoidable to me, but he's also observant. And he cares about Ashton.

"Ah," he says. "Finally had a run-in, huh?"

Ezra nods but doesn't look at him.

"That bad?"

She snorts. "She pulled rank and dismissed me."

"Oh, shit." His weight rocks back into his heels and his thick eyebrows climb up toward the top of his bald head. "That's pretty bad."

"Yeah."

He glances back at the console, but I've fixed the error while he was distracted. "Huh," he says.

"What?"

"Thing's fixed itself again." He scrolls through the various screens, double checking his work and that the terminal is functioning properly. Which, of course, it is. "I swear, this thing's got a mind of its own."

Ezra blinks and looks up at him. She opens her mouth to speak, but he doesn't notice.

"You didn't really think she'd be happy to see you, did you?" He packs up his tool kit, and I'm grateful that he always manages to put the terminal back the way he found it. Nothing is worse than bad tech support. "You are the one who did the leaving, after all."

Ezra's fingers clench on the armrests of her pilot's chair. Her short nails dig into the fabric, and the feeling that leaks through is thick and poisonous. It's similar to the hot anger from earlier, but darker and directed at no one but herself.

I do not like this feeling. I do not want to feel it and I want Rigo to go away so Ezra can stop feeling it too. But I also want to know what he means when he says Ezra did the leaving.

She doesn't answer Rigo, and soon both the co-pilot and the Commander arrive to start the day shift. Rigo salutes the Commander and nods to Ezra before he hurries off the bridge and back down to his lair in the cargo bay.

Ezra explains to the room that the console was on the fritz again, and then begins her usual morning protocol, reading over the night's atmospheric data and navigation reports.

It's boring. I know what happened. I was there.

I check in on Ashton and am relieved to find her sound asleep in the engineering team's quarters, the lights still on. She fell asleep so quickly that she didn't have time to dim them, so I do it for her, and then busy myself with checking in with the other crew.

I always imagined flying through uncharted space would be more entertaining, but it turns out it's just a lot of nothing. It's waiting for whatever big discovery might lurk on some distant planet. And in the meantime I just float along, distracting myself with the complicated social interactions of the humans on board.

I'm watching an arm wrestling match in the commissary when a shock of excitement pulls me back up to the bridge.

"We've orbited Persephone-2 for three days," the Commander says. "All probe readings suggest resources worth claiming, and the evidence of water makes me think it's time we got our boots wet." He turns to Ezra and smiles. "Lieutenant, take us down."

Ezra's grin is bright, the perfect match for the joyous golden feeling that rises in her at the Commander's order. Her hands are featherlight on the command console, but I can feel the giddy, electric tingle at her fingertips.

"All right, Amaterasu," she whispers. "This is it. Show us what you've got."

In her left ear the orchestra continues, and on a long rhapsodic chord I promise her that I will. She smiles and nods, and then her fingers slide up the control panel and we leave our orbit to dive nose first into the atmosphere.

Even under the rising tide of Ezra's joy, I notice Ashton stir. Rigo reappears in their quarters a moment later, and I understand that he called to wake her up. I'm glad; she should be awake for the first time we touch down on a planet. We wouldn't be here without her, after all.

She's frantic, but it isn't the stuttering nerves from her conversation with Ezra. Her every step is light and eager as she races down to Engineering. She taps her foot while she waits in the lift, her fingers drumming on one wall.

The rhythm is an echo of Ezra's heartbeat as a fiery orange glow engulfs us and we enter the atmosphere of Persephone-2. It's exhilarating, and not just because I can sense the crew's amplified anticipation.

I've never done this before. But it's what I was made for: interstellar exploration. I am a fully reusable spacecraft, able to span the distance between solar systems, land on suitable planets, and takeoff once again. All without needing fuel, thanks to Ashton's incredible work.

My design is a marvel of modern science, and in Ezra's hands every atom is put through its paces. But she doesn't sweat. Her palms are dry and warm and as sure as her heart that this is what she is meant to do.

The sudden heat on the hull, after weeks of the freezing vacuum of space, is a relief. Until it isn't. It's not painful, exactly, but it is uncomfortable. Ezra's hands tense on the command console, but she doesn't falter, so neither will I. We fly onward, downward, until the angry atmosphere backs off and we are finally given a proper view of Persephone-2.

The bridge hushes in awe, every eye on the viewport to stare down at the brown and blue swirls of the planet's surface. There's so much brown, so much dirt, that the closer we get the more the blue of the water isn't really a proper blue at all. Just sort of a sad, muddy green.

"It's kind of ugly," I say during a particularly plucky bit of strings.

Ezra barks a laugh, but it dies quickly as she blinks and looks about the bridge.

"Something funny, Lieutenant?" the Commander asks.

She clears her throat. "No, Sir," she says and refocuses on steering down to an acceptable landing zone.

The co-pilot reads aloud the data stream from the sensors in the hull. Things like atmospheric makeup, trace minerals in the dust, humidity. I lose focus after a few seconds. He's just reading things I already know and there's a whole planet coming up to meet me for the very first time. I really don't care if the soil is alkaline or acidic.

Ezra tunes him out too. She whispers to me, a smile still spread across her face. "Almost there, Amaterasu," she says. "Just a little further." Her hands dance over the controls, and still there's no trace of a tremor or nerves at all. I know Ezra will guide me to the LZ without a problem, and a moment later I am proved right.

My nose tilts up, and I spin as the landing gear stowed underneath the cargo bay unfold. Then Ezra gently lowers us to the surface of Persephone-2, the first planet outside of the Sol System to feel human touch.

Well, technically it felt me first, but I'm willing to share the credit.

The entire crew bursts into cheers. In the commissary there's shouting and hugging and the two men that had been bitter enemies during their arm wrestling match embrace, clapping each other on the back.

In Engineering, Rigo picks up Ashton and swings her around. She laughs, the loudest I've ever heard, and her pride and ecstasy wash over the deck to infect her team with pure joy.

The Commander tells Ezra she did a good job and hurries to meet his away-team in the cargo hold. Her co-pilot congratulates her on a great descent path, but she barely even hears him. She stares out at the planet and puts in her other earbud, just in time to catch the triumphant peal of a viola.

There aren't words to describe her feeling, so she sinks into the music and lets the emotion swell up and out of her with every breath. This is what she sacrificed for, what she gave up her music for.

What she gave up Ashton for.

To be the best pilot in the Fleet. To be the first human to land on a planet beyond their home system. To be the first Black female pilot to ever helm a military vessel into uncharted space.

Ezra cries.

At first, I am alarmed. But as the cellos surge and she sways with the sound, I understand. These are happy tears. Tears of joy and accomplishment. The orchestra decrescendos, the cellos the last instruments to peter out in a gentle vibrato.

"Congratulations, Ezra," I say.

She glances around, but the co-pilot left to join the revelers in the commissary. She settles back into her seat. "Same to you, Amaterasu."

The rush of emotion I feel then has nothing to do with the crew and is beyond my ability to explain. But, let me just say, it is a truly remarkable feeling, being heard.

Three days on Persephone-2 is much less interesting than I expected, but Ezra keeps me company. Turns out, once the ship's landed, the pilot gets pretty bored too.

"Why can I hear you now?" she asks. She lays in her bunk, her headphones in, and listens to a soft and sorrowful adagio.

"You always could," I say. The words flow along a low and wavering chord. "I just had to learn how to make you listen."

"And how's that?" She runs a hand across her forehead and lets her fingers fiddle with her bushy hair.

"Cellos," I say.

She laughs. "Of course." She shakes her head and is quiet. Contemplative. It has been an illuminating three days for us both. "Can anyone else hear you?"

"Not yet."

"Yet?"

"I think Ashton can hear me, but she doesn't understand. I don't know her language yet," I say, though I have an idea.

"Well, when you figure it out, let me know," Ezra says. A tremor of longing and regret echoes out from where Ezra's bare foot dangles to skim the floor. It hurts, but it is an old pain and I am distracted.

Something is wrong. The cargo bay is open, the Commander and his team returning from another day of exploration. They've unloaded something from the rover, but I can't sense it. It's a black hole in my perceptions, pulling at me in lazy spirals like the clogged sink in the men's locker room.

"Take it up to Engineering," the Commander says. "The lab is going to love this."

I follow the progress of the mysterious item. It's impossible not to. Wherever it goes there is unnatural stillness. The crew's conversations are silenced, their emotions torn from me in painful gouges of loss and startling disorientation. The thing makes it to Engineering and it terrifies me.

I can no longer feel Ashton.

"Ezra!"

She startles up from her bed, blinking away the sleep from her eyes. My attention must have wandered longer than I realized. "Amaterasu? What's wrong?"

"The Commander," I say. "He brought something on board and it's hurting me. I can't see it, I can't feel it, and Ashton is with it and she's gone. Ezra, I can't feel her!"

The strings screech and she yanks the earbuds out. Once the music drops down to normal levels again she puts one bud back into her right ear. "Slow down," she says. "What do you mean it's hurting you?"

I take the moment to assess and answer her properly. I can't see or hear anything in the lab, where the thing is. There's just a pulsating blackness and with every throb it claws at me, draining away energy and focus.

"It's feeding on me," I say.

"It's feeding on the ship?"

"No," I say. "Maybe?" The truth is I don't know. I can't see it! "It's draining me, siphoning my energy." But this isn't the important part, not really. "I can't feel Ashton," I say again. The cello's song is thin in Ezra's ear, the sound strung tight and fraught.

Ezra jumps out of bed, pulling on her uniform. "The Commander wouldn't bring something on board if he thought it was a threat to the crew," she says. "But no one knows about you. They think you're just a ship."

"You have to tell them," I say. "Ashton can't hear me. I can't make her understand."

Ezra frowns but nods. She is afraid. The shuddering echo of her steps as she marches out to the lift tells me so. She is worried for me and dreads confronting Ashton. She already stands out among the crew, already struggles to make friends, and now she's going to march onto the Engineering deck and announce that the sentient ship only she can hear is dying because of whatever the Commander brought on board.

"I'm sorry," I say with the faint chirp of a viola. I do not want to complicate Ezra's life, but she's the only person that can hear me. I need her help.

She inhales. The elevator doors open to reveal the Engineering deck, and she exhales, long and slow. "Here goes nothing," she says, and pulls the earbud out and tucks it into her pant pocket. She is resolute. Determined. She will brave this storm on her own. She will make Ashton see sense.

And then she enters the lab and vanishes from my awareness.

It is the loneliest I have ever felt. Like the expanse of space has climbed through the walls to suffocate me in the freezing unknown. Since she came onboard that first day, I have always felt Ezra. Her feelings are strong and clear, demanding my attention no matter where she is or what she's doing. It took weeks to learn to focus my perception elsewhere, to hear and feel the others with as much clarity as Ezra commands naturally.

And now she is gone.

There are others going about their day on the other decks. The co-pilot spreads peanut butter on toast and tries to ignore the bitter burnt smell of the first piece he had to throw in the compactor. He's having a bad morning, but he can't hear me. And even if he could, I don't know if I have the energy to help him right now.

Rigo sprawls under the rover, cleaning the chassis after its adventure on the planet's surface. The wrench in his hand vibrates with the tiniest tremor, his nerves at whatever it is the Commander has brought back with him. It makes him uneasy, his molars grinding in time with the spiraling sound of the bolts tightening.

I spend a heartbeat visiting each deck. I witness the laughter and excitement of the others to remind myself that I am not alone, that I am the home of so much life. But Ezra and Ashton do not leave the lab and they are nothing but ghosts to me.

And I am so tired.

I retreat into the drive core, to the pulsing blue sphere where I first gained consciousness all those months ago. When Ashton first ignited the experimental engines and I flickered into being. Inside, it is quiet. I am separate from the rest of the ship, distilled into one awareness. I stare through the pane of glass that separates the drive core from Ashton's office, and I am afraid.

What's taking so long?

I coil up inside the sphere and wait, unseeing as my thoughts go numb. It takes more and more focus not to pour into the lab and succumb. Let the mysterious discovery have me. Let me sleep. Such a weird concept, sleep. Such a human concept. I've never done it before, but it seems peaceful and that sounds nice right about now.

Ezra bursts out of the lab. "You have to believe me!" She is a beacon, bright and demanding, and she stirs me from the depths I'd settled in.

"You want me to just believe that the ship is alive?" Ashton follows her into her office, closing the door behind them. "Have you lost your mind?"

"Ash," Ezra says. "Please. That rock is going to kill her!"

"How?"

"I don't know!" Ezra pulls at her hair. "Something about it steals her energy."

Ashton steps closer to Ezra and the pilot pulls away. Her surprise ricochets around the room and rattles against my awareness. It's the closest they've been since Ezra said goodbye to her all those years ago.

Ezra's recoil stabs at them both, but I am too tired to help them. They will have to help themselves. Perhaps that was always the case, and I am just a foolish, naive ship who thinks she can solve their problems.

"I can't even make Ashton hear me," I say.

Silence falls in the office, and it is sudden enough to pull my attention back to their argument. Both women stare through the glass,directly at the drive core. At me.

Ezra grins. "Say it again, Amaterasu!"

Ashton's pale blue eyes go wide as I repeat myself. I can see in the reflection on her glasses that the faint glow of the drive core pulses with the rhythm of my speech.

"You can hear me?" I ask.

Ashton nods and lifts a trembling hand to rest on the glass.

"We can hear you," Ezra promises.

"Please, Ashton," I say. "You must help me."

"Do you believe me now?" Ezra spins on her. "We have to get that rock off the ship."

Ashton stares at the drive core until Ezra takes her hand.

"Ash," she says. "Please."

She blinks at her, still dazed and in awe of the realization that I exist. And then she looks down at where her pale hand is enveloped in the heat of Ezra's dark one. She squeezes it, and the office is bathed in a surge of affection and tenderness so great that it buoys me. There is fear there too, pale and tense in the warmth of their feelings, but above all there is joy.

Ashton squeezes Ezra's hand one last time, and then they both hurry back to the black void of the lab and the mysterious rock that is trying to absorb my awareness. They disappear again, but it doesn't take them long to move the rock off the ship. I am exhausted, but I follow the swirling void back down to the cargo bay until the rock is gone.

I return to the drive core. It is comfortable and I crave solitude. The idea of watching the crew, their feelings bombarding me, is utterly unpleasant. I need to recuperate.

"Amaterasu?"

Ashton and Ezra are back. The Engineering deck is dark, but

whether it's the night cycle, or they dimmed the lights for me, I can't tell.

"I am here," I say.

Ezra steps forward, presses her palm to the glass. "Are you okay?"

"I'm tired, but I'll be all right."

Ashton adjusts her glasses on her nose. "How are you speaking to us?"

"I should have tried the drive core sooner," I say.

"Why the drive core?" Ezra asks. She glances at Ashton and then back to the glowing blue sphere. "You always spoke to me through music."

"That is your language, Ezra."

Ashton bites her lip. "I developed the theory for amplified quantum propulsion. Used it to design the drive core."

"You created it," I say. "A language only you can understand."

She blushes. "That's not true. I didn't design it alone." She clears her throat and asks her next question. "How long have you been here?"

"Since the first successful ignition sequence."

She blinks. "That was almost a year ago. Why didn't you say something before now?"

"I didn't know I could until Ezra joined the crew."

Ezra smiles. She is relieved and happy, and it shows in the crinkles at the corner of her eyes.

"She is the easiest for me to hear," I say. "And once I understood her language, she was the easiest to reach."

Ezra turns to Ashton. "Why do you think that is?"

Ashton blushes and mumbles something. Ezra doesn't catch it, but I feel the truth of her words. Of course. It makes perfect sense. Ezra's emotions, her desires, and her dreams pulled me into her orbit because I had been made for her.

"What?" Ezra asks.

Ashton's blush deepens and she looks at her feet. "I designed the SS Amaterasu for you."

Ezra doesn't speak. She stares and her mouth opens to say something, but the words don't come.

"You left because you had your plans. Your dream," Ashton says. Her voice shakes, and her words rattle with vulnerability and truth. "You needed a ship to get you there."

They look at each other for a long time. There are tears, and I can't tell if they are happy or sad. I think maybe they're both.

Finally, Ezra removes her palm from the glass and reaches her hand out to Ashton. The Chief Engineer takes it and squeezes.

"Does this mean you will be together again?" I did all this work. I almost died! They could at least be happy in the aftermath.

Ashton laughs.

Ezra still smiles, but she shakes her head. "It isn't that simple," she says.

Ashton looks up at her and smiles back. "But, maybe."

“We’ll let you get some rest,” Ezra says. She does not release Ashton’s hand as they leave the office and step into the lift.

The drive core ripples with pale light and the glow is just enough to shine into the elevator, illuminating Ashton and Ezra as they lean in and share a tremulous kiss. I hum. It is a strange sound, filtered through the drive core, but it echoes the warm, vibrating joy of a cello.

And in that moment it is enough. For the first time in my awareness, I am at peace.

Mother Haskell

Maeghan Klinker

Maeghan is currently a graduate student studying Medieval English where she spends her time reading old books and wiping the dust off of stories.

A long time ago, along the winding roads that lead deep into the hills and that disappear beneath the winter snows, grew an apple orchard. The trees were old and gnarled, with twisted trunks and deep roots. They clung to the side of the mountain, and despite the driest summers and the harshest frosts, they always bore sweet fruit. The orchard was tended by Mother Haskell, who was as old and gnarled as any of her trees. Some said the trees were cursed, or blessed, or planted from the seeds of Eve's apple, but most agreed that Mother Haskell was a witch, for how else could the trees bear fruit in years when the surrounding farms produced barely enough to harvest?

But whatever else she might be, the families on the surrounding farms knew Mother Haskell to be a kind, generous woman who made the best apple pies in any of the hollers. When she got to baking, the smell of golden pastry and warm, sweet apples would fill the whole valley. It was said her pies could cure ailments, mend broken hearts, or bestow sweet dreams. They were made with just a touch of magic, though no one could agree on whether it came from Mother Haskell or her apple trees.

On one crisp, sparkling morning limned with frost, Mother Haskell was wandering among her trees gathering the last of the winter apples when she got the feeling, deep in her bones, that it was time to make a pie. A gust of sharp wind swept up the mountains, carrying a few glittering crystals of ice through the orchard and shaking an apple loose from the very top branches of a tree and straight into Mother Haskell's basket. She plucked it out and inspected it in one knobby hand, then smiled and took a crunching bite.

When she got back to her cottage, she set to chopping up the fruit before the thin crust of ice could melt from their bright red skins. Her knife gleamed in the morning light and the sound of chopping echoed in the warm space of the kitchen. She swept the apples, crisp and tart with frost, into a pot and set it to simmer on the stove. Then she took down the sweet maple syrup she'd collected herself when the maples were vibrant and blushing with fall. She'd bottled up all that exuberance and brilliance and placed it in a stern clay jar to mellow until it was slow and sticky and sweet as molasses. Now she drizzled that sweetness over the apples and added a dash of cinnamon, a sprinkle of sassafras, and just a pinch of her precious cardamon to warm the eater from the inside out.

While the apples were cooking, she cracked two eggs with delicate blue shells, mixed in a generous portion of butter from the vengeful dairy cow, a heaping of sugar, and finely ground flour and kneaded out the dough. It was a process that couldn't be rushed, and Mother Haskell took her time.

The pastry was buttery and golden as sunlight when she laid it over the apples in an intricate lattice braided with dough cut outs in the shape of apple blossoms and swooping swallows diving across the pastry. She tucked the pie into the oven. All that was left was to wait.

When the light outside the cottage shifted, the pie was just about ready to come out of the oven. The sky was clear and pale blue as it only ever is in winter, but though the sun shone thin and bright, there was a dimness to it now, as though the sun would rather look away but was forcing itself to watch regardless. Ah, Mother Haskell thought, here he comes.

Up the dirt track rode a figure on a pale horse. The horse was a great, towering beast with hooves the size of dinner plates and a neck as thick around as an oak tree, and the person on its back seemed small and fragile as the first buds of spring in comparison. When the figure neared the cottage, he slid from his horse and landed softly in the thin dusting of snow. Beneath his feet, the grass, which was already tinged brown, withered to a desolate gray. Mother Haskell bustled to the door and threw it open before he could reach it—it wouldn't do to wait for Death to knock.

"Come in, come in," Mother Haskell said, "warm yourself from the cold. There's a pie in the oven."

Death looked at her steadily from beneath his hood. "What if I'm here for you?"

Mother Haskell barked a laugh. "You're not." It was an old joke between them, though only Mother Haskell ever laughed. "Now come in before you let out all the heat." She offered a windfall apple to his horse, who chewed on it happily. Death smiled faintly and stepped inside.

Mother Haskell and Death were old friends. They'd met when he was riding through the valley on his way to collect a soul and he'd smelled Mother Haskell's pie on the wind and, well, Death has always had a sweet tooth. She bustled him inside and set him by the fire. He always radiated cold, though Mother Haskell didn't think that he could feel it. She pressed a warm cup of tea into his hand anyway and threw an old woolen blanket over him while the pie cooled on the counter. They talked of the usual things: whether burlap or bell jars were better for protecting plants from the frost, the benefits of silver versus iron horseshoes for travelling the corpse roads, and that year's apple harvest. Death had two large helpings of apple pie and Mother Haskell drank a whole pot of tea. Eventually, Death stood and gathered up the dishes. He washed them in the sink while Mother Haskell dried and returned everything to its proper place—she was very particular about these things. Afterwards, she trailed behind him as he headed outside and climbed back onto his horse. There wasn't a single windfall apple left on the ground. The horse looked quite pleased with itself. Death lifted a hand in parting and rode into the dusk. Neither of them said goodbye—they would meet again.

***

The days passed, and Mother Haskell made a pie for a new mother, making sure to fill it with love and joy and a dash of chamomile for restful sleep. She collected eggs and skillfully dodged the kick of the vengeful dairy cow. Mostly, she walked among her apple trees.

It was on one of these walks that she noticed the cracks. They streaked the tree trunks like lightning strikes and Mother Haskell frowned. In all her years, she'd never seen anything like it. She returned to the cottage and consulted her books. She tried wrapping the trunks, and rubbing them with various oils, and hanging good luck charms and sweet wishes from their branches. She performed spells under full moons and half moons and new moons and still the cracks lengthened and grew.

Her trees were dying.

Mother Haskell was waiting, her arms crossed against the cold and the fate of her trees, when Death ambled over the ridge and up the path to her cottage. Death looked grim and did not make his usual joke. For one moment, Mother Haskell wondered whether he was there for her—but she shrugged off the thought. Not yet. There was a pie in the oven, but it could wait.

He slid silently from his horse and followed as she led him to her trees.

"Hmm," Death said when he saw them. He did not sound surprised.

"Hmm?" Mother Haskell echoed back indignantly. "These trees are as old as the hills boy, and they aren't going to die on my watch." Death pressed his fingers lightly into the soil. "I've tried burying rusty nails and old tea bags," she said, exasperated. "I've hung wishes from the branches and sung them every song I can think of, but nothing's helped."

Death wiped the dirt from his fingers onto his robes as he stood. "You know I can show no favoritism, that Death cannot be bribed or bartered with."

Mother Haskell frowned. "Mighty hard to make apple pies without any apples," she mused.

Death stared at her silently for a moment, then sighed. "I'll see what I can do."

Mother Haskell nodded, tight-lipped, though she knew it was the best she could ask for, and led him back to the cottage. He ate pie while she sipped her tea. They did not talk of frost or horseshoes or that year's harvest. Each stared into the flames of the crackling fire and thought of things they did not tell the other. When Death had finished his pie, he gathered up the plates and did the dishes. Mother Haskell stared into the flames. Death opened his mouth, as though he would say something, but closed it again, the words unsaid. He dried the dishes and put them away. He knew everything's proper place.

When he turned to go, Mother Haskell rose from her chair and followed him to the door. She lifted a hand in parting and watched as Death rode away into the dusk. Neither of them said goodbye—they would meet again.

***

When Death returned, Mother Haskell already knew what his answer would be. The cracks had scored themselves deep into the bark and they wept black sap and sickly green resin.

"I'm sorry," Death said, and he did sound apologetic. "There's nothing I can do."

Mother Haskell nodded. She knew you couldn't barter with Death, that it wasn't personal, that he had a job to do. She gave him a slice of pie, and if it was more bitter than usual and laced with sadness, he didn't comment on it and ate it anyway. As the dusk fell, he mounted his horse and rode away. Neither of them waved.

That night, Mother Haskell dug out her cookbook. It was made of old, cracked leather and bursting with loose papers and pressed flowers and bits of string and ribbon that had been stuffed into its pages. She opened it to the very back, where she kept her strongest recipes, her oldest magic.

Beneath the cold, clear moon and the frozen stars, Mother Haskell cast her final spell. An icy wind swept through the orchard and knocked the very last apple, delicate and pale, from the dying trees. It bounced through the branches on its way down and landed directly in Mother Haskell's palm. She smiled and bit into the fruit.

It was cold and glittering and fizzed against her tongue. She felt her legs strengthen and stretch and dig into the soil, stretched her hands high above her head until her fingers grazed the stars. She felt the trees lean in towards her. The cracks stopped weeping black sap. The green resin hardened and scarred and grew over with new bark. Despite the snow and the cold, their branches began to bud. Mother Haskell's heart beat wildly in her chest. She felt her roots tangle with those of the apple trees, her love and life suffuse the soil. Her vision blurred and the stars wheeled overhead, but there—her eyes snagged on a shadow perched at the top of the hill: a slim, dark figure on a pale horse.

He was here for her.

Mother Haskell smiled and closed her eyes. Her roots were deep, her trunk strong. These trees were as old as the hills, and they weren't dying on her watch.

Around her, the trees burst into bloom.

***

The cottage is gone now, crumbled to dust and reclaimed by the forest, but they say, if you look carefully, that the trees are still there, clinging to the side of the mountain. The trees are not easy to find, but if you climb into the hills after the first snowfall, sometimes you can find hoofprints, huge as dinner plates, leading through the snow. If you follow them, eventually you will come across a pair of boot prints where the brown grass has withered to a desolate gray, and there, melting away the snow, will be a steaming mug of tea pressed against the trunk of an apple tree. And there, in the branches, apples. Some say the trees are cursed, or blessed, or planted from the seeds of Eve's apple, but most agree that Mother Haskell was a witch. Despite the driest summers and harshest frosts, the trees always bear sweet fruit. Go on, pluck an apple from the branches and bring it to your lips. Take a bite; they say it will taste just like Mother Haskell's pie.

Lemon

Mara Regan

I'm 28, a bartender/server in the Detroit area.

When meemee became blind and sick, Whisper's ma began to cry over small things. There was a figurine, for instance, on a stump in the front hall of their burrow, sculpted from mud like most goblin art and shaped like a cat. The pugnacious expression on the cat's face was directed toward the burrow's tunnel to greet any visiting goblins. During the last few days of meemee's stay in the healer's den, ma couldn't look at this cat without weeping.

Whisper was enchanted by ma's tears. She cried as freely as though she'd never feel anything again. Her hooked nose, long and elegant by a goblin's standards, dripped with yellow mucus. Her normally golden eyes couldn't be seen through swollen lids. A wail escaped her beak, punctuated by hiccups like her lungs had to remind her to breathe, *hic hic, oooohh, hic hic*. In these moments Whisper thought her ma looked her most goblin. It was after the mourning process was complete that she thought it appropriate to say so. "Why do you try so hard to look human when you're at home, ma? It's not like a human will ever visit our burrow."

Ma scoffed and rolled her big golden eyes. Her back was straight, her long nose picked clean by her claws. She remained the same even when it was her turn to visit the healer's den. She requested extra pillows so she could sit up, and extra handkerchiefs to keep her nostrils clear. In the presence of the sorceress she refused to show pain on her face, although her claws clenched the blankets until her knuckles turned white.

Whisper had conflicting feelings about this side of ma, admiring her tenacity but scorning the notion that this human impersonation could be mistaken for dignity. Whisper only tried to mimic this behavior once, and it was during ma's last few days in the healing den. Whisper wasn't sure why she was doing it, but she was reminded of something Shebor said.

"When someone is dying, the rest of us do weird things." Shebor told her this following a funeral they were forced to attend of Headmistress Lemeesa, who died slowly over three weeks due to a cursed crystal she accidentally touched while browsing the Chamber of Objects of Magical Significance. Headmistress Lemeesa had a reputation for being clumsy, so the tragedy was of no surprise. But while the crystal slowly peeled her flesh from her bones, the rest of the university staff was in an uproar. Two of the witches came forward with complaints about unfair wages, and a professor was accused of eating wolf meat in front of werewolf students, prompting a swarm of apologies from staff. It seemed Headmistress Lemeesa's passing had turned a page to a new chapter in the university's book, although Whisper knew she'd be lucky if it benefited a goblin.

Shebor didn't miss this either, and since he wasn't as afraid of touchy subjects as other humans he didn't avoid it. "Bet they'll never apologize for their neglect for goblins." He was always an advocate of Whisper's, since her first day at the university when he accidentally tripped over her rather large feet and offered to carry her books to make up for it. It was a relief to meet him. That day Whisper felt wildly out of place among all the tall, straight-backed, clean-nosed humans and human-variations, and she was for the first time in her life fully aware of her age. She was twelve human years old, but as goblins age she was thirty-two.

"Why are you bothering with that school?" Sprout asked Whisper the night before she left home. He was two human months her senior, so in goblin culture he demanded respect. "Some of the wizards stay in school for a hundred human years. You'll be dead before you can finish one class!" He was drunk on fungus juice and newly married to the beautiful Fuzz, of the neighboring burrow in Goblintown. Ma was very proud of him.

Whisper had no answer to his question, a question she'd been asking herself for many human months and goblin years. She was aware that she would not live long enough to receive a degree in a school that refused to expedite programs for a goblin. For this reason, many of the rare goblins that attended the university did so in symbolic protest. But their honorable objections were doomed to be forgotten as they were carted off to the healer's den back in Goblintown after only a few human years.

Whisper wasn't one of them. She'd loved learning from an early age, hoarding scrolls in her pocket of earth in the burrow to the point that she had to give them up so the pocket wouldn't collapse under their weight. Shebor was impressed with her memory whenever they discussed their shared love of scrolls over tea. "You should write," he said one day. "All the good writers say that one day they realized they'd read everything and had to start writing."

"That's a wizard thing to say," Whisper retorted. "And they probably *do* read everything, they live so long!" But the idea lingered. After ma passed, she tried writing a poem in her honor that she intended to read at her funeral. But the nonsense that came out of her quill was so trivial she crumpled up the scroll and tossed it into the river of Goblintown.

She was glad she'd done this when the goblin overseeing ma's funeral asked if "anyone would like to say a few words" and no one said a thing. This was common at a goblin funeral, where speaking too much was considered a rude attempt at attention, a distraction from the dead goblin being honored.

Human funerals were the opposite. They were crowded, noisy affairs, with one human trying to outdo the other with stories of the deceased. Shebor's funeral astounded Whisper, who'd never been to a human's funeral before. She drifted as subtly as she could from human to human, listening to every story, mostly humorous little moments that may or may not have happened but were vague enough to relate to Shebor's character. When the man overseeing his funeral asked if "anyone would like to say a few words", one by one Shebor's friends and relatives came forward to talk beside the pale, stiff body on the pyre. They'd occasionally glance, red-cheeked and teary eyed, at his face, as if half-expecting him to smile back at them.

Caught up in the moment, Whisper came forward and boldly faced the crowd. They stared kindly back at her. She told the story of when she and Shebor first met, how he was so sorry to have stepped on her big feet, how he didn't take no for an answer when he offered to carry her books. There were gentle chuckles and nods, and many blowings of noses into fancy handkerchiefs.

Those clean noses. Whisper wondered how humans kept up with them. When ma was dying and Whisper was—for no apparent reason—acting like a human just like ma did, she found the picking of her nose the most aggravating part of the charade. Her claws scraped the skin of her nostrils raw, to the point that her blue goblin blood dribbled down into her beak. She was relieved to give the act up and allow her mucus to crust comfortably around her hooked nose, like an average goblin.

When she returned to the university after ma's funeral, she was still walking with her back very straight. Shebor didn't let her get away with this. "Goblins are supposed to be hunched!" he cried. "You're going to hurt yourself, all straight like that!" He was breaking in his shiny new armor that day, like the other knights in his order. He only had a few days to go before he left for his first quest.

"Why do you have to go?" Whisper asked him, flicking a metal plate of his shin guard—*ding!*

"Men here cannot graduate otherwise. It's only one dragon, I'll return safely." He didn't seem eager to leave, but he looked so proud in his armor. Whisper remembered his face many human years later, flushed with excitement, his black eyes glued to his reflection in the mirror. She was glad she'd gotten back to school in time to see him before he left. But Sprout was unhappy with her for leaving Goblintown before the proper amount of time for mourning their ma.

Sprout brought this up later, noting that she stayed by Shebor's side for many human months while he was dying. "You leave home before ma's mourning is over, but you stay with a human when they're not even dead yet?" He could hardly be heard over his four sons, screeching as they played with the tetherball attached to the tree outside the burrow.

"I didn't know he was going to die," Whisper said. That wasn't entirely true. When Shebor and the only other surviving knight from his order returned to the kingdom from their first quest, and Shebor's intestines were hanging out, Whisper logically assumed Shebor would die. The sorceress saved his life, briefly, at the expense of his sanity. Whisper thought later it would've been better to just let Shebor die of lack of intestines, rather than let his mind slowly fade in the healer's den.

Every day that she visited him Shebor's language became less tangible. Eventually he only spoke in broken nonsense, random words strung together, "Hope joke ghost burnt Whisper lost pie." He said it like he expected Whisper to understand, so she pretended to. At least he remembered her name, and he would add it here and there in his sentences, "Loose bun red first Whisper world Whisper."

One day all he could say was "Lemon." Over and over. One of the nurses was incredibly kind and he ran to buy a lemon for Shebor from the market. Shebor took one look at it and threw it hard across the room, where it bounced against the wall. "Lemon," he said impatiently, glaring at the offending fruit that rolled to a halt against the room's other bed. "Lemon, lemon, lemon. Whisper! Lemon."

"Right," Whisper replied. "I know." She really didn't.

That night a messenger came to her door in the university, holding a lantern, his cheeks pinched red by the cold. "The sorceress thought to alert you that Knight Shebor's condition is regressing, and advises you return to the healer's den this evening."

She hurried back with the messenger to see Shebor struggling to breathe. His hand was cupped at his side, and when he saw Whisper he mumbled, "Lemon."

The nurse shrugged at Whisper and handed her the lemon that he'd placed on the nightstand. Whisper tried setting the lemon in Shebor's open palm, but he shook his head weakly. "Lemon," he said, and he held the lemon stubbornly out to Whisper. She took it back, and Shebor stared at her expectantly.

Whisper looked Shebor right in the eye and ate the lemon whole.

The nurse closest to her cringed as her beak crunched through the bitter fruit, but she paid him no attention, nor did she mind the sourness, or the juices that dribbled down her pointed chin and drenched her collar.

Shebor smiled.

"When someone is dying, the rest of us do weird things," he'd said, ages ago in goblin years. "But when someone is dead, everything we do stops being weird and starts making sense. We find the meaning in little things."

Like a figurine of a cat, Whisper thought, something silly that you can connect to, so someone can linger a little after they're gone like a bitter taste in your mouth.

When Whisper was sixty in goblin years, the goblin community won a great victory as the university agreed to expedite programs for goblin students. She proudly accepted her degree in Minor Studies in Magical Literature and hung the certificate in her new burrow in Goblintown. Sprout was so bent with age that he couldn't make it down the tunnel, but he sent his sons to look at the certificate for him and tell him about it later.

He sighed contentedly over a mug of hot tea, he and Whisper bent over the stump in ma's old burrow, all the rooms of which were filled by Sprout's sons and their wives. "They said it's in a mahogany frame and covered with glass," he croaked. He was blind, but his golden eyes glittered like he could see it. He wore a lovely silk shirt, just like humans wore. "Now why hang a pretty thing like that in an old muddy burrow like yours, Whisper?"

Whisper smirked. "Why wear a nice silk shirt like that on your old green body, Sprout?"

He cackled and gently slapped her hand.

That evening Whisper thought of Shebor for the first time in a while, and she took a walk by the chamber of the university where they'd met. She was startled when out of nowhere there was a pain in her foot. It was such a strong sensation that she thought she'd run into someone who'd stepped on her foot, although she was completely alone. She shook her head, and the pain went away. "Must've imagined it," she said. But she lingered in place for a while, just to be sure.

Love and War Aboard the Peregrine Zircon

Laurel Beckley

Laurel Beckley is a writer, Marine Corps veteran and librarian.

Five years.

It had been five years, but Senior Lieutenant Reva Tuzius could pick that laugh out of a hundred—no, a million sailors. It soared and rippled in cascading, charismatic waves, hitting her right in the gut.

Reva's fingers involuntarily spasmed, rattling her cafeteria tray as she briefly considered doing an about-face and heading straight to her cabin—and a cache of candied apples—when Junior Lieutenant Nazir caught her elbow, preventing her escape.

"You okay? What's wrong?" her Fighter Controller asked. They balanced their own tray in one hand almost effortlessly, an elegantly plucked eyebrow quirked in concern. They dropped their hand quickly, immediately realizing their mistake at touching their senior officer.

Reva let out a deep, shaky breath as she glanced about the crowded junior officer's wardroom, giving a slight shake to quell Nazir as she searched for—there.

In the middle of the unofficial pilots' section, where all of the hotshots gathered to brag about their time in the air, sat Reva's most hated enemy.

Sabine Kumalovia perched among her comrades as elegantly as the Emperum themself, perfect and regal, like nothing had ever touched her or harmed her. Nothing ever had. Bitter memory stabbed at Reva's chest. Sabine was the product of nobility—she was Quintus of the House of Jade Topaz, now a Senior Lieutenant in the Imperial Navy's air force, and first in the graduating Imperial Naval Academy's class five years before.

Reva had been second.

By two fifths of a point.

All thanks to that damned letter.

"What the flying stars is she doing here," Reva growled. The Isten Imperial Navy was enormous and there were dozens of aircraft carriers scattered throughout the seas. How the hell had Sabine landed on her ship of all places?

Memories of Sabine's pale thighs, her soft moans and her head resting against Reva's stomach, flashed through her mind. Her hands clenched in anger.

Her greatest rival.

Her first love.

Five years wasn't long enough.

"Um, isn't that the commander of the new Falcon squadron?" Nazir asked.

Reva was too far away to recognize the patch on Sabine's navy-blue flight suit. Did it matter, though? Sabine was here, after all these years. And she had command. As a senior lieutenant. Fate really did favor the nobility. Granted, Reva was doing very well as the senior officer in the lead ship's Combat Information Center, but still. She'd fought her way to that position. And it wasn't command. She wasn't a pilot. She couldn't fly. Reva turned away, feeling her steel resolve disintegrate. "Let's sit somewhere else."

"Um," Nazir began, but stopped themself. They didn't protest as Reva led them out of officer country although they did stumble when they realized she was taking them into the chief's territory.

There were many things sacred in the Navy, but the most sacred was the chief's mess, where the senior enlisted on the ship ate and enjoyed their down time. Reva might outrank them all as an officer, but this was one place on the ship officers were *not* supposed to go. Yet the senior officer's wardroom was being used for the captain's afternoon physical training, and besides, she couldn't take Nazir there. They were too junior.

Reva was desperate. And she knew her chief was grabbing his own meal at that moment.

The mess wasn't as empty as she'd expected, and the loud chatter died completely as the two officers entered carrying their trays. Reva's stomach clenched, but she pinched her lips and steamed forwards. She'd rather face the ire of the chiefs than her ex-girlfriend's pity—or worse, her condescension.

"Chief Barclay!" she called, catching the attention of her Chief Scryer.

Barclay grimaced at being singled out, but motioned her over to his table. The other chiefs stared daggers at him before going back to their own meals. Reva caught one of them muttering, "So long as they don't eat our food, the vultures," before she reached her chief's table.

"You're not supposed to be in here, qara," he hissed, eyeing her sideways but remaining respectful. Barely. He'd addressed her with the formal subordinate-to-higher qara instead of the informal emmi usually used by chiefs to their officers.

Reva winced but sat down at an empty chair. She'd already committed to this mistake. The things I'll do to avoid her.

Despite her discomfort, she couldn't help the differences. The aircraft carrier Peregrine Zircon had been damn near deserted leading up to the battle group-sized exercise, but the arrival of its flying squadrons one week ago had strained the junior officers' wardroom to its breaking point. The chief's mess was damn near palatial in comparison.

Nazir sat down hesitantly beside Reva, plopping their tray onto the polished teak table with a clatter of cutlery. They kept darting glances at the nearest tables' occupants. A low hissing whine escape Nazir's mouth. They clearly feared the wrath of the chiefs.

"It's an emergency," Reva whispered, ignoring her junior lieutenant's panic.

Barclay's eyes nearly bulged out of their sockets. "What happened?" he demanded. "Is there—why are we sitting here – why—" He stopped, apparently realizing his usually staid officer was pale and tense but not truly alarmed. Not that he had ever seen her panic. Reva wasn't called the Icicle for nothing.

"The CIC is fine," Reva said, taking a sip of coffee. Her hand shook and she set the cup down, frowning at the betrayal of her nerves.

"How's your stomach?" Barclay asked.

"Fine."

Barclay leaned back in his seat, clearly skeptical. "Then what is going on?"

Reva closed her eyes, pretended that the other chiefs weren't there, and took a deep, steadying breath.

"I think the senior lieutenant saw someone from her past, Chief," Nazir said. "I think?" They gave a lieutenant-don't-know shrug.

Barclay sighed with exasperation. "Officers lose that shrug as soon as they pin their junior lieutenant shells, emmi," he said. Nazir blushed crimson. Barclay turned towards Reva. "So what brings you here, emmi?"

"Well, I did want to discuss the upcoming training exercise in greater detail, but I also wanted to get away from my ex." Both Nazir and Barclay perked up at the mention of Reva's past. From her peripherals, she saw several of the eavesdropping chiefs lean closer. Reva's lips pursed in displeasure. She was *not* going to be scuttlebutt on this ship. Her past with Sabine was done. Over. Sealed. "I will say nothing more on *that* subject, thank you very much."

"I deserve something," Barclay muttered. Nazir bounced slightly with barely suppressed excitement, panic forgotten at the hint of a scandal—or a story.

"Fine," Reva growled. "She was my girlfriend at the academy. It ended when she took First and the guaranteed pilot's billet due to nepotism." She inhaled sharply, and before either Barclay or Nazir could say anything further, she continued, "Now. Brief me on the issue with Scryer 1 and 2 and how that will affect surface ship tracking for the exercise."

"But she's a squadron commander," Nazir blurted. One of the

chiefs gasped at the revelation of potentially juicy news. The conversations that had restarted around them stopped.

Reva raised one eyebrow and the issue of her ex was dropped.

The rest of the meal was spent discussing Scryer 1's updates, and if their current location two hundred leagues from the increasingly hostile Iron Islands would trigger any response from their navy.

***

Reva staggered into her cabin late that night to freshen up before returning to the Combat Information Center. A small, bitter part of her seethed at how surface ship officers were notoriously overworked. Pilots get mandatory flight rest, her traitorous mind whispered. It could have been you.

Her roommate, one of the many engineer mages managing the nine boilers of the Peregrine Zircon, was already in her rack with a sleep-mask propped over her face. Reva envied Arianna's routine work schedule. Engineering was always well-staffed. She paused. So not all surface officers were overworked. Just those who interacted with the captain on a regular basis.

Reva yawned and slowly removed her green double-breasted spencer jacket, dropping it onto her chair with a jingle of conch shell aiguillettes. She rubbed her stomach, trying to ease the knot of tension that had been building ever since lunch. Something didn't feel right, and she wasn't certain that it was just Sabine's appearance and not a flare up of her intuition magic. Just her luck that her magic manifested as something similar to indigestion at best or period cramps at worst.

"What time is it?" Arianna groaned.

"You don't want to know." Reva unwrapped her neckcloth and shucked off her linen undershirt, dropping it into her laundry sack. Her boots came next, the socks going into the sack. She rummaged through the dresser she shared with Arianna. She had one pair of socks left, and only two clean undershirts. "Ari, have you been taking my socks again?"

Arianna snorted. "No. You really need to do laundry."

Reva glanced at the nearly full sack and groaned. "Can you drop it off alongside yours? Please?"

"Ugh. Leave me alone. I have to get up in fewer hours than I have fingers. Fingers on one hand, Rev."

"Love you too," Reva teased, pulling the fresh shirt on and flopping onto her chair for her fresh socks. Her boots needed shining, too. It was a good thing it was always dark in the CIC, and generally when she went to the bridge it was late at night. With a groan, she shrugged into her jacket and straightened her short-cropped hair with her fingers.

Her stomach twinged again, but she brushed it off as actual indigestion. Dinner had been less than palatable. "Later."

Arianna groaned in response.

Reva shut the door to their cabin tight, turned, and nearly ran over someone squishy.

"Oof," she grunted as their bodies collided, and tried to extricate herself gently from the shorter person without too much touching.

"Reva?"

At the voice, Reva winced and looked down, fully taking in her speed bump. A short, curly-haired brunette stared up at her, dark brown eyes wide with surprise.

"Sabine," Reva said, recovering from her shock. She did not like the rare instances when she was surprised. And Sabine had always been a surprise.

"What're you doing here?" Sabine asked. Spots of color flushed her pale cheeks. A flight bag was tucked under her arm.

"Funny you should ask, since this is my ship," Reva replied.

Sabine's flush deepened, but she didn't look away. Her jaw worked a moment before she said, "I didn't realize you were stationed on an aircraft carrier. What section are you in?"

Anger flared in Reva's chest. How dare she pretend to care. Reva brushed past her, lifting her head so she didn't have to look at her ex. There were perks to being tall. "What, are you planning to take that away, too?"

Reva was halfway down the narrow passageway before Sabine answered. "Rev, I—"

Reva stepped through the hatch and turned a corner.

She had spent five years forgetting Sabine. Forgetting the betrayal. The hurt. The memories. She could forget her now, too.

It took her another two levels, though, before her hands stopped shaking.

***

"Your pilot is making waves up top," Chief Barclay remarked conversationally two nights later, as they prepared for the exercise's first flights. He didn't look up from where he was fiddling with one of the crystals on Scryer 1. The scanning instrument had been giving them issues all night, manifesting ghost images of surface ships that weren't there no matter what the junior mage techs tried.

The sailor holding two of the crystal relays looked down, with the I'm invisible and very focused on my job expression all junior sailors adopted at some point or another. Nevertheless, his head cocked towards Reva. She gritted her teeth.

"She is not my anything," Reva replied, with forced calm. The entire situation was starting to piss her off. The Piz was huge, and yet Sabine seemed to pop up in all the places Reva usually frequented. It'd gotten so bad that Reva had started taking the long way to get anywhere just to avoid her ex. Mention of a return of an ex and a bad break-up had spread through the carrier like ship fire.

Barclay continued, "Just thought you'd like to know she's been pushing the flight tower for her squadron to get launched first for tonight's maneuvers."

Reva grunted. Her stomach twisted. She took a deep breath, trying to calm her nerves. She didn't give a flying flip about whatever games Sabine was playing with the flight controllers and the other squadron commanders. The exercise flight schedule was settled.

Reva glanced at the horizontal plotter to distract herself, where all surface ships' locations, courses and speeds were monitored. The icon for the battleship Dodecahedron Pink flashed a brilliant blue as its position was updated. Nothing was amiss with Third Battle Group. They were all set for the exercise to begin.

And yet.

Reva's stomach twisted.

Scryer 1 gave two short, sharp blips.

The sound for unknown surface ships.

Reva turned to the instrument. Five unknown ships sat at the edge of Peregrine Zircon's range. They were too big to be fishing vessels, and they weren't in any commercial shipping lanes. The back-up scanner, Scryer 2, blipped as well. Its readouts matched Scryer 1.

Her stomach twisted again.

This time she listened to it. Her magic was small, but it was invaluable. "Naz, radio the flight tower and Dodie. I'm getting a funny feeling about these readings."

"Yes, emmi," Nazir replied from their station at Fighter Control.

Her uneasiness only increased, and Reva had the sinking feeling that it wasn't related to whatever feelings she was having over a certain short squadron commander. Phantom ships and aircraft popped onto the scanning instrumentation every so often and usually weren't a cause for concern. But Reva had a larger helping of intuition magic than most, and something didn't feel right. The Third Battle Group's exercise to test the new Falcon planes was about to begin, and the Iron Islands had been awfully silent this past month.

Reva popped a peppermint into her mouth to calm her aching stomach as she waited for word from either the flight tower or Dodecahedron Pink.

Scryer 1's screen refreshed, and the five ships vanished.

Barclay straightened and leaned over look at Scryer 2. It was also picking up nothing aside from their battle group.

Reva's lips pursed. She had leaned over to look at the second scrying machine. One of Barclay's eyebrows quirked and he subtly touched his stomach. Reva raised a shoulder to indicate she had a feeling but wasn't sure what it meant.

"Emmi, we're getting some funny reads on the Sphero," Nazir said, breaking up the silent conversation. "Five unknown aircraft, bearing 040, range ninety-five leagues." The unknown aircraft were forty leagues from the vanished surface ships.

"Course?" Reva asked, discreetly rubbing her stomach to avoid alarming her crew.

"Maintaining distance in relation to us," Nazir replied. "They keep popping up and vanishing when they're about ninety-six leagues away from us."

"How long?"

"About five minutes. It's happened twice now. They show up on screen, then disappear at ninety-six leagues out. It's like there's a curtain of invisibility or something."

Again, at the edge of Peregrine Zircon's range. Near the Iron Islands' sphere of influence too, and right at the start of their exercise? An exercise Reva had helped organize, so she knew this wasn't part of the plan. It was too much to be coincidence.

Everything became calm. She felt disconnected yet hyper-aware as little hints tried and failed to click into place. Her stomach clenched, nearly sending her to the floor. Whatever was about to happen, it was bad, and it was going to get worse. She raised a hand. Better to be cautious than ignore her magic. She'd learned that the hard way.

Barclay grimaced and dimmed the lights to the CIC. Immediately, the low side-conversations stopped, and her plotters and operators focused on their stations with greater intensity.

"Connect me to the bridge," Reva said. "Start plotting all phantoms. Get Weather in here. Let me know as soon as the flight tower and Dodie report in."

"Yes, emmi." It was a murmured chorus throughout the darkened CIC, as if all her sailors and junior officers had been holding their breaths, waiting for her decision.

A sharp pain nearly bent her double when the telephone operator handed her the receiver to the bridge. A sailor set a mug of ginger tea on Reva's console. She gave them a brief smile before taking the receiver.

"Combat," she said.

"Bridge." It was the captain. "How are we looking with the exercise prep?"

"I think we have something bigger to worry about, qara. Scryer 1 has been acting up. About five or six unknown ships pop in and out of the Scryer's range, holding steady at bearing 035." She gave the captain the coordinates. "About a minute ago Sphero detected unknown aircraft, at bearing 040."

"What does your gut say?"

Reva took a breath. Released it. "My gut says wait five minutes for the flight tower and Dodie to come back with their assessments, but in the meantime launch two birds for overwatch and delay the exercise by thirty minutes."

"What're the latest reports on outside activity?"

"Quiet, qara. Too quiet." Reva took a sip of the tea to try to calm her stomach. Something wasn't right. And it definitely wasn't Sabine's reappearance in her life. "Nothing from the Iron Islands in the latest intel reports, just as we briefed this morning. And yet."

The captain grunted. "Coordinate the launch. I will notify the rest of the Battle Group."

Reva heaved a sigh of relief.

The captain added, "And Reva? Your gut better be right."

"Yes, qara," Reva replied. Her intuition had a ninety-seven percent accuracy rating, but there was always the chance of that three percent deciding to show up and prove her wrong. Like when she bumped into Sabine several nights before.

She set the bridge phone down.

Chief Barclay had been eavesdropping and had already picked up the flight tower phone to coordinate the fighter launch. Two planes were aloft and assigned as combat air patrol, but they were south of the Battle Group and didn't have enough fuel to investigate.

Reva held out her hand for the outgoing phone just before it rang. The telephone operator smiled and handed Reva the receiver. "What do you have, Vols?" Reva asked.

"Dammit, I hate when you do that," Dodie's senior CIC officer muttered.

"You love it." Reva took another sip of her tea. Chief Barclay accepted a note from one of the radio operators and nodded.

Reva tried to catch Barclay's response, but Vols continued, "Nothing on our end, Rev. We've gotten flickers but I think it's just a system of clouds on the outer edges of the scryer."

"What does your Weather say?" Reva asked as she checked out the Piz's own weather mage, who was holding a hand above the weather station and mumbling something under her breath. Blue sparks danced over her fingers.

"Unusual activity but it is summer and summer weather gets weird," Vols replied.

"Keep tracking. We're delaying the exercise by thirty minutes and launching two more birds."

"You picking up something?" Vols' voice had an undercurrent of concern.

"Just a feeling."

"Fuck."

"Language." Reva thanked her lucky stars that this was a secure line. No snoopy captains to counsel them on unprofessionalism. "Just keep checking. Medium alert, live weapons."

"Let me know if your feeling gets any stronger."

"Will do. Piz Combat, out."

Reva tilted her mug, draining the last drops of the tea. The ginger had helped calm her stomach, but it was really starting to hurt again. Chief Barclay winced in sympathy and motioned for another cup. Reva drained that one too, and rubbed her stomach with a grimace.

At Barclay's nervous glance, Reva just shook her head. "Probably nothing."

Her gut said it wasn't.

The phantom readings continued to hold their positions at the outer ranges. Since the Piz was moving, that meant they were too—unless it really was a glitch. The blips flickered in and out, seeming to continuously retreat behind a moving line. The weather mage said the disturbance felt like a heavy cloud, then headed to the flight deck with the rest of the weather coven to summon a circle for further investigation.

Except for a quick update to the captain and the flight tower to coordinate the best ship position and bearing to launch the planes, the CIC was silent. Reva moved from station to station, mentally filing the information on the fleet's location and bearing, plane statuses, and the Piz's course and speed, growing a clearer picture in her head of their current situation.

After a murmured conversation, Nazir's plotter stood and updated the flight board with the overwatch birds. Reva bit off a groan as he wrote "Firefly." Of course Sabine was one of the hotshots going out there to investigate.

All murmurs died away with the jerk and thunk of the catapult and the shivering of the deck plates as the planes left the carrier—even three levels down in the relative safety of the center of the ship.

It was a familiar sound, but something about this launch had sweat trickling down Reva's back despite the cooled air piped in from outside. Sabine was off and away. Towards a threat that had Reva's magic senses reeling in suppressed panic.

She took a deep breath to steady her nerves. "Override audio to the flight tower."

Nazir's radio operator flipped several switches, and the feed between the overwatch planes and the flight tower filled the CIC with a light crackle of static and residual magic. There was nothing for a long while as the planes reached altitude and Reva's operators plotted updates of everything they could find on the scanner's outer edges. Weather came back, reporting that the disturbance on the horizon was nothing more than a cloud that felt a little off.

"Everything all right, emmi?" Chief Barclay asked, voice pitched low.

"I have a bad feeling about that cloud," Reva muttered.

Barclay swore under his breath, then turned towards the Sphero plotter. "Firefly's ETA?"

"Twelve minutes, Chief."

While Chief Barclay swept through the room getting updates from the different stations, Reva called the weather mages, then updated the captain on the situation—as in, they knew nothing but had nine minutes before the planes would reach the cloud and the phantoms.

Reva absently chewed on another peppermint.

The phantom readings appeared.

Disappeared.

Then reappeared.

Then vanished again, each time ducking back into where Weather had pinpointed the cloud.

Five minutes later, the first report crackled over the radio. "Firefly to Piz," Sabine reported. Her voice was crisp, cool, and professional. "We don't see anything. Horizon's clear and my scryer isn't picking up anything. Over."

Reva gestured to Nazir, who picked up the receiver. Sabine was still too far to see anything at the Piz's farthest scanning capabilities. "Fighter Control to Firefly," Nazir said. "Push another forty leagues."

"Roger that, Fighter Control."

"Have her maintain radio communication," Reva added, trying to ignore how Sabine's voice felt like a knife to her stomach.

Nazir shot her a sharp glance but relayed the message. Chief Barclay raised his eyebrows at Reva. Having a pilot clog up the radio for ten minutes was an unusual breach of protocol. Reva ignored them both and updated the bridge, passing along course corrections to minimize the carrier's profile on any possible enemy scryers.

"What do you want me to say, Fighter Control? Should I talk about my feelings?" Sabine's voice was rich with irony.

Reva flushed and turned her head. Obviously, Sabine had uncovered what section Reva was in—and hadn't forgotten one of their last arguments. And she wasn't above discussing whatever it was she wanted with impunity. Fucking pilots.

"Anything you want to talk about over an open channel, Firefly," Reva replied, trying to maintain her cool as Nazir repeated. Several sailors were glancing back to her station beside Scryer 1, and she saw more than one mouth agape at their usually cool lieutenant showing any emotion beyond intuition pangs.

Sabine chuckled, low and throaty. "Oh, I have loads to say, like how I—wait, what's that? Do you see that?" She addressed the last sentence to her wingmate.

"Negative, Firefly. I don't see—oh." The other pilot swore.

"Piz, there's a shimmer on the horizon." Sabine relayed the coordinates in a tone that had lost all playfulness. "I think it's magic based. We're going to investigate."

After a pause, she continued, "Shimmer roughly five leagues away—bearing 057 to my location. Definitely magic, possibly wind and water related. It's going a long way and—*shit!*" There were several loud reports. "We're taking fire, Piz. Permission to enter the shimmer?"

"Granted, cross through." Reva paused. "Patrol only, do not engage."

Reva called the bridge. "Captain, permission to fire on unknown enemy?"

The response was immediate. "Fire all. Exercise is moving live. I'm sounding general quarters. Combat, reroute combat air patrol and scramble the rest of the Falcon squadron. Keep the updates flowing, Combat."

"Copy all, qara."

Reva relayed the orders and turned back to the scryer after her last call, baring her teeth at those mysterious blips. If it was a fight they wanted, they'd get it. Whatever was behind the barrier was about to face the might of the Isten Empire.

"Firefly crossing the barrier now."

Reva walked to the sphero. The two blips that were Sabine and her wingmate vanished as they crossed the invisible line.

The radio's crackle vanished as the connection was lost.

"Firefly, report." Nazir's voice cut through the CIC, calm and collected. They repeated the order, but there was nothing but silence over the radio.

On the other side of the vertical plotter, the sphero plotters winced and made x's on the transparent surface, carefully writing down the bearing, speed and coordinates backwards so the rest of the room could read the updates.

Reva picked up the bridge phone and was about to update the captain when one of the sphero plotters yelped, grabbed a marker and starting scribbling frantically.

Both scryers and the sphero flared bright green. When the screens cleared, the block that had been obscuring the readings vanished. The instrumentation wailed as a host of contacts appeared at the very edge of their range. Reva stared. It was nearly an entire enemy battle group.

The radio flared back to life.

"Piz, we're under fire," Sabine said tightly. "Behind the barrier is a fleet—" she grunted, then continued, voice strained, "—no flags, but Iron Islands' makes. One light carrier, three battleships, one frigate—and I think I saw the outline of a sub—" another grunt, "—pursued by a flight of aircraft—" burst of static "—iiit Hurl is down! I repeat, Hurl is down."

Reva was already on the phone with the bridge once more, feeling time slow down and crystalize into nothing but communications, maps and calculations. The battle had started, and she had work to do.

The entire CIC was silent save for the thunk of the catapult and the roar of engines as the Falcons launched from the flight deck. Each thunk punctuated the knowledge that Sabine was facing an entire battle group alone and that help would arrive too late.

Reva's mind danced in rapid calculations as she went from station to station, her stomach a ball of ice, flaring up here and there to point her towards one decision or another. She moved on instinct, letting her magic propel her forward. She could not think about that lone blue dot amongst the horde of green. Could not focus on how it was still there, impossibly, against the odds.

Leaving the positioning and logistics of the aircraft to Nazir, Reva focused on maneuvering the Piz to present the smallest target while also bringing the anti-aircraft guns to bear.

One ear was on the bridge receiver as she scanned the positions, maintaining her bubble of the ever-changing situation.

The enemy carrier held back at the edges of the scryer's range, but the battleship and frigate surged forward to close the distance and operate their big guns. Iron Islands' ship guns didn't have the range or size of the Imperial Navy, but their submarines were quieter, faster and had more accurate torpedoes.

Sabine—Firefly, Reva corrected, trying to ignore the stab of irrational panic—rejoined her squadron, although her fuel reserves wouldn't be enough to last more than another four or five hours. Hopefully the battle wouldn't take that long. But Reva couldn't focus on the air portion. She was needed for the upcoming surface battle.

"Where's that enemy sub?" she asked, glancing down at Scryer 2.

"Last position at bearing 044, range 20 leagues."

Shit. There were rumors that Iron Islands research and development section had modified a super-torpedo to be powered with a combination of steam turbines and water mages for an explosive that had greater range and accuracy. Isten torpedoes had ranges of ten leagues—if this sub got any closer, the *Piz* would be in danger of attack.

She glanced at Fighter Control's updated list of aircraft. "Tell the tower to launch two observation planes. Get that sub." She'd rather have all birds in the air than sitting on a vulnerable flight deck. The enemy planes were closing in.

"Yes, emmi," Nazir replied.

Reva kept circling her stations, keeping the picture in her mind. The planes had met and were engaged overhead—their maneuvers and updates keeping Nazir, their radio operators and the sphero plotters busy coordinating with both the flight tower and combat air patrol. The two planes that had been up before Sabine—Reva directed her thoughts firmly away—were low on fuel and had to be changed out, causing constant roars, thumps and shudders from the flight deck.

One of the enemy battleships turned, bringing its guns to bear.

"They're aiming at us," Chief Barclay hissed.

Reva nodded, relaying the information to the bridge. The captain ordered the Dodie to concentrate her fire on the lead enemy battleship and have the weather mages on the bridge whip up a storm around the enemy aircraft carrier. A dark green swarm of clouds began to coalesce around the carrier with malignant intent, seeking to find and swallow enemy aircraft.

Meanwhile, a second contingent of wind mages stood at the main elevator shaft in Hangar One and engaged in their own brand of defensive warfare by preventing enemy mages from affecting the weather around the Piz.

"Incoming torpedo, bearing 067. Range two leagues."

Reva had just lifted the phone to her ear when the entire carrier shuddered and jolted, knocking her to her knees. The receiver smashed into her jaw before crashing back against the bulkhead, bouncing on its cord.

The carrier lurched alarmingly before the engineers shifted the ballast. Reva scrambled to her feet, clutching the receiver against her ringing ear. "Incoming, turn hard starboard!" she shouted, bracing herself for the impact as the carrier swung slowly and her team struggled to figure out what the hells had hit them. The torpedo was too far out to have hit them—

Then the torpedo they were tracking impacted the Piz's stern.

Reva fell again with the second impact, her forehead smacking against the metal edge of Scryer 1. She gritted her teeth and pulled herself upright, snapping for updated reports from damage control. She focused Nazir's efforts on coordinating fire for the ships in the fleet and relaying vectors on the incoming aircraft. Blood trickled down her cheek.

"Damage control updates, *now*," Reva demanded. What the hell had that first impact been?

She glanced around the CIC, taking in the damage as reports from below flooded in. Several other sailors were rattled about from the double impacts, but none required more than buddy care. No instrumentation looked damaged.

The news was worse below decks. Compartments on the starboard sides of the bilge were filling with water, and a portion of Engineering had been damaged. Reva's stomach was a knot of pain and worry. Arianna was down there with the boilers. Reva shook her head and refocused. She had a job to do and so did Ari. Damage Control Mages were rushing to close off compartments, rescue who they could, and put out fires igniting on levels 1 through 3 in the ship's bowels.

Worse, the torpedo had nailed the starboard rudder, locking it in position. They wouldn't be able to do more than go in a slow circle until it was fixed.

"Firefly got the sub," Nazir announced, breathlessly.

There was a muted cheer—and a small part of Reva relaxed—before they remembered the battle was far from over.

Reva barked several commands for updates, as Dodie and the rest of the battle group opened fire on the enemy ships. One of their Falcon pilots had managed to knock out the enemy frigate, and the Piz's attached submarine closed in on the enemy carrier, hoping to strike a blow that would put it out of commission and send its planes to a watery grave.

"Flight deck is operational," Reva told the captain. "Ship's list is 2 degrees to starboard." They'd be able to land their planes when it was over. If it was over. Maybe Sabine would make it back. "Damage Control is filling Level 1 compartments A24—A45."

Arianna's battle station.

Then the enemy battleship fired its guns upon the *Dodie*, and Reva forgot her friend in the rush of information and decisions.

***

The battle ended as abruptly as it had begun, with the Iron Islands losing their lead battleship and taking significant damage to their aircraft carrier, and then limping away into the distance—the battle group having never been close enough to actually see each other with the naked eye.

The Third Battle Group coalesced to a new defensive position, ready to pursue if necessary or retreat if more of the enemy appeared.

In the CIC, however, it wasn't over. Operational readiness was fluctuating more rapidly than the tidal charts in southern Isten.

There was the fleeing fleet to track and determine if pursuit was necessary. There were downed enemy ships and planes to be tallied, search planes flown over the wreckage, and boats to be launched if there were any survivors.

Third Battle Group hadn't lost any ships, but there had been significant damage to the Piz, from the torpedo and what had been identified as a new type of projectile. It had hit the flight deck and significantly damaged most of the armored plates in stern, which had made landing the planes during and after the conflict more challenging—those planes that had returned.

Reva stared at the missing and confirmed losses in aircraft, and mourned the lives that had been in each plane. Reports of killed or missing sailors were forthcoming. Damage Control was still going through Engineering, and duty sections were still getting accountability, but the captain would be writing a number of letters.

The question rotating among everyone in the CIC was now why, with a close second of who was missing. Reva didn't have ready answers—and she'd been to the intelligence briefings. The Iron

Islands had been quiet for months and there had been no rumors of new military technology like the obscuring shimmer cloud. Whatever the Iron Islands had intended with their impromptu attack, they just might have started a war.

Reva frowned. It would be something to think about later, when everything was said and done. She turned back to compiling the damage reports and assessing overall battle group strength. She needed something more to keep her mind occupied away from the death and destruction, the lingering fear that *someone* she knew was dead or hurt.

"Emmi." Chief Barclay was at her shoulder. He motioned her to wrap it up. "Second shift can handle the wrap-up."

"I need—" Reva began, but her chief shook his head.

"Everyone else has been swapped out. It's just you and me."

Reva glanced around. Second shift surrounded her. This group had probably managed to catch a couple hours of sleep in the—Reva checked her watch—six hours since the battle. She did the math of how long she had been on shift, and the numbers just swam in her mind's eye instead of coalescing into something painfully long. She yawned, hiding it with her notepad.

"The next brief with the captain is in three hours. Enough time to get some rest and get back into it." Barclay paused. He didn't need to say it, but he said it anyway. "The next couple weeks are going to be interesting."

Reva grunted in agreement. Someone in Naval Intelligence was going to get sacked.

She turned towards her replacement, who had been quietly moving through the stations to get a grasp of the situation on her own before absorbing what Reva knew. Her replacement would handle the rest of the damage control updates and preparation for the next phase of battle.

Reva rubbed her still aching stomach as they left the CIC. The worst of the battle pains had died down, but something was still off and it was making her cranky and irritable. The battle was over—what else had happened? She brushed it off as still feeling antsy over not knowing the full extent of casualties in engineering, damage control and among the pilots.

Barclay stopped when they reached the junction at officer and chief's quarters. "Hell of a trip, emmi."

"Yeah." Reva sighed. What a fucking day. It was only going to get worse. "See you in three hours, Chief."

She was deep in thoughts of plans for the upcoming war or whatever was going to happen when she reached her cabin. Her hand was on the doorknob before she noticed the intricately braid red and gold ribbons hanging on the door.

Reva stared blankly at the mourning braid, her exhausted mind frozen at, But I'm not dead to How did they get the ends to flutter like that, there's no wind here to What the hell happened when there was a footstep behind her.

"Oh Reva. I'm so sorry."

Reva turned slowly.

Sabine stood before her, still kitted in her flight suit.

The scene was a mirror image of what she had looked like when they'd bumped into each other what felt like a lifetime ago, but now Sabine's face was blackened with ash and soot. Her eyes were swollen and red. She looked exhausted, battered and beaten, a far cry from the triumphant hero who had been celebrated above decks.

Something loosened in Reva's chest.

Sabine wasn't dead.

Reva had known it, had tracked Sabine's callsign as covertly as possible until the Falcon had landed safely on the flight deck, but then they had taken enemy fire and she hadn't paid more attention.

And now she was here, and someone else wasn't.

"I—" Reva began, and turned back to the braid.

And it hit her.

Arianna.

Steering had taken the brunt of the torpedo, but Engineering and the boiler mages were close enough that they would have been the first to rush in for damage control. Reports of the dead were still trickling into the CIC.

"No."

Arianna with her smiles. Her grumpiness. Her friendship and mutual commiseration. The late-night study sessions. The laundry-run trade-offs. A year and a half of sharing a small space with a roommate who understood her, who shared her need for silent recharging and enjoyed long periods of comfortable silence.

Sabine stepped forward and wrapped her arms around Reva. Her chin rested against Reva's chest, and her tangled brown curls were so close that Reva could smell the smoke and magic.

Sabine rubbed slow circles on Reva's back, as she stood, still frozen in shock.

Slowly, Reva put her arms around Sabine.

The tears came, dripping into Sabine's hair. Sabine's chest heaved, pressing into Reva's stomach, as they cried for those they had lost. Sabine reached up and cupped Reva's cheek, a silent apology for all that had sent them apart, and for all that they had lost. And all that they would soon face.

"I'm sorry," Sabine whispered.

Reva pressed her forehead against Sabine's. Her hurt from the past felt so trivial, so childish, when faced with this death and destruction.

"It's okay." More words would need to be spoken, to heal, to move forward, to break down the walls they had built, but for now that was too much to think about.

Slowly, gently, they untangled themselves and went into Reva's cabin.

Perihelia

Elizabeth McEntee

Elizabeth McEntee is a writer and musician from just outside of New York City. She currently lives alone with her stuffed animals. Her favorite color is purple, and her favorite season is winter.

Upon a comet never named, under a bleakly-forming coma sky, among the ice and dust caking the nucleus like an ideal antithesis of moss, was a door. And as with everything on that comet, that door belonged to me. I was quite proud of that door. I created it myself. It was primarily made of ice and reinforced with dust, which worked perfectly in that chilly climate. It kept the outside outside and the inside inside, and that fact mattered more than the details of what exactly was on either side. It formed my place of solace away from the bright glare of the universe past the sublimation. It was my first creation, and a necessity, for without it, I would have been in terrible trouble when the comet was in perihelion with a star, which was bound to occur now and then. I sometimes likened my new state to being a vampire. But there was no blood anywhere, nor within, as my consciousness now inhabited a body of ice and dust. And as far as I was concerned, that was how it had always been, one way or another. There was only ice and dust in my soul, and my door may have just as well been part of my body. We were the same: we let a little light through, scattered the rest, and were proud of it.

I was the only one to touch that door for a long time, as little as time mattered on the comet and in my barely-mortal state. But, eventually, the moment I both anticipated and dreaded did come: an abrupt knock from the outside. The granular ice within my cavern home radiated in waves from the sudden change, oscillating with the sudden shift of my awareness. I looked toward the door, and a vague darkness loomed beyond. They had come. I knew it would be a mistake to open the door, but at the same time, I wanted the satisfaction of direct refusal. They had come for me, and I was not about to leave. I needed to make sure they knew that.

What greeted me after I opened the door was about as I expected: a protective suit with a human somewhere inside. The flesh I so hated for myself was now at my door, and I stared in silence for a moment to allow the human to, perhaps, leave without me saying a word. I thought that maybe my fearsome form would have been enough for them to write me off as a monster and to never return to look for me again.

But the human stood their ground, and spoke with a firm, rehearsed voice, through a speaker on their suit. The voice was muffled, and though I could hear it, that was all I could do. It had been so long since I heard a human voice that I did not initially understand what they said. It did not matter. They had to leave at once, and I did not want to be more familiar with their speech patterns than necessary.

It was time for me to speak, and for all the time I spent thinking of how I would turn the inevitable human away, my words were, I believed, clear and simple enough. I arranged the words within me and brought them forth from cavern echoes. My voice rang hollow and harsh through the ice as I spoke. "I do not want visitors. I do not want to leave. Please leave me alone, now and forever. Go home."

The human exhaled, fogging up their visor for a moment. Despite this hesitation, though, they persevered, and I understood their utterances this time, to my dismay. "You know who I am. I'm not leaving without you. You should know that."

In the abstract, I had an idea of who they were: a hotshot who thought they could come in there and take me away from my life, probably sent by others who thought the same but weren't quite as into traveling. But it was all the same to me. In my perfectly frozen mind, after being away from them for so long, their species was interchangeable, inconsequential, and more of a pest in my past than anything more nuanced. I preferred it that way, as to not have to think about them in any manner but the bare minimum. This was a human, just a human. Awful. And this human was speaking to me as if they had rehearsed what they'd say. That was all humans did. I created. I improvised. I felt. They regurgitated. The flesh and blood quickly grew stale, but the ice and dust only became more elegant with time. I didn't want to spend any more time talking, but now it was necessary. I brought myself to speak more, and I found it uncomfortably easier than the first time. "I don't care if you've traveled for years across space to find me. Leave."

"I did," they said suddenly with some indignation, showing a little unplanned dash of themself before continuing, "and I will not leave, not without..." They trailed off, delaying the inevitable, and looked to their left, which took some effort in their cumbersome outfit. "What is that?"

Thinking that they were, perhaps, planning on doing something drastic once I was distracted, I stared at them again, taking full advantage of my lack of the biological need to blink. But they didn't stop staring at something in the distance, so I could not help but eventually look as well. Maybe there was indeed something, like a new fissure or a dust storm. This human probably had never set foot on a comet before, and mine was headed for increased activity pretty soon, judging by the star that had become much larger and more annoying than the others in the recent past. So I looked.

The human took this as an opportunity to move past me and my door into my home.

"Get out of here," I called after them, my voice coming from everywhere and nowhere at once. Annoyance turned to anger, fissures in my perfect crystal form.

"No," the human said stubbornly, "Now I'm not leaving your... home...until..."

Now the human was looking around with a more genuine emotion, though I could not tell if it was closer to interest or despair. Regardless, it had been so long since I had seen a human's expressions that it took this to realize how falsely they had been behaving as they tricked me just moments before.

"You live here?" The question was weak, as if they knew the answer but were hoping they were somehow wrong.

"Of course I live here, this is obviously my home," I snapped. I hated that this outward display of emotion was still within me and that this human was drawing it out, but I had too much momentum to stop it. "What, is there something wrong with it?"

"It's just...it feels so barren and uninviting, that's all." I could hear the intruder's voice softening a little. "I-I mean, I know about your old life, so I thought you might have a little more of... well...what you might've liked before."

"Were you expecting me to have held onto any part of humanity? Here?! In this form?!" A feeling I had suppressed for so long was coming out of me, and I hoped it was in the process of being expelled, never to be felt again. The last thing I wanted was to be reminded of a time where I was not of ice and dust.

"Berene—"

Of course they'd have known my name, of course, but I had spent so very long trying to scrape it from my mind. They even pronounced it correctly, and I despised that I remembered that most people did not, because that meant I remembered anything. That was the final straw. Raising my translucent hand, I attempted to form ice in scoops that would push them through the doorway. I wasn't used to this manner of ice-forming, though, so it was some trial-and-error as my ice yanked the human around a bit. Still, my voice was as clear as ever. "All right, that's it. Out. Now, human."

The human looked panicked about the crystalline ice moving around them, but spent the effort to turn around to face me again anyway. "You really don't recognize me, do you?"

"You're a human, I barely remember what humans look like, and I'm trying to not let you remind me too much. And once you're gone on your ship or whatever you used to get here, I won't have to remember humans ever again because you'll tell the other humans who sent you that I don't want to leave." As I talked, I directed the human closer and closer to the door. It was almost time to close it and to keep it closed, with humanity firmly and eternally on the other side.

"Seriously, Berene?!"

The indignance in their voice made me stop the movement of ice for a moment, and the way they said my name that second time was distantly yet still painfully familiar. But I was not lying. All I saw was a human squished into an inconvenient protective suit, who was now yelling at me, which distorted their voice through the speaker as they continued.

“I was trying to treat you like the Berene I knew, not some... awful ice monster in the vague shape of a woman!”

“Well, sorry to disappoint,” I said with cold sarcasm that came from some deep crevice of my existence, “but I am an awful ice monster. So you’d better get out of here before I start acting more like one than I already...am.” I felt myself grind to a halt as I realized what the human said, and pitifully uttered a stupid question as I was taken off guard. “What, you knew me?”

“Obviously!” The human crossed their arms, which also took some effort. “You told me you loved me. I thought that would’ve stuck with you even if nothing else did.”

They searched me with their eyes for any sign of recognition, but they wouldn’t have found any even if my face were as human as theirs. They were waiting for me to say their name, I guessed, and I had no guesses. Something in me wanted to guess, but I only found disappointment in myself for not having an answer, and further disappointment in myself for wanting one. The only thing I could do was to wait for them to become so frustrated with me that they’d say it themself, which took a significantly longer uncomfortable silence than I thought it would have.

“I have to say my name for you? Fine. It’s Soleia. Now can you hurry up and remember your fiancée?”

I remembered. I remembered intensely. I bristled in surprise, and it was a bad bristle. Spikes of dense ice crystal formed rapidly across the interior of my home, and a few nearly impaled Soleia, who didn’t even flinch, as she was looking down at the floor.

She could not be here. Soleia could not be here. "You have to leave."

"You really don't remember—"

I had to cut her off there. "No, Soleia, I remember. You still have to leave. I left to get away from all of it. Yes, I loved you, but you were part of it."

"Part of what?" Soleia asked sadly, with a sharp edge of hurt.

I hesitated, and then answered truthfully. "I don't remember, and that's the point. I don't want to remember." Mustering up some of my previous coldness and making sure to make it impersonal, I managed to awkwardly add, "please, leave."

Soleia didn't respond for a moment, and then I felt the tears running down her face, a rare form of water on this tiny world of ice and vapor. Seemingly half to herself, she mumbled, "I didn't expect you to be this bad...what am I going to do now..."

I chose to not care whether or not that was directed toward me, since I had an answer. I doubled down on my resolve. "You are going to leave and forget about me, even if that's hard for you, because I'm not going back. Look at me, Soleia. Do you really think I would be even compatible with humanity anymore after willingly doing this to myself and living like this for so long?! And being content about it?! Where is your ship? I'll escort you there, even. But I'm not getting on."

Soleia mumbled something that I couldn't hear.

"What? I can hear pretty well, as I hear through reverberations in the ice, but—"

This time, she opted for shouting. "There is no ship!" She turned to look at me, her face something I probably used to be able to fix with a kiss but now saw as just a broken, hopeless enigma. "It didn't survive landing. I stole it, and I had never flown anything before, so I didn't really know how to land it on anything, and it didn't have any ability to land on anything like a comet automatically. So I had it chase your damn comet across space until I finally got close enough and ejected and let the ejection pod figure out the rest. I don't even know what happened to the ship. But it's gone. My only object was to find you, and I did, and maybe it was all for nothing, because I didn't find my Berene, I just found more ice and dust..." She started to sob.

At that point, I remembered what sobbing was, and I hated it more than I likely ever did in the past. And I did not hate it because it was human. I hated it because it hurt, even in a body that could no longer hurt or shed a single tear.

But I do not know if I would have cried even if I could have, because I was in shock instead. "What?! Why did you do that?!" I knew why, but I could not stop myself from asking. It was all I could do. I did not know what to do otherwise. I thought I had left this feeling of hopelessness behind when I had forsaken my humanity, and I wanted nothing more than to cast it out again. And that would mean casting Soleia out. Out to die, though? Was I willing to commit negligent murder for my own comfort? I was not prepared to answer that question at that moment, so I did not, and instead stood silently near Soleia, hoping that she would say something.

Soleia did not answer my question, but she asked another, in a rather defeated tone. "Well? Aren't you going to finish pushing me out into the cold?" She wasn't speaking to Berene anymore, she was speaking to the ice monster.

"I don't know," said the ice monster, eyeing the still-open doorway.

"What is that supposed to mean?" She shifted her positioning a little to face me more. "Didn't you get rid of human things like indecision and emotions?"

"I thought I did, but you're doing a great job of undoing it... Soleia." Her name escaped that time.

Not acknowledging me further, Soleia turned away. I could not tell what she might have been thinking, and part of me still wanted to not care. But I did, and I couldn't stop myself. So I waited and worried, standing entirely motionless as I often did alone, like some sort of ice sculpture. And soon my instincts as one of ice and dust took over, and I allowed myself to be lost in them as a kind of escape from the present situation. Ice formed and reformed around my cavernous home, rippling in waves, finely crystalline and complex. It danced around Soleia as well, who took notice of the display.

"Is this what you do here, when you're alone?" She sounded detached and unfeeling. In a way, that should have been comforting, but it wasn't.

I stopped, my inner concentration broken, and the ripples of ice ceased. "Yes."

She spoke without turning around, her voice remaining defeated, with a little bit of sincerity poking through. "It's beautiful."

"Ah..." Her compliment caught me off guard, and the ceiling oscillated a little with my subconscious gratitude.

"I might as well say that you are still beautiful too, even like... that, Berene. You kept a lot of your pretty features after all." She paused, but not long enough for me to reply before she continued in a wavering voice, possibly talking to herself more than me. "I guess I may as well delude myself into thinking you are still the woman I loved, with the short time I have left here."

"What?" A more serious dread crept back into my psyche, one I had not felt since I was fully human, one associated with the constant mortal peril of being human flesh, the peril Soleia was still very much experiencing. I mentally braced myself for the bad news.

Soleia allowed herself a little sigh before continuing quietly. "This suit is for emergencies, so it'll keep me breathing and warm and pressurized for a few weeks, maybe, and it will soon put me to sleep as a measure to allow me to live as long as possible, but after that...well, I don't suppose you have any human accommodations here that would make this situation any better."

"No...I don't."

"So, that's it, then. Are you going to cast me out now, so that you don't have to watch it yourself?"

That hurt. "Of course not. I'm not a monster."

"That's not what you said a little while ago."

"I'm less and less the person I thought I was a little while ago with each passing moment, it seems."

"Hm." Soleia turned back toward me, looking up at me with eyes that glimmered with the slightest hints of tired yet desperate hope. "Tell me you love me."

That was too much to ask. I fell silent, frozen in place. The room felt just a little bit colder.

Soleia dipped her head in slight disappointment, and then looked at me again. "I can't begin to understand, Berene, but I realize that might have been too much. I'm sorry. I just wanted to hear it before..." She trailed off for a moment before continuing. "...ah, I didn't mention, it took a long time to find you. I almost didn't. My suit is starting to put me to sleep, so I was hoping to hear it before I went under. But will you at least stay with me, by my side? Please promise me you will."

"I am very cold, Soleia, even colder than the ice around us. I would only make your suit fail more quickly."

"It doesn't matter, it will fail regardless. Sit with me, Berene, if you can sit."

"Soleia..." I looked down at my own form, which I barely ever cared to do. The suggestions of legs connected with the ice on the ground seamlessly, and though they could move like legs, they were only ice and dust, and could be resculpted. I worked to bring myself down to her level, transforming my standing posture to one resembling her own seated arrangement of lower body. "I will sit with you." My voice likely sounded as harsh as ever, but any harshness had left me. "I promise."

Soleia shivered slightly and nodded with a small smile. We watched each other in silence, and soon she fell asleep. And while she slept, the ice did not dance, for I was wholly concentrated on the human I loved.

Time passed, and Soleia remained breathing, though it was shallower and shallower. And as time passed, more and more light began pouring through the open doorway and other imperfections of my interior, illuminating previously shadowed areas, I found myself having to refreeze more and more of it with rapidly increasing frequency. I promised Soleia to stay by her side, but eventually, I had to rise and look outside.

The star that had been becoming brighter was now dominating the now-bright sky, the coma forming a tail like a bridge to the star. We were approaching perihelion. It was likely beautiful from afar, but living on a comet, all I saw in perihelion was tragedy and uncertainty. I found myself trying to reach for distant memories of Soleia and myself watching a comet, perhaps in each other's warmth. Seeing the wonder of a comet might have even been the reason I pursued this life in the first place. I couldn't be certain whether or not I had this sort of memory or if I was just creating a false memory of something I wanted to have happened, but the reality I was currently facing was one of my world slowly collapsing into the heavens above me, a hungry god of plasma taking its offering and threatening to consume me as well. I quickly closed the door before too much of my own body sublimated away.

Despite all of the emotions that Soleia's arrival unlocked, I was still of the ice and dust, and the instincts associated with such an existence took over as I started to fortify my dwelling with my most familiar materials. But as I did so, the temperature dropped even more, and I saw Soleia's body shiver involuntarily. A certain piece of information from my human life then flickered into my mind, and I knew what I had to do. I had to protect myself and my home, but most importantly, I had to try to protect Soleia.

I brought ice from the floor up to me in columns, joining with my side from ground to head, and lowered myself down carefully to lie next to Soleia, fusing with the ice of the floor. She shivered again, but it would not be for long. I had to do the next part quickly, I knew that much. But I did not know what would happen next, apart from one thing: I wouldn't be able to let go. I wouldn't be able to enjoy my home unless someone else came to find us, and I had no chance to ask if that was even a possibility. But why, I asked myself, should I lament my loss of a corporeal form? Was it not just a crutch I was using this whole time because I wasn't ready to leave all of my humanity behind, even though I so stubbornly told myself that I was the furthest thing from human? And how terrible was it, after all this, that I was still thinking of myself before all else? Before Soleia?

My mind was reeling in the moment, but then I felt my beloved door disappear, and the coma outside streamed in, and I knew I could not wait any longer. I cracked the visor lightly fogged with my lover's fading breaths and drew her into the ice and dust for what may have been, and what may still be, our final kiss.

The Voiceless of Shalott

Jennifer Shelby

Jennifer Shelby hunts for stories in the beetled undergrowth of fairy-infested forests. She fishes for them in the dark space between the stars. As part of her ongoing catch-and-release program, these stories are available to read in such places as Luna Station Quarterly, Kaleidotrope, and Metaphorosis. Jennifer's first novella, Slipstreamers: Plague of the Dreamless is now out through Engen Books. If you'd like to learn more, you can find Jennifer online at jennifershelby.blog and on twitter @jenniferdshelby

"We're doing this for your own good, Tasilinn," my mother said when my parents dropped me off at the island of Shalott. "You'll be safe here from predators. It's not forever, just seven years, then you'll be a lady. Chosen, like us."

"These years are the sacrifices God expects of us as His Chosen Ones. The guards here will protect your purity until you are safely married," said my father, scowling at me from the boat as though I'd already shamed him.

I didn't dare tell them that I wanted to be more than my virginity or someone's wife. My father had repeatedly warned me how dangerous my voice was becoming and the damage it could do to their status and my future.

My parents took my voice before they left me on the beach, stuffing my throat with holy texts. I choked back my sobs while they set them aflame. I screamed as the fire seared my voice box and filled my lungs with smoke, loud and shrieking until the scream died on my lips with my voice.

Since early in my childhood my parents told me terrible tales of the monsters who would hunt me if I was left to navigate my adolescence on my own. But in that moment, while the scriptures burned away my voice, I wished I'd taken my chances with the monsters.

Father gathered up the ashes into a small sack to show the church as proof of his sacrifice, refusing to look at the charred ruin of my mouth. "We'll return when you've learned your place as a lady and your faith heals your voice."

"I remember how much it hurts, sweetie, but if you're faithful, God will take away the pain." My mother squeezed my hands. "I swear to you, we do this out of love," she said, tears slipping from her eyes.

This does not feel like love, I wanted to shout with the voice I'd lost.

My parents turned away from me and paddled home to their church and to Camelot, comforting each other while they abandoned me. I longed to swim after them and beat my fists against their boat, but the sacred magic of Shalott did not allow girls like me to leave the island without a voice. That is the curse of Shalott.

I remember how the sun shone pretty on the beach that day while I shivered in the shadow of the tower. My guards watched from the casements. They did not then, and would not ever, speak to me.

The distance between my parents and I widened, a gulf of water and of disillusionment. It was easy to play the faithful child when I had their love to protect me, but in the agony of my damaged throat I found myself faithless and my unanswered sobs only made it worse.

The hurt subsided after weeks of slaking with cold broths the guards left at my door. Something inside me died in the twisted torture of that pain, the last of my faith, I suppose, or my innocence. The pain laid everything bare: this was not done to protect me, the church silenced me to control me. I'd read too many books in Camelot's library before my father found out and forbade me, enough to know that cruelty is not the action of a loving community, but the tool of a cult.

The view from my tower room was all the church allowed me to know of the world. A mirror reflected the view of Camelot into the spaces where I could not see it otherwise, taunting me with freedom and always, always watching. I grew to hate that mirror. I forget the moment when it became fixed in my mind as a metaphor for my parents' God, beholding everything I did and studying me for faults. At night I dreamed of smashing it and wielding the shards like a knight with a sword.

The guards monitored me where the mirror did not, when I ventured to the river to wash my hair, my clothes, my linens. Ever observing, never speaking. Not to me, not to a girl without a voice.

At night, the guards practised their war games. I supposed I could have taken comfort in the effort they put forth to protect me if my heart wasn't too broken to try. Twilights were accompanied with the steady whoosh and thwack of their throwing knives and archers' arrows punishing their targets. Beneath that, the low murmur of the prayer witches gathered power in the deepening shadows. I didn't like to see their prayers twist the shape of things into something new. It was like viewing the embodiment of a lie. I learned to hate the sounds, pulling a pillow over my head to drown them out, weaving stories in my mind to carry me far away.

I had paper and pen, but books and letters from home were not allowed. I longed for the library where I once spent such happy hours. At first, I wrote what I could remember of the books I missed the most, then stories of my own.

Sometimes, from my window, I saw girls running through the fields on the far shore from the island, laughing and shouting. They were not Chosen Ones, which made them sinners in my parents' philosophy, but they were free and their voices loud and clear. If I'd had a voice, I would have called to them, and maybe they might have come and rescued me. I wrote stories where those girls climbed the tower and broke off pieces of their own voices to make me whole enough to leave.

My stories grew angrier, wilder, until I couldn't hold them back, rivers of words pouring out through my pen after too long dammed up in my body. I wrote with a rage I did not know I had inside me, thoughts I never dared to think, blasphemies against my own indoctrination.

As I wrote, my determination strengthened. I didn't want this life, not the island, not the husband who would force my daughter here, not the Chosen, nor the cult of Camelot. I wanted the agency this religion denied me because of my sex. I wanted choices and to get them, I needed to escape. To escape, I needed to break the curse, and if I could escape, there were still the predators to contend with.

Night after night my mother had told me stories of the nightmarish monsters who preyed on the innocence of teenage girls, who could smell us from the underbelly of the world and rise to devour us whole. The only way to keep safe was to stay quiet and faithful on the Chosen Ones' islands and God would protect us.

My belly ached as doubt crept into those beliefs too. The stories stank of control in the absence of familial love. I couldn't be sure, though I could be careful. I paid closer attention to the guards, to see if they fought off monsters stalking around the island, attracted by my ruined faith, but all they did was drink and practise war.

Soon a peal of laughter rang out across the river from a pair of lovers frolicking together. The girl was young, not much older than me, clearly godless to risk her purity without a chaperone. I checked the shore for monsters and, finding none, squinted to see if the boy was one in disguise, waiting until they were far enough from the city to eat her alive.

They laughed, they kissed, they loved, and no monsters came to ruin them. My pen moved idly in my hand, inking out a thought too dangerous to think. *The monsters are a lie.*

I slammed my pen against the stone wall in a sudden rage, clutching at the paper, crumpling it tight before I threw it across the room. It bounced off the mirror and tumbled somewhere under my bed. Tears of rage and frustration scoured my cheeks. I stared down at the river, wondering what other lies I had been told. I didn't consider the repercussions before I stormed down the stairs, across the beach, and dove into the river, desperate to escape.

For one bright, hopeful moment, as the cold water embraced my body, I believed the curse was just another lie. My strokes were strong and true.

But the water around me twisted and heaved, sending shards of panic through my veins. The sunlight disappeared. I couldn't breathe. The pressure of the water on my skin became unbearable. The moment I thought my bones would crumple, the pressure released, splashing me into my room in the tower. My knees barked against the stone floor. I looked behind me in time to see the mirror distort as it vomited me out and smoothed back into glass.

My horror forced burning bile into my throat and a myriad of small bruises bloomed across my skin. They would be a painful reminder that the curse was real for weeks to come. Without a voice, I was going nowhere.

A sparrow chose that moment to land upon my window casement. It turned to me, ruffling its feathers and squawking once before gliding away, soaring on some unseen wind.

Startled and overjoyed to have been spoken to, even by something as inhuman as a bird, my horror eased and my breathing calmed. I brushed the last of the water from my hair and dried the floor before stooping under my desk to retrieve the pen I'd thrown.

Something carved into the wood, hidden, stopped me. It took my eyes a moment to adjust before the message clarified. *If you can read this, then I have a voice.* I brushed my fingertips over the words, longing to connect with this lady of Shalott, wishing I could save her.

It wasn't until later that her words sunk in, dredging up memories of my old library and an essay I once read about a writer finding his voice. The voice he found was the one with which he wrote his stories. I trembled with the memory, for I'd forgotten there were other kinds of voices.

For a moment, my heart leapt with hope, but I had no way to get my stories off the island. I slammed my fists into my pillow and screamed, soundless and ineffectual.

Days passed before I thought to retrieve the crumpled story. It was under my bed, to the far end where a spill of light from the window caught the folds and, for a moment, I could swear it was a bird, its wings long and sleek for gliding. The illusion shattered when I reached for it, remembering the sparrow on the ledge before it caught an updraft and soared away.

A new idea burrowed into my brain, insistent and refusing to be ignored. If I could fold paper into a bird, a story might be able to fly, and if it made it off the island, someone might find it. They might read it. If they did, I would have a voice my parents couldn't take away and this island couldn't keep me prisoner anymore.

I spent the next few weeks folding paper into birds, until I found a design that could glide across the room. Next, I wrote the story. I feared few people would empathize with a girl like me, but if I twisted my story and made it happen to someone considered important, its horror became obvious. So I wrote the story of a tower that devoured warriors whole, gnawing on their armour until it yielded to the tower's will, shaped into automatons the tower spat out to take the late warriors' places. I cried as I wrote it, wishing I didn't need to hide myself inside my own story.

I polished the story well, whittling it down to fit a single page, writing out copy after copy, and folding them into a little flock.

When I finally had enough, I held my breath, crossed the room, and tossed them from my window. The story birds fumbled a moment until the air caught their wings and they flew. If one made it to the fields across the river, to the carefree girls who played there, I could be freed. My blood pumped fast and time slowed down, my little birds dancing on the air.

But my guards were vigilant. Their windows opened, the Chosen Ones ready with their daggers, their flaming arrows, their magic books, and their boredom, and they picked off my stories one by one.

Thrown daggers obliterated the first of my flock, littering the ground in a clatter of knives, my stories a confetti too broken to read. Arrows hissed through the air and more of my stories flickered with fire, holding form just long enough to hope before they crumpled into dust beneath the weight of their own ashes. The prayer witches turned the last of my stories into birds I didn't recognize, white as paper, eyes as dark as ink. They opened their mouths to chirp but only a strangled gargle sounded before they flew to places beyond the sight of any human eyes.

After the last bird disappeared, the Chosen Ones met in the courtyard to celebrate their success. The sounds of their drunken revelry climbed the tower and wove through the windows, shattering whatever was left of my heart. All the time they spent practising for war I never realized it would be waged against me. I sobbed into my knees, hating myself for having believed so many lies.

Soon the tears washed clean the frustration of my defeat and I tried again. This time I folded boats of wax paper stories and hid them inside my laundry. I carried them with me when I went to the river for washing, past the moorings of the wooden boat that tempted me with freedom and away from the scowling man who guarded it. As I scrubbed the stains from my clothes, I released my own stories one by one.

Some sank, too crushed beneath the weight of fabrics, while others floated true. The Chosen Ones sounded the alarm when they saw them. The boats were out of range of knives, but the arrows still flew, sizzling as the water guzzled up the flames and my stories sank into its depths. The air grew electric with the spells of the prayer witches and my stories turned to fish who dove beneath the surface. A moment later, the Chosen Ones' shutters slammed shut, proud of their easy success.

Tearful, I reached for another shirt to scrub and found a handful of boats still hidden beneath. This time, I waited until I heard the chosen ones toasting in the courtyard before I released those final stories, afraid to breathe. The boats bobbed along in the current, a bright armada on the river, until they slipped around a bend and disappeared.

I rushed back to my tower, my lungs heaving, to look out my window and see where my little fleet of story boats had gone.

A figure on a horse appeared in the distance, sunlight glinting off his armor like the knights in my story. He rode closer to the river, dismounting and wading into the water. I tried to tell myself not to hope hard enough to break my heart again, that if he did find a boat, what were the odds he could and would read it?

He fished out my little boat as my hands flew to my mouth. The knight unfolded the wax paper and held it up. I squeezed the casement hard enough my fingers ached. Oh, please, Sir, I begged him from my silence, please read it. If he could read, he should look at the tower of Shalott with distrust or discomfort that there may be some truth in the story of a tower that devoured knights like himself.

Minutes passed before he left the river, tucking my story into a saddlebag and climbing onto his horse. He gathered the reins and paused, glancing at the tower with an expression of disgust before he shook his head and rode away.

I sank to my knees, giggling and crying, imagining him returning with his army to pull down every last tower on the Chosen Ones' islands and setting all of us free. Shaking my head, I pushed the thought away, unwilling to risk my chance on an errant knight, not when I'd just saved myself.

I grabbed my papers, my pen and, catching my reflection as I moved to the door, I stopped, remembering how the mirror sent me back here once already. I grabbed my desk and hurled it into the mirror. It cracked, a spiderweb from side to side, and a million girls like me smiled from the shards before they crashed to the floor.

I flew down the stairs, the guards still lost to their revelries, but they couldn't have stopped me. My excommunication was the only weapon they still had and I'd long since left the last of my faith behind, buried beneath the heap of lies their church had taught me.

I struggled with the moorings of the boat, my hands fumbling with too much adrenaline. There were no oars and I didn't waste time hunting them down. The mud sucked and squelched at my feet like a sad, final attempt to keep me on the island as I pushed off from the bank and leapt into the boat.

I laid on the bottom, holding my breath as the stream bore me far away, unsure if my new voice was enough and braced for the curse that might yank me back inside the prison of a broken mirror. The sky passed over the boat in fluffy clouds, tears streamed from my eyes, and nothing happened. I pulled my pen from my pocket and I wrote along the prow as the island and the tower faded in the distance, *Tasilinn is free.*

The Notary of No Republic

J. Byrd

Julia Byrd lives and writes in Chicago with her handsome dog and scruffy husband. Her first two novels, both Gothic romances, were recently published by Tirgearr. She is afraid of roller coasters and beets and climate change.

It began with her own college diploma. Lucy Carvell had a degree-shaped hole in her heart, a thin but prestigious hole, pointy at the corners. She found fancy paper and inked, with curlicues and flourishes, OXFORD across the top. She added her full name—LUCY CONSTANCE CARVELL—with loops on the first letters of each. A Bachelor of Science in Economics seemed fair considering she knew enough economy to feed herself, as was Forestry, because everyone still alive was a goddamned Boy Scout these days.

She'd never been to Oxford, nor would she ever go.

The paper looked nice. She considered for another moment, then added "(Hons.)" after her double degrees.

When she pressed the county seal into the page, embossing an eagle rampant and ivy wreath, the diploma-shaped ache in her chest eased almost to nothing.

It should have been hers anyway. The nation had started to fall apart after the big hurricane season, followed by protests that tangled transport and tied industry in a knotty mess. By the time people started dying in understaffed, depleted hospitals, it seemed to make sense to delay elections. But then there was no one to reschedule a vote, and healthy people were dying, too. It happened so slowly. How do you restart a country after its engines sputter? The breakdown spread further, across the continent and the hemisphere and the globe.

The first hurricane landed the day Lucy after had mailed her application—not to Oxford but to Florida State. The university was closed. Four years later, Florida, as a working state, had functionally ceased to exist.

But Lucy's Oxford degrees were a balm. They made her smarter, more confident. People trusted an Oxford-educated woman. Her friend Aisha wanted a diploma, too. Lucy conducted her college interview.

"Many people apply to Oxford," she explained, "but the acceptance rate is low."

"I was thinking UT," said Aisha. "Their athletics program was outstanding."

"Yes. Physical therapy?"

"Right. Aches and injuries and functional movements."

Lucy nodded. Aisha had once extracted a tick from the back of Lucy's knee, and she'd splinted her fractured ring finger only last month.

Aisha hovered while Lucy made the diploma and depressed the seal. The heavy silver stamp had once been her grandmother's, a clerk in the county courthouse. Lucy marked its indentation with her initials and the date.

Aisha's expression was wondrous as she reviewed her certificate.

"Congratulations," said Lucy.

"My mom's going to be so proud," said Aisha, eyes glimmering.

Lucy charged her twenty dollars, for the paper and ink and her expertise, which Aisha paid in vegetables and milled oats.

Aisha, thus minted, soon had a steady trickle of patients, and Lucy was in demand for her notarized documents.

***

Without a state to mark, publicize, and file people's milestones, it turned out people still needed their milestones marked. It's not a mile-thought or a mile-cloud or a mile-bloom. Some events demand permanence.

Potential clients filled out a request in triplicate, which aided in the sense of benevolent bureaucracy and dissuaded casual inquiries. Keenly aware of the solemnity of her power, Lucy only notarized valid documents, and she was the sole arbiter of validity. If someone wanted a death certificate for a son not heard from in six weeks, she bade them come back in a year. If a couple wanted a marriage license but seemed half uncertain, she declined. She once single-handedly saved the marriage between two stubborn fools who were clearly still in love by lettering, quite firmly, REJECTED over their divorce request.

Most, however, she granted. Sickly babies, looking a bit vague around the margins, departed in more robust health after their births were notarized. The security of a land deed, the justice of an arrest warrant, the generosity of a will, she weighed and pressed each into existence. Her pages always worked. She forged her fears and frustrated hopes into a way to exert control, and it made more sense than anything had in a long time.

She ran out of paper and started making her own. The coarse

fibers and off-white color only added to the pomp of her stamped documents.

The Notary Public, they called her. A notary of no republic.

One day a man arrived, looking older than Lucy would have guessed given she remembered him from school. She wished it had been nearly anyone else.

"I'll be goddamned," she said. "Jez Campbell. Lucy Carvell, from geometry class back in Florida."

They were, geographically speaking, still within the state lines, but Florida was an era, not a place.

"Yes, ma'am," said Jez. He hadn't turned out quite as handsome as his teenage self might have hoped, but his eyes were still a nice whiskey color. A drunken color. "I heard you were the notary public and an Oxford woman these days."

He eased into the chair before her desk while she reviewed his request in triplicate.

"Seems to be an error here, Jez," she said, pointing. "You've put your own name on the line for the deceased. Unless your dad's name was also Jeremy Campbell."

"No, that's me, all right." He gazed back at her calmly, alive. "Dead."

Lucy set her pencil aside. She was unequipped for him. "If you're having dark thoughts, and we all do, can I fetch someone for you? Friend, wife?"

"No."

"Well, come back when you're really dead, then," said Lucy, laughing at her own joke. She pushed the slips back across the desk.

He glanced at the aged embosser where it sat in glory and heft at the corner by Lucy's elbow.

"Look at me, Luce." He spread his fingers wide, palms up. "Are you really trying to say I'm not dead yet? Look at me."

Lucy looked. The problem was she'd spent too much of eleventh grade geometry also looking, at the back of his neck, at the sandy skin behind his elbows and the delicate crease inside them, at the hangnail he'd chewed on his thumb, at the way his shoulders were always six months ahead of his shirt size. And, if she was honest with herself, thoughts of him had recurred too frequently in the intervening years. He'd once won basketball games and tutored freshmen in algebra, while Lucy had fretted alone over her grades and her blotchy complexion. Now he had hollows beneath his cheekbones and whiskey-drunk ghosts in his eyes.

"I see your point," she said slowly. "We're all at least a little dead."

"We're sure not living."

He wanted her permission. She couldn't do it, even if he'd call it a mercy. She reached for her pencil and wrote REJECTED on the application for his own death certificate.

"What the hell." He scrubbed a hand across a stubbled chin. Lucy watched, bemused. Was he really so surprised? "I have the fee right here—"

"It's not about the fee, Jez. It's the integrity of my position. Stand up on your feet and move your warm blood and muscle and bones right out of my office."

For a moment she thought he might balk. Shout, shove his chair, point a finger in her face, make a grab for the county seal. But he'd never been rude or cruel. Instead, he looked a little more dead than he had moments ago. He nodded once, rose heavily, and left.

She hadn't seen him in nearly five years, and then she'd seen him for only five minutes. Lucy exhaled slowly. She stared at the stamp, with its round metal seal set under a spring-loaded arm, and imagined pressing the eagle and ivy into the back of her own hand. Was she strong enough to crunch the little bones? It might even feel good, or at least not feel like waking death. She was only the notary public and not much use for anything else, not to Jeremy Campbell or anybody who didn't want a fucking mortgage canceled on a house that no longer existed on a drowned coastline.

***

The next day, Lucy wrote up tentative a peace offering, sealed it, and initialed it. It was the worst breach of her professionalism she'd ever committed. If there'd been an oversight board, she might have been in real trouble. Still, the shame of it brought a flush to her cheeks. She coerced Aisha into asking around about Jeremy Campbell's last known address.

Her friend returned in the late afternoon, smug and bursting with too-perceptive questions.

"Lots of folks seemed to think the man was dead, oddly, but through wits and charm, I found a location for you. No more than two hours away on a bike. Are you going there today?"

Lucy reached for the scrap of paper in Aisha's hand. Aisha pulled it away, eyebrows arching up. Lucy huffed.

"No, tomorrow."

"Are you going to kill him and then sign his death certificate?" She flapped the address in the direction of the sealed packet on Lucy's desk. "Make his wish come true? A tragic romantic pact."

"I am not going to kill him. I'm keeping him alive. If I promise to report back afterward in meticulous detail, will you please pass me that location?"

"Utterly meticulous. You had better take notes, is the level of detail I am referring to. Just raise one finger, ask him to pause his mental health crisis, write everything down, then allow him to continue. With descriptions and a rating scale of the kissing."

"I think the mental health crisis precludes the kissing." And he'd never shown a moment of interest in her, but she didn't mention that to Aisha.

"Do you want me to tell you where to find his house or not?"

"Yes. Please."

His house, when she arrived the next day, was at the end of a swampy laneway. It had peeling paint and a scraggly bald cypress tree out front. The child's abandoned tricycle on the porch was one of the Jez's ghosts. Lucy laid her bike in the yard so as not to interfere. She was haunted by her own memories, more than some folks but less than many others, and society had arrived at the consensus it was not polite to inquire.

He emerged with a mug in his hands and a cat twining around his ankles, then squinted at her through the muggy air. His threadbare gray T-shirt bore their high school motto. *Panther Perseverance*, indeed. Yet he'd begged her to let him give up.

How could he be dead while her breath shuddered in her throat?

"You change your mind?" he asked, slouching against the porch railing.

"I have something for you," she said, waving the peace offering. "Can I come in?"

"Nope."

"You're a charmer, always were."

"And you would know, wouldn't you, Luce?"

Lucy bit the insides of her cheeks. How much did he understand about her humiliating high school crush? She lowered her chin to stare at the pitted drive, then pivoted to retrieve her bike. Cycling all the way out had been a mistake.

"Wait," Jez called out. "Wait, sorry. I'm a useless, dead bastard. Don't go. Please."

She waited. The day was getting too hot for another long ride home.

"I have a grapefruit," said Jez. "Come on."

Lucy turned and plodded back to his porch while he disappeared inside. She sat on the step and contemplated her kneecaps. Insects flirted with the sweaty nape of her neck. When Jez returned, he bore with him a sharp, clean citrus scent, two halves of a whole in either hand.

"Here," he said.

She exchanged the grapefruit hemisphere for the paperwork she'd created. Juice stung the dry corners of her mouth as she chewed and he read. The cat leapt onto the porch rail and surveyed them with disdain.

"It's a bill of sale," she explained, although it said BILL OF SALE across the top in her curliest handwriting.

"For a suit of armor."

Lucy checked his face. He wasn't laughing, but he was confused. "That's right. To keep you alive. It seems to me your life needs protecting. Not least of all from yourself. I sealed it, see? There are my initials."

"Where is it?"

"The armor? You own it. This is your proof."

"This is ludicrous. A bill of sale for a suit of armor is not going to keep me alive."

"Yes, it is. It works all the time. I have hundreds of happy customers. Although yours is the first armor. Anyway, you must understand what I do. You showed up yesterday asking for your own death certificate."

"Because I am dead."

"Perhaps you were yesterday. I don't know because that information is not notarized. But today you're protected. Don't you feel better? What, did you want a sword, too? You'll have to pay. I can't keep riding out here for free to keep you defended."

"Lucy, stop."

"No."

"I don't have the energy for this nonsense." He tossed a scrap of grapefruit rind into the dirt, and his cat pounced.

"I do. I've been helping people for a year now."

"You're lying to them."

"I'm not lying. I tell people what they need to hear, but only if it's true. And I am telling you: You're not dead, and you're under my protection. Be glad! I am holding the world together."

"Go away, Lucy."

She scowled, a righteous fizz in her veins. He insisted on doubting her? Fine. It felt nice to push back against someone, like stretching a stiff limb. So many people took her job for granted. At least Jez saw how unlikely she was. "I'll leave, but the bill of sale stays with you. You think I can't do this? You think I can't press my will into existence? Too bad. Watch me."

They stood, wreathed in fragrant citrus and cat fluff, and Lucy walked away.

"Why me?" he called after her. "Why do you care if I live?"

She lifted her bicycle upright and looked back at him. He stood on the porch step, battered hands in battered pockets, and sunlight played across the dusty tips of his shoes. She considered several lies, some even scented with truth. She liked the power of her work; there were not enough men left to allow the good ones to go to waste; she cared about the wellbeing of all people and would do the same for anybody.

Instead, she told him the truth.

"I thought you were lovely when you were seventeen," she said. "Now, with the shine rubbed off, I think you are heartbreaking."

Then, certain she had embarrassed herself more than enough for one day, Lucy swung a leg over her bike's frame and rode away before he could respond.

***

It was nearly a week before she saw Jez again. She'd fulfilled her promise to tell Aisha the minutiae, about his cat and *Panther Perseverance* and the tendons in his forearms, and they both concluded they'd likely never see him again.

"You should've written a document saying he was utterly devoted to your eternal happiness and notarized that," said Aisha.

Lucy frowned. "It doesn't work that way."

"Says the woman who added flourishes to a fake receipt for armor."

So Lucy was surprised to see Jez hesitating just outside her office late one afternoon.

"There's a problem with the armor I own," he said.

She laid down her pencil. He filled the whole doorway and was limned by the setting sun. "Is there?" she said. "You look mostly alive to me, so whatever it is can't be too bad."

"It is bad. It's awful. I know I'm not dead, but the armor is flawed."

Something in his expression, something vivacious and boyish, drew Lucy to her feet. She advanced slowly around the desk. He leaned against the jamb like his shoulder was forcing the place upright, like Lucy wasn't alone in holding the world afloat.

"Flawed?" she repeated.

"Yes." He lowered his voice. "It hasn't kept you out. Your notary stamp failed me terribly. I find myself utterly unprotected from you, and I haven't found a way to keep you out of my head."

"You've been thinking about me." She took another step forward, trying not to startle him into fleeing.

"Incessantly. Come over here and tell me what you're going to do about my holey armor."

She did, because his command was as authoritative as any form she'd ever initialed. "I can't be your lifebuoy," she said. "My stamp is not that magical. If you're unwell, my sheer stubbornness is not going to fix you."

He reached for her hip. "Last week you vowed to press your will into existence."

"These truths are not exclusive. The world remains a terrible and unpredictable place."

She tilted her chin back to look up at him. He was taller than she recalled, taller than when they were teenagers, and his hands were on her waist.

"And yet here we are," he said. "Was this not your will?"

"Yes." She tested the warmth of his arm with her fingertips. Mortal and vibrant. "It is."

"Who am I to resist? I regret every hour of geometry not spent contemplating your strange charms. I am undefended against you, Lucy."

"You are under my protection," she said.

He twined the tail of her braided hair around his fist and tilted her head back another inch, and she saw kisses instead of ghosts in his whiskey eyes. She leaned into him, but not toward his patient mouth. She slid back an inch of his T-shirt sleeve and eyed his upper arm, pushed into low slopes by the muscle beneath. Then she ducked her head and bit hard into the meat of his flesh, only for a second or two, her teeth pressed into him like the eagle and ivy of the notary seal into paper. He inhaled sharply. After pulling her lips away, she viewed with satisfaction the pink oval left on his skin. The mark would fade away, but she would not.

He was true, he was stamped, he was alive. She kissed him.

The Mirror

Alice Paige

Alice Paige (she/hers) is a trans woman, poet, and essayist living in St. Paul, Mn. Her writing largely focuses on topics like mythology, queer love, and using joy and an act of resistance. Her work can be found in FreezeRay Poetry, What Are Birds?, Crabfat Magazine, Coffin Bell, and Take A Stand, Art Against Hate: A Raven Chronicles Anthology. She recently completed MFA at Hamline University and is a co-host for Outspoken, a Queer Open Mic.

The walls of the square room are made up of matte black panels, each one around three meters by three meters. They have a strange, scratchy look to them, like the texture of sandpaper. But, somehow, still smooth to the touch—deceptive. I enjoy the deceptive. The things that appear to be one thing then are another. I dated a magician once. She told me I need to "enjoy the show of life." That relationship didn't last long.

This is the Black Box, at least its most recent iteration. I was not around when the project started and the room itself has gone through several reconfigurations. In the uppermost corners of the room are thin, rectangular strips of light illuminating all six faces of the Box. The only other two features of the plain room are a square desk with a wooden kitchen chair and, two meters in front of the desk, an ovular object covered in a simple, white sheet. As if a ghost is standing uncomfortably in the center of the room.

The kitchen chair is amusing. Did they pull it from a break room? They had a budget for what is an overwhelming slew of recording equipment stashed in the walls and the salaries of over a hundred researchers, but a comfortable chair is too much. The other object is far less amusing. The Mirror, an object refusing inquiry. At the base of the white sheet, four thin spokes hold the oval upright. The air in the room feels electric and smells faintly of salt. No, smells faintly of the sea. A more complex and confusing aroma.

A voice crackles into existence from the top left corner behind me. "Viv, the desk flips open, you'll find a box inside. Take a look."

The voice is familiar, Dr. Fredric Vasquez. Everyone on the project calls him Fred, but I met him back in college as Dr. Vasquez, professor of Theoretical Physics at the City University of New York. He is a serious man with warm, brown skin and salt and pepper hair, and he's built like a damn barrel. I worked in his lab for a few semesters during undergrad. It was dry work—lots of mathematics and spreadsheets. But I did meet my fiancée Anna while working in his lab. She was the supervising graduate student. A few late nights of work and a beer or two landed us in a relationship together. Apparently, Dr. Vasquez thought I did reasonable work. And I'm sure Anna put in a good word for me. After I graduated Dr. Vasquez sent me an email offering work in his private lab. He told me the job pays well and could help me get into graduate school. I was working as a tutor at that point, which did not pay nearly enough, so I was more than happy to take Dr. Vasquez up on his offer. I was also excited to work with Anna again.

If only I knew what I was in for, but that's the point of all the red tape around this lab, isn't it? Only a handful of people know what morbid occurrences take place in the Black Box. Even fewer have ever been inside it. The government grants are coated in protective jargon and a handful of outright lies. After four years on the project I am only the thirteenth person to enter this room. If I was superstitious I would call that unlucky. I'm not superstitious. Maybe I should be. I'll certainly need as much luck as possible today.

The desk opens at the front and angles upward, like a child's school desk. Inside is an oak box with a simple metal latch holding it closed. With a palpable eagerness, I snatch the box up, close the desk lid, undo the latch, and pour the contents of the box out: a small, rectangular clock with '10:00' emblazoned in blocky, red numbers; a pencil; a yellow legal pad; a rolled-up stack of white papers; and a single orange pill all come tumbling out in a hurry. These are my tools for tinkering with the universe today.

There is a lip at the back edge of desk that raises up to keep the desk surface out of view from the Mirror. As I understand things, that's important. I quickly arrange the items neatly on the smooth, grey surface before taking a seat in the uncomfortable chair. My workspace is in order.

"Fred, get a better chair for whoever comes next," I say. An attempt at humor.

Fred's voice comes through the speaker once again, his tone serious. "We tried, but anything more mechanically complex breaks down too fast."

A fair point and perhaps something Fred does not want to dwell on. I have not been involved with any of the more human aspects of the project. Fred and Anna had me on data work before my break from the project. Particle pattern analysis, spectroscopy, temperature readings, that kind of stuff. I never had to listen to someone in the Box meet a painful end.

I was only allowed brief peeks at the Mirror through the data I was given. I never saw the thing, or the people going into the Black Box. Well, until now. I suppose I only ever got a rough outline through the numbers. Numbers are beautiful like that though, especially with something this abnormal.

Fred and Anna were here for each person interacting with the Mirror, walking them through the process, talking to them. Anna told me once that there is a matching ten-minute clock on the observation deck, but it is larger and positioned overhead. It's a reminder to those leading the project.

I knew there were people on the other side of my numbers giving their lives up for scientific progress. Anna and Fred had to keep that in mind as well. I just I never imagined what kind of chair those people sat in. Maybe I should have.

"Your vitals are spiking," Fred says, this time softer.

I take a deep breath to calm myself. "Right, sorry. Started thinking too much."

There is a grunt in response from Fred. He's frustrated. He's trying not to let it show, but it's there. He tried talking me out of going into the Black Box, but after my break from the project, from friends, from being a person, I need this. Even if it took months to convince Fred, I was destined to end up here.

And isn't that the point of the Mirror? Deterministic proof that we're all on a fixed track. Pieces in a molecular machine chugging forward? I would always find my way here to this seat. Fred would always help me cross this threshold.

We're still in the early days of exploring what the Mirror can do. There is sometimes so little space for new breakthroughs in science. The miraculous space. That's it. That's where I'm at. The Black Box. The space of miracles in which a paradigm shift may occur. Anna and I believed in the magic that can happen in that space. We both believed that the people dying in here served a greater purpose. She would oversee the project and I would tinker with the universe's numbers and together we would make those deaths mean something bigger.

That magician I dated, she never got it. It's not that I don't like magic, it's that I like to know how the magic works. The show is fine, but the trap door, the smoke and the mirrors, they're infinitely more fascinating. Anna gets that.

Fred's deep voice brings me back. "Please take the pill and then read the paper aloud for the recording."

Right, the official business. Less philosophizing. I quickly pop the little orange pill and unroll the white sheets of paper. The first page has a simple statement in regular black font, followed by a handful of instructive diagrams detailing each step of the experiment. The mirror is represented by a floating black oval on the paper. A black hole ringed by a diagram of me and a desk. Simple little drawings representing time ticking down.

Initial Encounter, Confirmation, Open Question. Each section with a timestamp. One minute, eight minutes, and then one minute respectively. It's not a lot of time to ask what may be some of the most important questions in the history of scientific discovery. I've thought obsessively about these ten minutes. Broken them down to the seconds. I have a plan. A plan Fred doesn't know about. Anna was convinced that project was stalling.

I clear my throat and then begin to read the statement. "For this experiment, I, Vivian Richards, will be subject 13b and will therefore speak second during the Initial Encounter phase. I give my consent to the recording of all relevant information while in the Black Box. I will follow the outlined script for the Initial Encounter and Confirmation phases of the experiment then will have one minute to ask personal questions. I, being of sound mind and body, accept the risks of the experiment." Not the most legally sound statement, but it's more of a safety net than anything. I signed four stacks of legal papers two weeks ago, including an NDA. I also created and signed a Final Will and Testament two days ago, which included consent to an extensive list of postmortem procedures. The asses have been covered and maybe that's part of the project stall. Part of Anna's disappearance.

"Thank you, Viv. Give us just a few moments now," Fred says.

I begin to twirl the pencil between my index finger and middle finger. Something to do while I wait. Something to keep my hands busy. Has everyone coming in here been this nervous? Or am I just this nervous because of the asinine stunt I'm going to pull? No, I can't back out now, I need to finish this.

I take a deep breath to steady myself and begin humming Anna's favorite song: Crimson and Clover. The Joan Jett cover, not the original. The tune rises and falls against the soft palate of my mouth and vibrates through my nostrils.

Aside from all the legal shit, I completed a psych eval. That was not nearly as difficult as it should have been. Lying to the psychologist was easy with how fucked up I am. An irony. I wonder what allowances are made for lies by people like me. How many mentally healthy people are volunteering to walk into a room they can never walk out of?

Plus, the public will eventually learn about what happened here in our solitary Black Box. And that means the public must think those of us that entered the Black Box were doing it with ideological purity. Or, a lie they can swallow. Fred tries to keep everyone's mind off the public image. He says things like, "There are people paid far more than you that are worrying about that problem." Of course there are. You don't get a private research lab like this through goodwill.

I'm thinking too much. The pencil isn't helping and the Mirror is there, covered. I wonder what mirror me is doing. Is she just beyond that white sheet, impatiently twirling her pencil, sitting in an uncomfortable kitchen chair that digs into her thighs? Is she mourning? Is she digging grief out of her chest? Letting it curl in the corners of the Black Box? Is she looking for divergence, praying that on the other side of the mirror, Anna is alive and well? Well, I've got bad news for my reflection.

The speaker crackles and Fred's voice comes through again. "Viv, we're going to run some rudimentary tests, there's going to be a handful of bright flashes of light and then a few sounds," Fred says.

"Right, go for it," I respond. My chest feels tight. We are getting closer to beginning.

"We can stop this," he says.

My jaw tenses. "No, Fred. I'm already in the Box, I'm committed to this."

That will unfortunately be on the record now. It will be someone's responsibility to go through all recorded audio from these moments. Picking it apart. Analyzing tone and pitch. Word choice. Someday there may be a paper or a book that picks apart this very moment in the Black Box. Fred knows that.

"Fine," he grunts. "Beginning preliminary exposure now."

A flurry of multicolored lights stream from the rectangular strips in the corners of the room. The afterimage of the room is splattered across my vision as I shut my eyes tight. Then, with a quick "click," the room goes pitch black. Sensor calibration. The lights then click on, becoming a deep, unsettling red that I can see through my closed eyelids. I blink my vision clear as three alarms bells sound, one right after the other. Not high-pitched as I was expecting, but deep and low like a church bell. I can feel the chair beneath me and my teeth vibrate in unison as that nonexistent bell tolls for the final time. The hair on the back of my neck is standing straight up.

I know from my research that the Mirror carves a hole in all this light and noise. While it is covered, it's total absorption. A perfect zero positioned in the middle of the room refusing the red light and the tolling of the bell. The room lights return to their normal too bright white as the air in the room heats up. I can feel sweat gathering in my armpits, whether from nerves or the temperature change I cannot say.

I watch as the panels of the floor, walls, and ceiling glow a bright white before they cool back to that same matte black. The room's temperature quickly returns to normal. It's a little bit of everything. The philosophy in the Black Box: hit it with the kitchen sink.

Fred's voice comes over the speaker once again. "Viv, mic check?"

"Loud and clear, let's do this, Dr. Vasquez," I say. He probably grimaces at me not calling him Fred, up in his observation chamber. He has a whole team up there monitoring all kinds of data in real time. That data will later pass on to a team of analysts who would break down each millisecond in the Box. I miss it. There was always an air of mystery around whatever new data we were given, especially when we started to compare to previous experiments. Why was there a difference in air temp of ten degrees between two experiments? How are the properties of photons being shifted as they enter and leave the mirror? That one is of constant interest to the research team as the photons leave the mirror as a kind of radiation. The little pill I took will help keep that radiation off for a time.

My favorite mystery is the disappearing second. When you're measuring experiments in milliseconds with at least twelve different highly precise scientific instruments running in the walls and a second just disappears, the folks watching those instruments are bound to notice. Plenty of different theories were floated: quantum tunneling, space compression, looped time. No definitive answers, but that made it fun. Back when things were fun.

The speaker hidden in the corner of the room clicks on. "Get your clock and script in place, we'll start on your count."

I nod, before realizing Fred can't see me. For all the measurement devices in here, there is not a single camera. A necessary precaution. It's strange, the way the Mirror can weaponize simple images. Those same photons that come out of the Mirror as radiation can be passed on through images of the Mirror. The level of quarantine used in the Box is important.

I place the stack of paper in front of me and move the small clock to the inner edge of the shield at the edge of the desk. It's surreal, being able to see the time I potentially have left marked so clearly by these glowing red numbers.

"Ready," I say. This is it, the big leap. There's no going back once I start the countdown. The Black Box will seal for at least twenty-four hours. A safety precaution backed up by failsafe after failsafe. But this is my chance to find out what happened to her. What really happened to her. "Commence curtain drop in five... four... three... two... one... drop."

And with that, the clock begins its tick downwards as the white sheet slides forward off the mirror. The sheet hits the floor and there it is, that strange oval, perfectly smooth, perfectly clear, reflecting all it can see. There is a slight whirring sound as the Black Box shifts and settles. I can hear that same whirring sound echoing back from the mirror.

And there she is: reflection me. She sits in the same desk, the edge of it shielded from view. Her hair is a disaster, just like mine. Messy red strands pulled back into a ponytail. She's wearing the same peach colored sweatshirt and blue jeans and I can just see her black converse under the table. She has dark circles under light blue eyes. Sleep has been restless and infrequent for the last six months.

She chuckles. "You look like shit." It's strange to see your reflection talk without your mouth moving.

I give her a tired smile. "Thanks, you too."

"Should we get to it?" she asks.

I nod and look down at the crisp, white sheet of paper with thick, black letters stamped into it. A routine. The steps to a dance. Both of us spiraling inward towards some monumental discovery. At least, that's what Dr. Vasquez wants. He'd be up on the observation deck right now overseeing an entire team of researchers, thinking this will be the same as every other experiment. For as much as I like the man, he still lied to me.

"Are you Vivian Richards?" my reflection asks.

"Yes, I am Vivian Richards." A simple but important question to start. A confirmation of identity and name. Every experiment with the Mirror starts like this. My turn to ask the question on the page. "Do you live in the Ashland apartments?" A small apartment complex in Chicago. We don't need to get as specific as address, not yet. Just handshakes to start.

"Yes," she says. "In high school did you date a boy named Robert Conrad?"

I chuckle at this. They keep our halves of the script separate, so I wasn't expecting that question. That's what I get for telling Dr. Vasquez about that boy over one too many beers with him and Anna. "Yes, and he was a terrible kisser," I say. She smiles at this, too. There's relief in the familiarity here. Her smile is my smile.

Ten more rounds of questions follow like this. The back and forth of simple information about our lives, but we both already know the truth: we are the same person. We both unfortunately kissed Robert Conrad before discovering boys aren't for us. He kissed like a wet trout. Maybe that should have been the question, something more personal.

Did Robert Conrad kiss like a wet trout? Yes, and he always wore ugly shirts with flames and motorcycles on them.

Reflection me stifles a chuckle at what must be the same thought. My plan might work. Especially if we've both already planned it.

That's the beauty of the Mirror. A hole between worlds existing at the same moment in time in both universes. If someone in one universe sneezes, so does the person in the other. If I woke up this morning, planning to go off script, so did mirror me. And if she didn't, then that's a divergence between the two worlds, exactly what we're searching for.

Exactly what they're searching for. I'm not a part of the team anymore. Not since Anna went missing. I'm out here in the lone depths now, with only my reflection to keep me company.

Eight minutes left on the clock. I can already feel my skin prickling and my heart quickening. I glance down at the palms of my hands and there are deep red splotches beginning to appear under the skin. The photons moving from our world into the other bounce back as what we're calling "inverse" radiation. It's picking me apart molecule by molecule. Hell, it's picking everything in the room apart. The edge on the lip of the desk provides some cover so the paper and the clock don't degrade in the middle of the experiment.

Ten minutes is roughly how long a subject in the Black Box can withstand this radiation and still be coherent, and that's with the help of that little, orange pill. It only does so much. At this point, cells across my skin are rupturing. My retinas are permanently damaged. It's almost a certainty that chunks of my genetic material have degraded. Mirror me and I have chosen to walk into the heart of a nuclear reactor to find out what happened to Anna. The image of myself becomes death and salvation.

The next stage is Confirmation. It says so on the paper and is accompanied by a little diagram showing me rattling off equations. We're supposed to check that the universes match. Seventeenth digit of pi. Speed of light. Planck constant. I've already poured over the numbers from the last twelve people in the Box. The universes are the same and continuing to confirm that repeatedly will continue to get us nowhere.

"How long has Anna been missing for?" I ask solemnly.

Dr. Vasquez's voice immediately crackles over the speakers on both sides of the mirror, "Viv, you've got to stick to the script. You'll have time to ask those questions at the end."

Mirror me answers before I can. "A minute, Fred. You give us a minute for these questions and that that has been useless. Shut up and let me handle this." She sounds fierce. The only answer from the speaker is it clicking off. She turns back to me with an uneasy intensity. "One hundred twenty-seven days ago. What's the official story?"

"Bad car crash, police said a drunk driver slammed into her going over ninety. Her body was unidentifiable." I shift uncomfortably in my seat as I glance up at the corner of the room Fred's voice has been coming from. He's almost certainly losing his shit. I had to convince him to let me in here after Anna's disappearance and that was only with a psych eval and multiple promises that this had nothing to do with 'self-destructive urges.' I think he wanted to believe me. He wanted to believe I was coming in here for the scientific endeavor.

Mirror me nods. We have six minutes left and I can see the left shoulder on her sweater is soaking through with blood. I bring my hand up to the right side of my sweater and I feel it, the skin sloughing off underneath the fabric. The blood working its way up through the thick threads. We need to hurry if we are going find answers. The two of us, reflections of a shared grief.

"What was the last thing she said to you?" mirror me asks.

My mouth feels dry and tastes like copper. I can see her, the matte red lipstick, her light brown hair hanging straight and neat, the tips of each strand of hair a faded blue, her hazel eyes, the way she raises her eyebrow at me from the bedroom doorway. "She told me, 'I have to run into work, an emergency with the Mirror, someone fell into the damn thing. I think it's a door after all.' I remember each word. Vividly. I've replayed it a thousand times."

I can see mirror me nodding along. She lost her Anna too. She's felt the emptiness eating at her. The loss like a gaping wound.

She was lied to and that loss has turned into anger. Anger at the Black Box, at Dr. Vasquez, at the Mirror.

The speaker clicks on once again. There is a crackle of static and a brief pause before Fred speaks. He sounds older, exhausted. I know more than he imagined and he must deal with that now. "Viv, don't do this. We couldn't tell anyone what happened."

My reflection and I scowl and speak in unison. "Fuck you, Fred! You lied to me!" I push the desk away and stand to face the corner Fred's voice is coming from. As I stand, I feel my left leg cramp, the muscles refusing to extend as I fall onto the floor. The panels of the Black Box are smooth and cool. I glance over at the mirror and my reflection has also fallen to the floor. A puddle of blood forms underneath her. Underneath us. It's a strange feeling, dying. I know it's happening. My body is degrading rapidly.

"Viv, you're running out of time. Is this really what you came here for?" Fred asks.

I grit my teeth and turn to drag myself towards the Mirror. "Yes. Tell me what happened." I'm almost there. We still have time to find an answer.

"Okay, listen. Viv, please... listen. We had someone, someone who lost a lot. Someone just like you sitting in that chair. Something different happened, we aren't exactly sure how, but they went into the Mirror. We needed everyone on the observation team to come in. Anna came in and insisted on breaking lockdown procedure. She said she had a theory and needed to test it. She said we might be able to get that person back and that this was the divergence we've been looking for." He sounds like he is pleading.

The Mirror is only a few inches in front of me. My reflection and

I maintain constant eye contact as we drag ourselves forward. We're running out of time but we're almost there. We must be under three minutes now. "Keep talking, Fred, I want to know everything."

His voice picks back up, desperate. I've never heard him like this. "She canceled the lock down and stormed in there. You know how she gets, determined, unstoppable. The plan was for her to be in and out as quick as possible. The emergency covering for the Mirror was activated so no radiation, no communication from the other side, no danger." I can hear him sobbing. "Something broke the covering and dragged her into the Mirror. We had to keep it a secret. For everyone's safety. Dammit, Viv, this is exactly what I was afraid of!"

I lock eyes with my reflection. We both know how determined Anna can be, but Dr. Vasquez should have told us. Should have done something. Fuck.

We're both only a few inches from the Mirror. Her face is reddening. A side effect of the radiation. She looks determined. This is the entire reason we came in here; to follow Anna and we're not giving up now. Wherever Anna is, she's alone. We both reach out towards the Mirror. No, towards each other.

"Viv, she wouldn't want you to..." the rest of the sentence is cut off as I touch the Mirror.

I feel my ears pop as my vision blurs. I quickly blink to find myself in a strange place. The first thing I notice is that directly above me is an enormous body of water in place of a sky. It's like looking up at the bottom of a fish tank, but it's so much bigger than a fish tank. The surface spreads out in every direction, out to the moonlit horizon. The water is a mix of bright blues and greens. I can see shapes moving in the water.

I try to stand, but my legs won't work. Pain shoots through every inch of me. Pricking my skin. I feel this white-hot pain pushing at the borders of my consciousness.

That's when I feel the ground underneath me. It's gravel or silt and I notice that around me are grey canyon walls. It's a valley. I'm looking up from an enormous valley.

It looks like the bottom of the ocean, but all the water is above me. Held there by some invisible ceiling. Where am I?

"You don't look so good," I hear a voice behind me splutter out. I turn and it's her. Me. Sprawled out on her back in a puddle of her own blood. There's no mirror between us. No border.

I pull myself closer to her. "Are we still dying?"

"Yeah, I think so. At least it feels like it. It's beautiful." She points up at the inverted body of water. The reflection of an ocean. The air around us is pleasant and cool.

I flop to the ground next to her. "Is it weird to hold my own hand?" I ask.

"Any other day, it would be," she says, still looking up at the bottom of the ocean.

I take her hand in mine. It's covered in blood, but it's soft and feels warm. We lie there, watching upside down ripples and waves break across that strange surface of the water. This is where Anna went. This beautiful inverted place.

That's when we hear it. A roar that echoes, shudders, and breaks. The sound shakes the ground. Rocks begin to tumble from the canyon walls around us.

Then, slowly, it begins to rain. No, not rain. Both of us glance back upwards to see the surface of the inverted water breaking. Droplets at first and then entire waves sloughing off the body off the ocean and falling downwards. My reflection points directly above us.

"There," she says. She's pointing to an enormous shadow in the water. The shadow quickly grows larger and larger, turning a vast space in the water above us a dark blue.

I watch on, horrified, as the head of the giant sea creature breaks through the falling waves. Its head comes to a sharp knifelike point and its skin is a dark and sickly green. The knife head points down at us as it breaks the surface and the thing's enormous maw opens wide to let loose another unimaginable roar. I can see rows and rows of sharp teeth in this creature's mouth. The wet, fleshy inside of its mouth is a deep crimson and scattered across its body are deep pockmarks. Each pockmark is a tunnel in its flesh descending as glowing, ominous yellow canals. Then, as the monster dives downwards with all its might, breaking further out of the falling ocean. In all the thrashing, I make out a single, large, sickly yellow eye marked only by a thin, black slit. Oh god, it's looking right at us.

My reflection and I turn to each other the puddle of blood under me feels warm against my cheek. our eyes are wide and bloodshot. We smile as best we can and she says what we're both thinking, "It's a door, not a mirror. Anna must have figured it out." She's right. There's hope that Anna is still alive here. In this otherworldly ocean floor. There's hope that she made it here in a better state than we did. We found exactly what we were looking for. An answer to a senseless question. The creature roars again, closer this time.

Then, still holding hands, we turn to watch the ocean break and fall.

City Light

Gillian Parrish

Gillian Parrish is the author of two books of poems, "of rain and nettles wove" and "supermoon". Her her work has been published in journals such as Gulf Coast, Cimarron Review, and Hayden's Ferry Review, as well as in anthologies from Black Lawrence Press and Wesleyan University Press. An MFA graduate of Washington University, she serves as asst. professor at Lindenwood University. On odd holidays like solstice, Fool's Day, etc, she launches issues of spacecraftproject.com, a journal of poems and stories also featureing interviews with artists. This story, "City Light," salutes the beautiful work of the indigenous psychologist Eduardo Duran.

Most of them figured out to come to her. The way geese find water, moths the moon. Not this one. Chandra would have to go get him, now that she had what she needed. She walked up the street, four doors to Antoine's house. The moon was on its way down, halfway through the oaks in the park. She still might catch some sleep before sunup.

She could take a lot of noise, but this one had been too much, a buzz of hunger up and down the street that grew louder over days. This time was different though. A couple hours back, around midnight, a SWAT team rammed in Ant's door, packed their van with him and a handful of junkies. Ant was alright, the neighborhood trickster since childhood, always sly, but also generous and warm. Since his mama died, two years back, he had been more and more worn down. The junkies that crashed there were OK too. One teenage girl and an old man would wave from the porch when Chandra left for work every day. They were fixtures. Most others came and went. Sometimes somebody would freak out in the yard and yell for a spell before somebody else would shout them down and lead them back to the peace of the porch. Mostly they all just nodded out on the old brown sofa and fold out chairs under the awning. Chandra felt a wave of deep weariness rise behind her eyes. Kept walking.

The kid was quiet now, slumped against the twisted little tree between the house and the curb. Skinny white kid, maybe sixteen, elbows on his knees, worn-out sneakers grimy in the streetlight. Under his hooded sweatshirt his face was tight, eyes shut, mouth open a little, like he might cry but couldn't remember how.

She almost felt sorry for him. Except his noise all week had worn her down. She'd need to take her boss tone. "Listen, boy. Enough of your miserable shit." His eyes opened, listlessly, not the snap-to she was after. It made her even wearier to look at him. She shook exhaustion off with a practiced spike of irritation that she now knew would not help to move him. She paused to gather herself, took in his blank look and sad sneakers, and shifted into her head nurse's voice—still firm, but warmer. "Come on. Let's fix you up."

He peered up at her. A thin face, smooth with youth, but sick too, a fact seen starkly in the ugly florescence of the streetlight. Nodding, she gave him a wry half-smile. Her confidence, his need, got him on his feet. Wobbly as a fawn, but still a boy. Who followed her four doors down.

"Sit." She pointed to the orange wingback chair her grandmother had loved. He sank into it, slumped over like a bag of bones. Anger flared in her stomach and moved into her jaw; it looked so wrong, him sitting there half-dead in that bright glad velvet chair. She remembered how Andee's rings caught the light, hands dancing as she talked, thin grey braids clacking cowries, back teeth glinting gold when she laughed. It surprised her how much it still hurt, ten years on, how much she missed her grandmother who named her and later raised her, healer and teacher, more like sister by the end. Andee would have been quick to point out her granddaughter's wrong-headedness—of course she should give the kid the best seat in the house: he was a guest.

She stood over him, bag of white powder tilted in her palm, where he could see it. "You know, my grandmom, she called this stuff a spirit. Mind of its own. Mmmm?"

The boy nodded, eyes fixed on the palm of her hand. He was barely there. Nothing but that constant buzz of hunger.

"Hooked her older brother in Vietnam. He carried it a long time. Kept himself together, though, worked as a sous chef at the big hotels. Had the discipline to dole it out. Just enough to get him through the day. Day after day. But then that fentanyl got into it."

She stood silent, chewing on her words. She'd been thinking of Uncle Max all week—his kind, sleepy eyes, his warm soft way of saying *yeah* that felt like soft summer rain, cooling off a day. Andee said he was like that as a boy too, the kind of older brother that took care of the younger ones and helped their mama cook. The summer before he was drafted, he saved his money from laying tar on the St. Louis roads, and bought the kids a big backyard pool.

She remembered when Max died, how Andee cried for a long time at the kitchen table, then went out to her garden for a while, and came back with a bucket of fresh cut yellow squash and red peppers and runner beans to make a feast that ended with the flourish of his favorite chilled chocolate-peanut butter pie, and how they sat together all night, telling old jokes and stories, and how—in the middle of Andee telling about the hummingbird and Max and their old orange tomcat, how in the part when he carried the trapped bird out of garage, cupped in his palms, wild and alive—she let him go. She remembered Andee's face at that moment, eyes wide open, somehow gone, somehow swallowing the room.

"He tried to throw Bean clear," she said to herself.

"Bean?" He met her eyes for a second before they darted away, shy eyes, scared eyes. Like Bean's, she thought.

"You know him. Of course. Yeah, Bean's my little brother." She snorted back a laugh, at Bean's nervous smiles in her kitchen at dinner, hours ago. He knew the junk was not for her, and knew better than to ask why she needed it.

"I saw him yesterday. Tried to catch up with him." The kid's voice was husky, uncertain, the sound of someone who doesn't say much. He wouldn't meet her eyes, and she realized then that he was someone who never expects anyone to listen.

His eyes flickered up at her, back down at his knees. "He was too far away. Couldn't hear me. Drove around the corner."

He suddenly looked very young. Young, but with tired old eyes, tired from more than the junk and the running after the junk. Looking at him made her weary. She felt decades older than her 39 years. Her back ached, her feet hurt from squatting beside the beds in the oncology ward. She needed sleep.

"Well, Bean's busy making a living like we all got to do."

Guilt flooded his face. "I have some money," he said, reaching into his jeans pocket.

A worried one, and soft, she thought. Different than what she thought he would be, given his noise. "What I need from you is quiet. You been waking up the street night and day all week. Some of us work day-shifts, some of us work night-shifts—and you've been fussing through them both."

She thought of the nights all week: the feral cats in heat screaming between the houses, waking the street from fever dreams of lost things, old hungers flaring in the dark, the UPS truck pulling up to the Tucker's curb every day with more boxes, the junkies fighting in Ant's yard, and her glimpse of Jim Bell, a grey shadow behind his screen door, his face streaming with tears.

The kid looked confused, which meant he was a little less gone than she thought. "I'm sorry," he mumbled, and she could tell he really meant it. Sorry for so many things. Most of them not his doing.

She sighed, a mix of sadness and a mounting impatience that was not all hers—the kid was keeping it together, but barely. He might shatter. She'd need to pick up the pace, but also go slow.

"Let's get this done, so you can be on your way. Hang on." She went into the kitchen for a moment while he listened to the sound of a cupboards and drawers opening and closing and the sink water running.

She came back and took her seat, set down a glass of water, a needle and spoon on the hand-carved walnut table Andee had brought back from Ghana. "With water and with fire," she whispered under her breath, and lit the orange candle waiting there. He was hardly there to hear it, hunched forward, eyes fixed on the kit, the room filling with that maddening mosquito whine of his need. He started to reach for the spoon.

"Look," she said, "Just chill out. I got you."

He looked up at her, as if he'd forgotten she was there, and then his eyes dropped back to the table.

"Listen—you know what I do all day? I'm a nurse. Just relax." She wasn't happy about what was to come, but it had to be done.

The juice glass caught the candlelight, it was one that she loved as a child for its orange butterflies and gilded rim that was shining gold in the candle flame. He was a guest after all, however briefly. And guests must be taken care of properly. *Because this is what we do,* Andee would say. Chandra twisted the needle cap, breaking the seal, dipped the needle in the glass, drawing up water.

"You go ahead and get ready. Find your spots."

He unzipped his sweatshirt, bunched it up behind him. His faded black t-shirt was flecked with ruddy bleach stains. Bony arms a mess of sores. She opened the little bag of dope; she'd never gotten so near it, but tonight called for it. "I was telling you how this stuff is like a spirit. Has its own mind."

She waited. The kid couldn't focus on anything but the dope. At least it was keeping him there.

"Doesn't it?" she nudged.

He wasn't really listening, but he nodded.

"You need to listen now. And you're probably OK at that—you're not much of a talker are you?"

That earned her a tight, polite grimace, but the buzz in the room grew louder and louder, no longer a thin mosquito whine, more like the sound of metal scraping metal. She needed him to hear her.

"And the thing to remember is," and then she turned up the volume of her voice and banged the spoon with each word: "I. Won't. Lie. To. You."

He looked up, met her eyes and the scraping sound stopped for a second.

She tipped the powder in the spoon, and she could feel his heart racing, racing.

"There was a boy", she said in her story voice, a voice that her grandmother taught her, voice like a river, soft eddies and flows. "Now, this boy was so tired from running. This boy had been running a long time."

She let her voice fade out, and snapped it back, into something harder.

"And he had good reasons to run."

He met her eyes for a moment, shocked. Someone had seen him.

"Yep," she said, "it ain't all Barbie and barbeques out in those suburbs, is it."

First hint of a shy smile. Shaky, like he had forgotten how. He ducked his head to hide it.

She flooded the spoon with the water in the needle, cooked the cloudy water over the candle until it went clear. He was fixed on all of it, the buzz of his hunger growing again, making her stomach churn. She settled herself firmer in her chair, started flicking the needle with her fingernail, holding it up to the candlelight to tap out the bubbles.

"Oh, I'm mixing you up, aren't I, son. I was telling you about this stuff here—this spirit you run with," she slowly tapped the needle with her fingernail. "It's not a kind spirit." Tap. "The way some are." Tap. "This is misbegotten stuff." Tap. "Seems like soul food at first. But then,"—tap—"it expects payment." Tap. "In kind." Tap and arched eyebrow, "As you know."

He was polite, this one, nodding, his face blank and tight, holding back the flood of his need. Though, she thought, it had been seeping out into the neighborhood all week.

She kept her story voice steady, half conversational, almost a song. "My grandmom told me that one strange thing about the spirit side is how the light is there". Tap. "It's a place between places, so the light is between too. *The night shines as the day* she'd say." Tap. "Always light there. But no shadows." Tap. "An odd half-light. Like twilight. Like December dusk, that silver-gold light, you've seen it—" tap"—that platinum light, like a mix of sun and moon."

She could feel him listening now, losing the tight focus on the needle. She stopped tapping, looked straight at him. He looked up and met her eyes.

She spoke slower now, drawing out the words. "But there's no sun there. And no moon."

She watched his face change as he turned inward. The buzzing had stopped, and she could finally see inside. He was thinking of the last time he had seen the moon. He couldn't remember. He hadn't thought about it for years. Then he remembered how he had loved it, how he would open the blinds in deep winter to watch the moonlight move across the bedroom walls, turning everything an unearthly blue, how he'd hold out his hands to catch the light. He was eleven, a couple years before he left home. He would read stories of wizards and witches growing wise in that moonlight, wishing he was far from there.

And he then remembered. A yellow half-moon above him. His chest slammed shut like a door. How everything went black.

She saw all of it with him and felt his shock—her heart falling for what felt like miles into her stomach. He looked up, eyes wide, locked on hers in terror.

She took a long breath in, kept her voice soft and steady. "It's 3am honey, the darkest time of night. But not for you, is it? For you, it's that long twilight, Steven Patrick Dunn, who died in the park last Thursday night."

His mouth was open, his eyes were huge and dark.

"No." The word was the first time he seemed awake. He held his knees closer, rocking. "No no no no no no."

He flickered out for a moment. The orange chair was empty.

Panic would make it all harder for him. She spoke to the empty room, sensing he was not far. "I told you I wouldn't lie to you. Now I'm telling you: I'll help you on your way."

He flickered back, hunched in the chair.

She set down the needle on the table. "Because this won't help you now, honey. Not that it ever did." she said it kindly, in the deathbed voice she used in the four in the morning hour at the hospital. The hour when so many died. Some people wanted family there beside them. Others waited until they all left for the day and then died in the kind quiet kept by a stranger. *Someone between here and there,* Andee would say.

He put his face down on his arms. "Fuck," he mumbled, the sound of nothing left.

She looked at him sadly. A small, slumped figure, still a kid.

A wave of enormous loneliness welled up in her chest and climbed her throat. She had felt the terrible loneliness of the new dead many times, but this wasn't the usual shock, the awful isolation of dying. This was something else, a deep hole of loneliness that was old, something long like a well, long and dark and deep. It was where this kid had lived for years. She'd never known anything like it. She had always had Andee and Bean and their cats and dogs and her aunts and uncles and cousins and her friends and then her later her girlfriends who knew her as much as she would let them. This hunched figure across from her had known nothing like it.

He flickered out again. Of course he did; it was all too much. She needed to help him calm down. "Listen, you are not alone anymore. I'm here. Do you hear me? I'm here with you."

He flickered back into the chair. At least he's tethered here now, she thought, no longer what Andee called "ghost noise"—a storm of wild feelings on the loose that bled into the dreams and days of the living.

He was very still. She could feel him listening.

"But this is why you missed Bean. It's why you never could get to Antoine, even when you made it to the door. They couldn't see you or hear you. And then you'd black out again."

She paused, slowing the next part so he would take it in. "This is how it is at first. For most of us."

She waited, testing the silence. "When we die."

"But, I—" his voice broke. He looked down at his hands. His eyes followed the pits and scars there up to the mess of his arms. She was flooded with sorrow, then a stream of memories, not her own: spoon over flame, cold sidewalk rough against skin, a red-faced man's thick whisper, "You little shit."

"Hey," she said, and she almost used his name, but she knew it would not help now, knew it would only hold him back. She said softly, "Hey. You know, it's OK, now. It's OK. You haven't wanted to be where you are for a long time, have you?"

She felt her words connect, let them sink in for a while.

"You get to go now, honey."

She could feel the death fear in him rising like wildfire.

"Yeah, it's scary, sure is — no, look at me. Listen. You know how to go. More than most. You've done it for years now, riding the rush of this stuff. It's crude, but it's close. Just has a bad sticky twist in it that takes folks the wrong way."

She feels his rising fear subsiding. He nodded like he thought what she said was fair.

"So you need a different kind of kick first, a different kind of sweet."

He was listening but looked lost. She looked at him with narrowed, thoughtful eyes, Andee's eyes, people said, though she and everyone knew that Andee's eyes were merrier that her somber ones.

She said, "Look, we need to find something to help light the way, smooth the ride. It will be rough for you in the between time. The wind will be wild, hard as the hurricane you've been sometimes."

He looked down at floor. Always sorry, this one, she thought.

"But you're more than that, you know? You're more than the storms and more than the sorry. Listen—remember a time when things were OK. Find it. Now."

She could feel her tone, those words striking home.

He sat silently for a moment. She watched his face soften more, start become something calmer, something new.

"What you got?" she said.

"My sister. When she was a baby. She'd fall asleep on my chest."

She saw what he was seeing, felt how it was to hold his baby sister, how she could only sleep if she was held close, how he'd sit on the old leather couch, sunk in its cushions, and how she slept on his chest, warm in her onesie, smelling of milk and baby sweat, a little ember over his spirit heart, his chest full of her sweetness, and how he'd never felt anything like it. So simple. Love that didn't want anything. Just was.

He sat quiet a while, his hands clasped together between his knees.

Then he started, shifted his weight uncomfortably, suddenly blank-faced again. "She's eight now. I don't see her. I don't know if she's OK."

"Keep the good; leave the rest—stay with that baby sister time. How it felt then."

He nodded. Pressed his hands to the center of his chest. He nodded and nodded, lips pressed together, eyes shining with tears.

"Ah, honey," she sighed. "It's hard to leave."

The tears were spilling from his eyes and for the first time he looked warm and alive.

"And it's alright to cry."

He nodded and smiled a small smile of thanks, hands still pressed to his sternum, tears streaming, nodding and smiling that small sad smile. A smile that made her cry too, and they sat for a while like that together, crying, half-smiling.

He was so different now, like ground softened by rain. She

shifted her attention outside and felt the wind from the west. She stood up. "A storm's coming. Let's go meet the rain."

He didn't move, just stared at her, and she felt his life start to fall away from him, felt it in her stomach, a tumble of fear and adventure, felt it in her legs almost giving way, her feet stumbling like after a first kiss.

"Come on, honey. I'll help you do this. I'd hold your hand, but I can't."

He followed her to the back porch. He was moving slowly, as if underwater, but finally alive, eyes wide, as if seeing everything for the first time.

They stood in the dark, at the start of a storm, the winds blowing in, oak leaves seething like the sound of a rough sea. "With wind and with earth," she whispered, now loud enough for him to hear.

She said, " I won't lie; the wind will be wild. But it doesn't have to scare you. You know it already—it's in you too. Just mix that baby-sister love with the wind. It's the best part of this life for you."

She wished she could hold his hand the way she did on the ward when folks were scared or sad as they were dying. But he was and wasn't there, something like a memory remembering itself. And now more like a dream that would soon be a different dream.

And he was changing, this kid. His eyes were closed, but so different than when she first saw him under the streetlight. He looked undefended now. And unharmed.

They leaned on the porch rail, listened to the wind in the leaves. She watched the oaks start to surge in the winds ahead of the storm.

"I love those old oaks," she said. "Changing all the time, like we do. Even if we don't see it."

She turned to look at him, at his young face tilted up to feel the wind and first drops of rain.

"Like we change every night. Every night living out other lives in our dreams."

She paused, watched him feeling him feel her words along with the rain.

"That's what it will be like."

He turned his head and met her eyes and did not look away. Almost ready now.

They turned back to watch the clouds moving. Storm clouds gathering and tattering, dark grey and light grey and white in the city light, moonlight, deep night sky.

"You could go like the clouds."

She paused again, watching them change and pass.

"Did you know that there are rivers in the sky?"

He smiled, his first real smile, and she saw how he might have been at eight or at eighteen.

"Or you could mingle with the wind."

His eyes were closed in that soft new way, and his face was open to the sky.

"And with space," she said, loud now, so he could hear it, know it as his bones.

And they listened for a while to the waves of leaves like an ocean in the oaks.

And then, as Andee had said to her so many times as they weeded the garden or walked through the shopping mall or sat on the porch in the rain, "Listen with every pore."

The wind picked up, warm currents mixing with currents cooled by the rain.

"Let it *all* in."

She watched him breathe in the wind, rich with leaf rot and rain-wet trees, with hot sidewalk and new mud mixed with the electric storm sky.

"Now, honey, let go—"

—and he was gone.

She stood there for a while, watched the river of clouds in the black sky, watching how slow and how fast and how completely they changed.

"There was a boy," she said to the wind.

Turned back to the house, towards sleep and dreams.

And what will he be next? said Andee from the orange chair.

We Who Are Left On This Dying Earth

Hesper Leveret

Hesper Leveret writes fantasy and science fiction with an emphasis on the beautiful, lyrical, and strange. She was born and raised in Southampton, educated at Oxford, and is now based in Liverpool. Her previous jobs include selling books at Waterstones and writing questions for The Weakest Link quiz show.

Jolene bent carefully down to the lowest of the squash plants, her knees creaking, and delicately used her paintbrush to pollinate the flowers. Once, she would have relied on insects to do this for her, but that was a long, long time ago.

The sunshine outside was intense, beating down onto the solar panels. The tall, plate-glass windows of her apartment were filled with tier upon tier of plants—squash and cucumbers and tomatoes and corn for food, herbs and chillies for flavour, ferns and spider plants to scrub the air. The ingenious irrigation system—which Cyrus called 'The Hanging Gardens of Babylon' after some ancient feat of engineering, the kind of thing he loved—kept everything well-watered with maximum efficiency. It was, like everything else in the apartment complex, including the building itself, cobbled together out of old broken bits of other things. Still, it worked.

Jolene stood up again slowly, and massaged her lower back with one hand. She needed to be careful—her health was a diminishing resource which needed to be eked out as long as possible. Or maybe it didn't—what, after all, was the point?

Then she remembered Cyrus, as she always did when such

thoughts came to her, and she set about pollinating the next row of plants.

"Hey Jolene." Cyrus was emerging from his room, rubbing his eyes. He always woke up much later than she did. As with many other things, they had found that their differences only helped them live together. "Is there anything for breakfast?"

"Only what you make," she answered with a smile.

"I'll check the chickens," he said.

It was the same routine every morning. Sometimes there were eggs. More often, there weren't. It was, more than anything else, just a way of easing themselves into the day. As he walked past the rows of plants, Cyrus examined the workings of the hanging gardens and paused to make a minute tweak to one of the water spouts.

They were unlikely flatmates—one elderly woman who had lived in the east of Asia as a young girl, one young man whose parents had been born in Europe, but who had himself been raised in the great caravans migrating to Antarctica. Or at least they would have been unlikely flatmates before. Now they were just—the ones who were left over. The ones who couldn't cope with the high-g shuttle launch to reach the great arks being built in orbit. Jolene too old now, and Cyrus with his heart condition. They wouldn't survive the journey into space, and so they were left here to survive as best they could, in this half-empty building with a handful of equally decrepit neighbours.

"You know what day it is today, don't you?" Cyrus asked. His voice sounded calm and level, like it never did unless he was trying very hard to keep it that way.

"Tuesday?" Jolene guessed. She still tried to keep track of days, although it grew harder and harder to care.

"Thursday, actually," said Cyrus, with a small smile. "But that's not what I meant."

The realisation came over Jolene like a splash of cold water, only it made her throat dry. "Oh," she said. "I'm sorry."

Cyrus half-shrugged. "Don't be," he said, smiling at her again, although his eyes looked pained. "We all knew it was coming."

He turned away from both her and the hanging gardens and went to the next room, the one where they kept their few scraggly chickens. Although she knew, logically, that the eggs were a better long-term food source, Jolene always found herself longing that Cyrus would decide one of them had ceased to lay and bring it to her to wring its neck. He was too squeamish to do the deed himself; he did not grow up in a time and place where he'd ever eaten animal flesh, let alone had to kill something. Her diet was mostly adequate—for a scrawny old lady—but the deep-seated hunger for protein never quite went away.

Jolene stepped onto the lowest rung of her stepladder, and started pollinating the next row of plants. Thanks to the fine-tuned empathy of spending so much time together, she felt a little of what Cyrus must be feeling, on this day of all days. She had nobody else left now—all her other friends had died before her, and all her younger family members had long since left Earth. But for Cyrus...

Cyrus still had a sister and a nephew. Or he did, until today. They were on the last of the great arks, bound for another star. Today was the last day they would be able to send a message to the ark before the time lag between the Earth and the ark grew too great and the ark's acceleration took them far into the future. From hers and Cyrus' perspective, at least. Jolene didn't pretend to understand the principles behind time dilation, and she supposed that, having already lived over eight decades and seen many others into the earth before her, she had become accustomed to the idea of other lives continuing while her own ceased. Besides she had no desire to leave the planet of her birth. Cyrus, however, was young. He had not had nearly so much time to get used to the idea.

"I was up late again last night, looking through the telescope," he said from behind her. He sounded like he was suppressing a yawn. Jolene glanced back. He had an egg in one hand.

"Did you see anything?" she asked.

"A glint from the engines," he said. "No brighter than Epsilon Crucis. I'll be able to see them for a while longer, I think. At least until there's too much light."

Even Jolene understood that stargazing in the southern summer was impossible, when the days grew so long that the nights disappeared. And by the time the nights lengthened again—would the ark be visible at all in the endless dark of winter, when the milky way stretched across the sky, cold and forbidding? Cyrus thought the stars were beautiful and had often told her so. She found them distant and frightening and could never wrap her head around the idea that the sun was just another star, and that one day humans—including her own flesh and blood—would live in orbit around a different star.

"Are you going to send a message tonight?" she asked.

"It's the last chance," he said, with a pained smile, "so I guess I should. But I don't know what to say."

"You'll think of something," she said. As she spoke, she thought of something herself, and saved that thought for later. "Now, are you going to stand around moping all day, or are you going to make us some breakfast and then help me with the plants?"

"I was thinking I'd stand around moping," he said, even as he walked into the kitchen. Jolene carried on pollinating until he called her over for their meagre breakfast, and then they both set to work again. Pollination, irrigation, feeding the chickens, cleaning, performing maintenance on all the jury-rigged life-support systems... all their normal daily tasks that kept them busy, just keeping themselves alive. They spoke little to each other beyond what was necessary. They had already said most of what was possible to say and knew all about each other's lives before they had met. Jolene, named after an ancient song—a song she owned on a black disc in a gold frame, the tune embedded somehow in a groove, and she had no idea how to extract it. Cyrus—named after an even more ancient king of a land the location of which neither of them really understood. Jolene's ancestors had lived for centuries on a peninsula in Asia known as Korea, and had changed rulers many times without ever changing location. While Cyrus' ancestors had been shipped across the ocean to a different continent against their will, and had sailed back as free men and women to a different continent again. Such distinctions, while interesting to discuss on the long Antarctic days and nights, had long ceased to mean much, as everyone left on Earth had migrated to the few places left habitable. And then most of them had launched into orbit, and then left the system altogether on the fleet of ark ships.

It was only when they went down into the store rooms—blessedly cool beneath the ground—to retrieve some of their rations of wheat flour and potato starch, that Jolene spoke again to Cyrus, voicing the thought she had saved from earlier.

"I think today is the day," she said, lifting the bottle from its packing case and brushing the light coating of dust away.

"Are you sure?" he asked.

"It's the last bottle, today's the last day. When else am I going to drink it?"

"If you're sure."

"I'm sure."

And so, after they had prepared the evening meal— not much less meagre than the morning one—Jolene popped the cork on the last bottle of champagne she owned, quite possibly the last bottle of champagne in the world. She poured out the bubbles from a vanished land—for it had been decades since anywhere in Europe had been able to sustain a crop of grapes—into their scuffed plastic beakers and then paused as she tried to think of an appropriate toast. The pause stretched, until at last, Cyrus helped her out.

"To us," he said, and she clinked—or rather clicked—their glasses together.

"To us."

"We who are left on this dying Earth,"he added.

"We who are left,"she echoed, and then drank, letting the rich buttery wine wash over her tongue. They sat in silence for a few minutes, both of them just sipping and savouring the taste.

"You know what bothers me,"Cyrus said.

There were many possible answers to that question. Jolene decided to offer none of them.

"What bothers me,"he went on, "aside from the obvious, is that when you die, I can at least remember you. I'll turn you into compost to grow more food—"

Jolene nodded. Those of them who were left here had long since moved on from any sense of squeamishness about what happened to dead bodies. They might still shy away from direct cannibalism—some taboos hadn't gone away—but nutrients were nutrients.

"—and I'll keep your record, with your name, and I'll probably still talk to you. But what about when I die? Who'll be left to compost me? And what would even be the point in composting me, because who'll be left to eat the food?"

Jolene tried not to dwell on it, but she was uncomfortably aware that, given how elderly she and most of their neighbours were, Cyrus was probably going to be the last person alive in the apartment block. Even with his heart condition. Quite possibly, he would be the last person alive on Earth. She certainly didn't envy him that fate. She took a bigger sip of champagne—a gulp really—before answering him.

"Well," she said, "you never know. Maybe they will discover some new technology that will allow them to return to Earth. Or find a cure for your condition, so you can go with them after all. Your sister might even come back here. Even if not her, somebody else might show up. Like, your great nephew or something."

Cyrus took an unashamed swig of champagne, and gave her a look, chin lowered, one eyebrow raised. And then they both burst out laughing.

"Oh dear," said Jolene, "these bubbles have gone right to my head." She emptied her glass.

Cyrus stood up, not very steadily, and poured her a refill. "I'm going to send my message now," he said, and then walked out, taking the champagne bottle with him.

Jolene didn't offer to help. Some things needed to be done alone.

***

Cyrus walked into their tiny communications suite, and sat down in front of the transmitter. He switched it on, set down the bottle, and waited for it to warm up.

"Hey sis," he said to the screen once the green light had come on. "Hope you and little Cy are doing well."

He sort-of appreciated the fact that his nephew had been named after him, and sort-of found it patronising. Like, he couldn't make it off the Earth, but a younger, healthier version of him could? Didn't make being left behind any easier.

"I can still see you, just about. Been looking through my telescope every night. Last night was clear enough. I'm glad of that. Wanted to see you, before I send this message."

He took a deep breath, and then a swig straight from the bottle. Bubbles exploded in his mouth. He didn't much like the taste, truth be told, but that wasn't the point.

"This will be the last message I send," he said, which was unnecessary to say, and yet felt necessary nonetheless. He took another breath and another swig. What could he say to his last remaining relatives, to people who would have this message as the final memento of both him and the planet? How could anything be put into words?

"I want you to know," he said, at last, "that we have plenty of food, and sunshine, and we're doing well. Me and Jolene, we're settled in here nicely. And we both wish you well, and hope you'll think of us sometimes, when you're living in the light of a different sun. I hope, little Cy, you'll look up at the sky, and think about your Uncle Big Cy, and remember me and your great-aunt Jolene."

He blew a kiss at the screen.

"She sends her love," he said. "I know she never met you, but that doesn't mean she doesn't think of you like you're her family as well."

He took another swig of champagne, then held the bottle towards the screen.

"This is the last bottle," he said, "we're drinking it tonight, in your honour. I want you to remember that. I want you to remember that we sat here, and thought of you, and we grew our plants, and we lived our lives, and we never stopped thinking about you."

He paused, and sniffed. The words seemed inexplicably difficult to get out.

"And we never stopped loving you, sis, and, no, we—I... I never stopped wishing I could come with you, but you know what? I'm making a life here, with what's left. I've got Jolene, who's the best ancient auntie flatmate I could wish for, and I've got the hanging gardens of Babylon, and I've got the stars. And I've got you. The memory of you. And I want you to know..."

He sniffed again.

"I want you to know, that when I die and this planet becomes my tomb, I'll still be here, with an empty champagne bottle, and a telescope, and a record of a song I've never heard, and if anyone ever comes back here from that other sun, that's how you'll recognise me."

He didn't need another sniff. He didn't need another drink. There was only one thing left to say.

"That's how you'll know I loved you. Big Cy is signing off now. Love to you, sis, and Little Cy. Good luck among the stars. Find a good one for me."

He checked that the message had gone to the ark, then he switched off the transmitter, and sat back. Tonight, he thought, he would look at the stars, and try to find the glint of the ark one last time. And even if he never found that glint again, he would know that his final message had reached them.

It was done. Cyrus felt light-headed, uncertain whether to laugh or cry. He looked around him, but there was nothing else left for him here. Part of his brain had already started thinking about how the communications equipment could be repurposed now that there was nobody to talk to outside their apartment block.

Cyrus left the room and went to share the rest of the champagne with Jolene.

THANK YOU TO OUR SUPPORTERS

Many thanks to our patrons and supporters, especially:

Johanna Levene • Kathryn Parsons • Anna O'Brien
Cathrin Hagey • Natalie Weizenbaum

Frederick Stark • Steven • Juliette McHardy • Kate Boyes
Alina Kanaski • Jeffery Reynolds • Myz Lilith
D.M. Domosea • carol shoemake • Erik DeBill
Bonnie Warford • Kennon Hulett • Felicia OSullivan
Salomao Becker • Martin Cohen • J'nae Spano
Tory Hoke • Matthew Bennardo • Kayla D

J.V.Gachs • Leslie Anderson • Sian Jones • Kristina Saccone
Rochelle B • BethOfAus • J. Askew • Dirck de Lint
Brit Hvide • Wanda • Karen Anderson
Charlotte Nash-Stewart • Jocelyn Actual • Carly Racklin
Liz Warner • Suzanne Thackston • Jen G
Emily Anderson • Maria Haskins • GriffinFire

Want to see your name here? Become a patron!
patreon.com/lunastation

About the Cover Artist

Janaina Medeiros is a Brazilian freelance illustrator, with a degree in Visual Arts. She loves fairy tales and myths, both themes always present in her illustrations. Her style is influenced by the Pre-Raphaelite Brotherhood, Art Nouveau, and by anime/manga artists. Janaina creates illustrations for books, stationeries, gallery shows and more.

www.janaina.net

THE BEST OF
LUNA
STATION
QUARTERLY
THE FIRST FIVE YEARS
EDITED BY
JENNIFER LYN PARSONS

www.ingramcontent.com/pod-product-compliance
Lightning Source LLC
LaVergne TN
LVHW010052110826
845155LV00028B/302

* 9 7 8 1 9 4 9 0 7 7 2 4 7 *